For Top and Commander

I hope you and the rest of
the unit have the chance to
enjoy this

ANGELS RISING

HARRIET CARLTON

Harriet Carlton

A big thank-you to my two editors who helped me polish the rough edges of Angels Rising: Gail Higgins for streamlining the story, and Kim from Kover to Kover Editing for putting on the finishing touches!

$\mathcal{C}$ROLOGUE

The baby's nursery was still and quiet. The windows were latched tightly shut, and outside a small flurry of midwinter snow settled on the windowsill. On a dresser near the baby's crib was a monitor. The device was dormant. There was no sound in the still nursery, save for the small breaths of the sleeping infant.

A soft *whoosh* of air did not trip the monitor, nor did the muffled footsteps that followed. There was little more than a whisper of wind as a figure crossed the room from the window, and made its way toward the baby's crib. The footsteps and the figure belonged to a man, who seemed to be in his early thirties. As he walked forward, he was illuminated by the child's nightlight. While somewhat taller than other men, with unusually striking, pale green eyes, it was neither his height nor was it his eye color that marked him out as being different. It was the pair of huge, powerful, green-feathered wings that curved up from his shoulder blades and arced high above his head.

When he was next to the wooden crib, the man looked around the nursery, getting his bearings. He took note of the baby monitor on the dresser near the door before looking down at the child in the cot.

"You are all such funny looking things at this age," mused the winged man, sounding as though he was talking to himself.

In the crib, the baby woke crying as though taking offense to the man's words. The winged man glared at the baby's monitor as it squawked and lit up. The device, though unable to catch his quietly spoken sentence, had detected the baby's sharp cry.

"It seems that this is my cue to leave. How insensitive you are to the fact that I have only just arrived," said the winged man with a small, gentle smile. Very softly, he touched the tips of his index and middle finger to the baby's forehead. There was a momentary glow of low, white light that wavered between the man's fingers and the baby's brow. It lingered for only a heartbeat then dissolved, allowing the room to return to muted darkness once more. The man's smile faded as the handle of the door to the nursery twisted slowly. A soft rush of air swept through the room, stilling only when the door swung open.

A woman clad in a white nightgown entered, rubbing her eyes, she seemed to have just woken. She crossed the room to her son's crib. When she looked down, she saw that he was once again sleeping soundly. Tiredly, she checked the room for anything that may have woken him. There was nothing amiss.

"Must have been a bad dream," she mused quietly. The woman sighed softly and made her way back to the door.

"Sleep tight, honey," she whispered pulling the door shut.

The infant's mother had not noticed the single emerald feather resting next to her son's pillow.

CHAPTER
1

It was half past seven on a Friday morning when seventeen-year-old Imorean Frayneson raced out of his house toward his vehicle. He was built like an athlete. Tall without being lanky, and slim without being thin. He had dark brown eyes, eyes that seemed much darker than they really were as they contrasted with the stark, prematurely white hair that just brushed the tops of his ears. It was Imorean's bright, white hair that drew the most attention to him. Attention which was often unwanted.

Imorean launched himself into the front-seat of his pickup truck. He hated being late for anything. It didn't matter whether it was for work, school, or an appointment. Ever since childhood, his mother had told him that being tardy was disrespectful, and Imorean often prided himself on his ability to be polite and courteous. Another reason Imorean tried his best not to be late was because of his white hair. It was much easier for people to forget a brown-haired person walking into an event late, than it was for them to forget a prematurely white-haired person. Truthfully, it wasn't his hair that he hated, it was being noticed, standing out.

"Come on. Come on," he pleaded, turning the key in his truck's ignition. The engine sputtered and turned over, refusing to start. Imorean gripped the steering wheel in frustration. He cursed himself for buying a used vehicle. The fact of the matter was though, that this truck was all that Imorean had been able to afford.

"Why must you do this to me?" groaned Imorean, pulling the key out of the ignition and reinserting it. "I really hate you sometimes."

Imorean took a deep breath, rested his foot on the brake and turned the key. He whooped in gratitude as, after some deliberation, the truck's engine grudgingly started.

"I take back what I just said," he said, putting it in reverse. As he pressed the accelerator and backed the truck out of his gravel driveway and onto the road, he glanced down at his watch. The watch itself was nothing special, but it had belonged to Imorean's late father, Christian Frayneson, and Imorean valued it more than anything else.

"Oh, great," Imorean murmured, frustrated. If he didn't hurry he would definitely be late for school. Today of all days. He had a presentation due in his first class, and at nine thirty he had an interview with two representatives from a scholarship company. He couldn't afford to be late. Quickly, Imorean glanced in his rearview mirror. There were rarely speed traps on this road. With that in mind, Imorean stamped on the accelerator.

"I'm surprised that junk heap is still going," said a voice as Imorean grabbed his backpack off the backseat. His truck was parked crookedly in the last space he could find, but then again, many of the other cars in the student parking lot were also skewed. A majority of the other high school students were in their first years of driving, and were still random with their parking effort.

"Thanks, Roxanne. I know it needs to be held together with duct tape, but you don't have to rub it in," replied Imorean dryly, slamming his truck's door and turning toward the speaker. Leaning on the back of an old, pale blue car was his best friend Roxanne Daire, better known as Roxy. They had been friends with each other since they were both small children.

Roxy was naturally dark-haired, and typically wore it loose around her shoulders. She constantly dyed her hair different colors and because of it, reminded Imorean of a parrot. She enjoyed showing her individualism by dyeing her hair, but something about it also helped Imorean feel less alone for having an unusual hair color. Imorean had often warned her that, as a result of the dyeing, one day it may all fall out. Roxy never seemed too concerned. It was Roxy's general lack of concern that made Imorean more comfortable with her than with most other people that he knew. Imorean knew that she didn't care what people thought as far as how she dressed or looked. Roxy was shorter than Imorean by more than six inches, and her short stature made her look heavier than she actually was. Another thing Imorean liked about Roxy was the dynamic of their friendship. It was quiet and uncomplicated. He was her best friend, and she was his.

"I just thought I'd point out the obvious," she shrugged, tossing this week's hair, black, tipped with pale brown, over her shoulder. "And don't call me Roxanne. It makes me sound like I'm seventy not seventeen."

"I just do it to annoy you," said Imorean, elbowing his friend in the ribs as they walked toward the school doors.

"It's something you do very well. You always have," replied Roxy, trotting quickly next to him. She looked at him fondly. "You forgot to brush your hair again this morning, you airhead."

"I did?" asked Imorean, reaching up to touch his short, white hair. He ran his fingers through it in horror as he felt knots. "I can't go in for an interview with bed hair!"

"Calm down. You're so lucky your best friend is a girl,"

said Roxy with a grin, reaching into her purse and passing
him a comb.

"Thank you, Mother," said Imorean, gratefully taking the
comb and running it through his pure white hair. As a child
he had brown hair, but at age twelve it began to go gray, and
then at fifteen, his hair had become completely white. Now,
at seventeen, Imorean had adjusted to the odd color of his
hair, and thought that the color complemented him quite
well. When it had started graying, he'd dyed it back to brown.
It had taken him a few years to come to terms with the fact
that he would have white hair for the rest of his life, and
would always stick out like a sore thumb in crowds. After
that, he hadn't bothered dyeing it again. He had learned to
accept and live with it. In an odd sort of way, he liked it.

"Shut up. You have English first period, don't you?" asked
Roxy, holding the door open for Imorean.

"Yeah, with Ms. Dillard. Thank God we're graduating in
June. I don't think I could stand much more of her. I heard
next year she's going to be teaching English for juniors *and*
seniors," said Imorean, not bothering to conceal his dislike for
the teacher as he passed Roxy's comb back to her. He glanced
down at his watch and his heart leaped into his mouth.

"Yikes. I pity them," said Roxy, shaking her head. "When's
your interview?"

"Nine thirty," said Imorean, glancing at his watch again
anxiously. "Rox, I have to go, I'll meet up with you at lunch,
okay?"

"Sure, sure," replied Roxy, waving her friend on. "Good
luck!"

Imorean grinned at her and jogged away quickly,
desperate to make it to Ms. Dillard's class before the tardy bell
rang.

Imorean's foot was just crossing the threshold into her
classroom when the bell rang. He looked at Ms. Dillard,
wondering if she would make him go to the front office and

get a late pass. She generally ruled that students had to be seated when the bell rang.

"Just go and sit down," she snapped, glaring at Imorean.

"Thank you," said Imorean, breathing a silent sigh of relief.

"Imorean," said Ms. Dillard as she turned to the board.

"Yes, Ma'am?"

"The front office has asked me to remind you about the interview that you have at nine thirty."

"Yes, Ma'am, I remembered."

As Imorean placed his backpack next to his desk and got out the notecards he needed for his presentation, he couldn't help but hope that this upcoming interview would help him get a scholarship of some sort. He had been to several interviews for scholarships so far, and had always come away empty handed and disheartened. It was frustrating – and strange – to say the least. After all, he was in the top ten percent of his senior class and his grade point average was one of the school's highest. He was pretty sure that he should have received a scholarship long ago.

"Mr. Frayneson," said Ms. Dillard sharply, jerking Imorean out of his thoughts. "We're waiting. Your presentation."

"Yes. Sorry," said Imorean with an apologetic smile.

Imorean walked into the front office, tucking the pass Ms. Dillard had grudgingly written him into his pocket.

"Good morning, Imorean," said Mrs. Parker, the school's friendly receptionist.

"Good morning, Mrs. Parker. I'm here for the interview with …" Imorean's voice trailed off. He couldn't for the life of him remember what his interviewer's name was. He had applied for so many scholarships already that they all seemed to blur together.

"The representatives have been talking to students all

morning," replied Mrs. Parker in a knowing voice. "They're in the conference room behind me. Just go in whenever you're ready."

"What's the name of the scholarship again? I can't remember," said Imorean, lowering his voice and grimacing guiltily.

"I believe it's called Saving Grace. Go and talk to them. I'm sure they can tell you much more than I can," replied Mrs. Parker, offering Imorean a reassuring smile.

"Thank you," replied Imorean, giving Mrs. Parker a broad grin and walking toward to the conference room. The door to the room was ajar, so Imorean knocked lightly, pushed it open, and stepped inside. Two men sat next to each other at the conference table, talking quickly and covertly. From the body language, it appeared to Imorean that one of the men was irritated. They both seemed to be oblivious to his presence.

"Good morning," Imorean said, wanting to get their attention. The two men fell silent and looked up when they heard his voice.

Imorean was slightly taken aback. They were almost identical in appearance. Each had dark brown hair, but where one had green eyes, the other had hazel. There was a slight difference in height, but it was barely noticeable, as both men were sitting down. They were both broad shouldered, and seemed athletic. Both had fine, angular features that made Imorean feel somehow heavy and clumsy by comparison. There was also a hardness to the way they held themselves that he couldn't place. The shorter of the two had a thinner, more youthful face, and shining hazel eyes. The taller one was slightly darker, as though he had spent more time in the sun, and his squarer face was lined with the beginnings of early onset wrinkles. His pale eyes were still slanted in annoyance.

"You must be Imorean Frayneson. Please, sit down," said the smaller of the two with a broad grin. "My name is Gabriel

Archer and this is my brother Michael. We're representatives from the Saving Grace Scholarship."

"Thank you for offering the interview," replied Imorean, taking a seat across from Gabriel. "I first applied for Saving Grace back in December. I can't say I know too much about it though, only that it is a full ride."

"Good, good. That's a start," Gabriel replied with a broad smile. "Saving Grace is relatively new. It was founded only a few years ago, so naturally not many people have heard of it. Tell us, have you applied for any other scholarships?"

"Well, several, yes, but so far I haven't had any luck with them," said Imorean, glancing between the two brothers. Gabriel seemed quite open and friendly, whereas Michael was positively glaring at him. The taller brother was holding a pen between his fingers and was fiddling with it, taking it apart and putting it back together. He seemed to be doing it absentmindedly. Imorean pressed his back against his seat, squirming slightly under that aggressive, pale green stare.

"If you don't stop glaring, you're going to get wrinkles," said Gabriel, glancing at his brother. Michael's eyes darted away from Imorean for a second as he listened to his brother, then he looked out of the window, freeing Imorean completely from his uncomfortable jade stare. The absent twiddling of the pen continued, but Imorean had a feeling that he was still listening intently.

Imorean fought the odd urge to smile. He understood the close relationships between twin siblings all too well. His younger half siblings themselves were twins.

"So, Imorean," said Gabriel, bringing Imorean's attention back to the present. "What scholarships have you applied for?"

"All the scholarships I could really. Any that have been available to me," replied Imorean. "Like I said, I haven't had luck with any of them, so now I would do just about anything to get a scholarship. God knows I need one if I'm going to be able to go to college."

"Is that so?" asked Gabriel, inclining his head. "Would you mind if I asked why?"

"My financial situation isn't the best. My mother is a single parent, working and trying to support three children," replied Imorean. He wondered for a moment if he should have added more or less to his statement when Michael quickly looked back at the papers in front of his hands.

Imorean frowned slightly when the two brothers glanced at each other. Michael's glare vanished for a brief moment, but he still did not stop fiddling with the pen. Imorean furrowed his brow. Perhaps Michael was just someone who had nervous energy.

"Well then, Imorean," said Gabriel. "I think Michael and I might have something that you'd be interested in."

"The Saving Grace Scholarship."

"Precisely. That is what we're here to talk with you about," said Gabriel, his tone turning businesslike. "Saving Grace is a full ride scholarship. It'll pay all your college bills for four years. Housing, meal plans, tuition, uniforms. Everything."

"What do I have to do? These kinds of scholarships are rare," asked Imorean, giving Gabriel a half smile.

"I like him," said Gabriel, glancing at Michael. "The scholarship itself is highly competitive. This year, Saving Grace is only available to Virginia, North Carolina, and South Carolina students. Only a hundred of those who apply will be chosen for the scholarship. Those hundred students will then be given the opportunity to continue their academic careers abroad. Saving Grace is based on need and merit, and nothing more. We're looking for clever students, those who are driven, work hard, and who can think for themselves. The minimum grade point average to apply is a 3.7 and for the remainder of your senior year those numbers must be maintained. Those chosen must remain in good academic standing with the university that they will eventually attend.

Imorean, what is your grade point average as of right now?"

"It's a 4.0 unweighted, sir," replied Imorean.

"Fantastic," said Gabriel with a grin. "Are you active in your school and community?"

Imorean nodded. "As active as I can be. I'm involved with a few teams and several clubs that do community service."

"How many hours have you tallied?"

"Over three hundred, sir."

"Excellent, and in what field did you volunteer?"

"I've worked lately with food banks, disabled children, and veteran services."

"Perfect," nodded Gabriel. "I think you may have the potential to be a good candidate."

"Thank you, sir," replied Imorean, smiling. He knew that Gabriel was simply trying to put him at ease. It was a trick he had seen other scholarship representatives use.

"Well, I suppose you are reasonable," said Michael, propping his chin up in one hand.

Imorean was taken aback slightly by the man's voice. While Gabriel's was smooth and gentle, Michael's voice was somehow rough and carried a tone of command in it. There was something severe about the words, and Imorean felt an odd chill in his blood. He resisted the urge to frown. What Michael had said wasn't something representatives usually said, and it was not encouraging.

"Pay him no mind," said Gabriel, reassuringly. "Imorean, in reviewing your internet application, we can tell that you're keen, and have already met much of the criteria we are looking for. Are you interested in entering the final stages of applying for Saving Grace?"

"By God, yes!" said Imorean. "If I could get the scholarship it would be like the answer to a prayer."

"Good. Well, I'm glad we could extend the offer of help," replied Gabriel, reaching down under the table. His hand reappeared a second later, and he passed Imorean a thick packet of paper.

"If you could fill this out and mail it back to the address on the second page by March fifteenth we will complete the processing of your application and contact you by April tenth."

"That's not long before graduation, and that only gives me ten days from now to finish it and postmark it," said Imorean, taking the stack of papers that Gabriel had slid across the table.

"Then we suggest you hurry," responded Michael curtly.

"We know. If the packet is received on the fifteenth, but is postmarked no later than March first, you will not be disqualified," said Gabriel, brushing aside his brother's words. "If you are one selected, then we will contact you again and explain what you should do next."

"Okay," mused Imorean, his brown eyes dropping down to the papers in his hands.

"Any questions?" asked Gabriel.

"How are students selected for this scholarship?"

"As I said earlier, we base it on grade point average and financial need."

"Right. This is a chance at a fully paid college education. Don't I have to pay it back in some way? I know there are some military scholarships where you have a mandatory period of service."

"That's true. We do ask for a form of service to the general public. Typically, it is community service hours throughout the duration of your college education. Some of our alumni have made generous monetary donations to our foundation."

"Okay," murmured Imorean, frowning slightly. He felt for a moment that there was something unusual going on. Then again, it was probably nothing. All scholarships had their strange quirks, and he was desperate.

"We should probably tell you now," said Michael. "That Saving Grace is not recognized by all colleges, so there are places where it will not apply. We, as the representatives of Saving Grace, are finalizing the establishment of a contract with a particular college where the scholarship will certainly be recognized, and all students with Saving Grace are guaranteed entry into said university. We urge you to apply also to colleges of your choosing, but if you receive Saving Grace, you already have a college you can go to."

"Okay, cool," said Imorean, nodding slowly. "That's interesting. I've never heard of that before."

"Anything else?" asked Gabriel.

"No, no, I don't think I have any questions right now."

"Brilliant. In that packet, you can find my and Michael's cards with our contact information if any questions come up. If you have any trouble or questions in general, please, don't hesitate to get in touch with us," said Gabriel, flashing a grin at Imorean. "Now, I do actually have a question for you."

"Yes, sir?" asked Imorean, slightly taken aback.

"Are you an albino? Just out of curiosity. I've been wondering ever since you walked in."

"No, sir," replied Imorean. "I was actually born with brown hair, but it went completely white when I turned fifteen."

"How interesting," said Gabriel, grinning. "Well, Imorean, it was a pleasure to meet you. I certainly hope that we'll eventually be sending you a letter saying you've received the scholarship."

"So do I, sir," replied Imorean, standing up and crossing the room to the door. He paused with one hand on the knob and turned. "Thank you."

"You're very welcome," replied Gabriel, nodding and grinning.

Imorean barely saw the smaller man's gestures, though. He

was transfixed by Michael. Surely it must have been the weak, morning sunlight of early spring shining in from the windows behind the man, but for a moment, Imorean could have sworn he saw an oddly shaped shadow flickering on the walls behind Michael's head and shoulders. Michael leaned down to grab something out of a briefcase and Imorean chuckled humorlessly. The sunlight was blocked by a small statue, casting an unusual pattern of shade just behind where the man's head had been.

"Is there something wrong?" asked Gabriel.

"No, no, sorry," said Imorean, smiling at him. "I just thought... never mind. Thank you."

"You're welcome," said Gabriel again, his grin widening.

CHAPTER 2

"You need glasses," said Roxy.

Imorean yelped as her finger prodded him hard in the ribs.

"I'm only telling you what I saw," replied Imorean, adjusting his pack on his back and pulling his truck keys out of his pocket. He had just finished telling her about his interview and the strange experience with Michael.

"Well, it sounds to me as though you need glasses," said Roxy, sounding unconcerned. "I'm sure, like you said, it was just the sun and the shadows making Michael's shadow look weird. When I went in to talk to them I didn't notice anything strange about them at all."

"You spoke to them as well?" asked Imorean, turning and walking backwards for a few paces.

"Don't sound so surprised," replied Roxy in mock hurt. "You're not the only one who's scholarship hunting. My GPA isn't that much lower than yours, and our financial situations are similar."

"True, true," mused Imorean, turning again and walking

the rest of the way to his car. He frowned as he studied the beaten, red, pickup truck in front of him. It probably wasn't safe to drive anymore. Briefly he wondered how much he could get for it. Seconds later, he cast the thought from his mind. The truck wasn't worth anything, and it was his only means of transport aside from his mother's car which was equally as unreliable.

"You might get a pack of gum for it if you're lucky," said Roxy, as though she was reading his thoughts.

Imorean smiled and laughed mirthlessly.

"Yeah. If I'm lucky. Roxy, I've got a lot to do, so I probably won't be free this weekend. I'll see you on Monday," said Imorean, unlocking the truck's door.

"See ya," replied Roxy, waving and getting into her own car.

"Please start," prayed Imorean quietly, putting the key in the truck's ignition.

Imorean hummed in surprise upon seeing his mother's car parked in the gravel driveway. It was unusual for her to be home during the day.

"Mom?" he called as he opened the door to their house. It was a small house, yet comfortable, and would always feel like home to Imorean. He had grown up here.

"I'm in the kitchen making coffee. Do you want any?" came the reply.

Imorean smiled in confusion and made the short trip from the front door to the kitchen.

"That would be great. You're home early," said Imorean, leaning on the door frame and watching his mother bustle quickly around the kitchen.

Amelia Watson was a slight, willowy woman who worked as a veterinary technician, and who tied up her curly, brown hair in a bun far too often. She was only in her thirties, but her hair was graying at the roots, and Imorean knew that it wasn't just due to the stress of her working life.

"I took half of today off," replied Amelia. "Are Isaac and Rachel here yet?"

"No," said Imorean, shaking his head. "Their bus gets in around four."

"Of course it does," said Amelia, smacking a palm to her forehead. "Honestly, sometimes I think working in that clinic addles my brain."

"It wouldn't surprise me," replied Imorean. "You spend some very long hours in there."

"So, what's new with you? How did the interview go?" asked Amelia, pouring some coffee from the pot into mugs and passing one to Imorean.

"Thanks," he said, taking the mug then placing it down on the counter top. "It went pretty well. I have some news about it."

"Oh, do tell," said Amelia, beaming at him and sipping on her own coffee.

"The two representatives I had an interview with today were from the Saving Grace Scholarship Foundation and they told me that they wanted me to continue into the second round of application for the scholarship."

"They did?" cried Amelia, her eyes lighting up. "How much is it for? Where's it to?"

"Slow down," said Imorean, grinning. "Apparently there are a couple of loopholes in the scholarship itself though, and it's not valid for all colleges."

"Keep applying for it," urged Amelia, beaming at him. "Imorean, you'd be a fool not to. You know how much the two of us have been worrying about paying for your college. This development with the Saving Grace Scholarship sounds like an absolute Godsend."

"There's no guarantee I'll get it," said Imorean.

"No, but at least you would have tried," replied Amelia,

sounding encouraging. "How many other students are you up against?"

"I'm not sure of the number, but I'm going to assume that I'm up against all the other qualified high school students from Virginia, North Carolina, and South Carolina."

"Oh, nothing too much then," said Amelia, turning and putting sugar in her coffee.

"There's only a hundred possible slots for Saving Grace."

"Then you better get started," replied Amelia, smiling at Imorean. "Honey, you're smart. Your grades are amazing. You'll get it, just go for it."

"Thanks, Mom," said Imorean, smiling at his mother's words. She always had such great confidence in him.

"So, you said that there were two scholarship representatives. Were they nice? Were either of them married?" asked Amelia with a wink.

"Really, Mom? I wasn't looking to see if they were married. They were actually brothers. Twins," replied Imorean, smiling. "One of them was really nice and courteous. He was a real easy guy to get along with. The other one though... I didn't really know what to make of him. He seemed kind of standoffish, and nervous somehow. I didn't really like the way he was looking at me."

"What do you mean?" asked Amelia, sounding defensive.

"He was sort of glaring, but it can't have just been me, right?"

"Some men just have a resting glare," replied Amelia, rolling her eyes slightly. "You know your step-father used to be like that."

"Oh, yeah, I remember that all too well," said Imorean, nodding and frowning at the memory. "Well, I should probably go and get started on this packet. I want to try and get my application in before most other people."

"Good idea. I'll tell Isaac and Rachel to give you some

space."

"Thanks," replied Imorean, turning and exiting the kitchen, making his way down the narrow hallway to his bedroom.

Imorean frowned at one of the questions in the packet. The first half of the paperwork had just been filling in his personal information again. His social security number, number of family members, all the normal things he had done many times before. Now though, he was completing a questionnaire. Most of the questions were normal ones that he had seen on other scholarships, but there were some that confused him. *Have you been skydiving at any point during the last four years?* What on Earth did skydiving have to do with a scholarship? Imorean shook his head and wrote beneath the question that he had never been, assuming that it was simply a survey question.

Imorean glanced up at the clock on his desk and was shocked to see that it was already eight o'clock. He grimaced. He was exhausted, and he hadn't done any of his other homework. Perhaps he should put the application aside for the rest of the night. Quickly, the white-haired boy flicked through the remaining papers. There were only five pages left, and the only things he had to write on them was his signature. For a few seconds, Imorean deliberated. This scholarship could be the key to help unlock the rest of his life. Perhaps he should read the fine print. He glanced guiltily at his watch.

'Who really reads these kinds of documents anyway?' thought Imorean. Hastily, he scribbled his signature in the blanks and checked a box saying that he agreed to the terms and conditions of Saving Grace Scholarship Foundation and its affiliates. The teenager shook his head and smiled as he slid the thick pack of papers back into its manila folder. He could send this off tomorrow. He was certain that he would have to go into town for something anyway.

Imorean sighed tiredly as he pulled a thick, geography book out of his backpack. All the students in Imorean's geography class had been assigned a country to do a project on. Imorean had been given Norway. Although he had all weekend to work on it, he wanted as much of a head start on it as he could get. It was a project, after all. Imorean rubbed his eyes and did his best to push away his tiredness. He needed to get to work.

Imorean was falling. On either side of his body he could hear a strange, fluttering sound, like wind through a bird's feathers. He couldn't open his eyes, the lids were too heavy. Air rushed past him, and he knew that soon the ground would race up to meet him. Imorean's head rolled forward, and he began to fall head over heels. If only there were some way he could pull out of this terminal dive. Something inside his mind told him that the ground was coming closer and closer and would eventually put a sudden stop to his fast fall. Closer. Closer. Closer.

Imorean sat up bolt upright with a cry, knocking a stack of notebooks onto the floor. His heart was racing and his mouth was dry. As Imorean caught his breath, he realized that he was shaking and had broken out in a cold sweat. The nightmare of falling to his imminent doom was one that had haunted him many times before. He was terrified of heights.

Imorean groaned and ran a hand through his hair, realizing that he had fallen asleep on his desk again. He glanced at the clock that rested on one corner of the desk. It was three o'clock in the morning. The idea of bed suddenly sounded extremely appealing. Not giving his homework a second thought, Imorean stripped his clothes and replaced them with pajamas, then flopped down heavily on top of his bed. He was incredibly grateful that it was now the weekend and, aside from his project, he had nearly two, full days to recuperate from the hectic week. Imorean closed his brown eyes, and the boy was asleep in only seconds.

CHAPTER 3

Imorean rolled over in bed, lying so that he faced the wall. Outside, even though, it was quite sunny, it felt early to him. Considering it was the weekend, and that he had stayed up late the night before, Imorean didn't particularly want to wake up. Then he heard a giggle and his eyes snapped open. There was someone else in his room. Two someones if his intuition was right.

"Shh," hissed a second voice.

Imorean buried his face in his blankets slightly and hid his smirk. Quickly, he closed his eyes again and cleared the expression from his face. The teenager felt the edge of his mattress dip.

"He's still asleep," whispered one of the voices. The first voice laughed again. A finger poked him.

Slowly, Imorean rolled again, adjusting so that he was facing the rest of his room. He kept his eyes closed, but kept listening for any other signs of activity. He heard both voices giggle again and a few hushed whispers. The edge of his mattress dipped again as more weight was put on it.

"And just what are you two planning to do to me this morning?" asked Imorean, opening one brown eye. Two horrified gasps rose from the children who sat on the edge of his bed, a bowl of ice cubes held between them, poised to be dumped.

"Ice cubes? In March?" asked Imorean, sitting up and plucking a handful from the bowl. "That's kind of you."

Imorean laughed as his two younger half siblings squealed and jumped off his bed, dropping the bowl of ice and scrambling over one another in their hurry to get away. When the door slammed shut behind his twin siblings, Imorean dumped his handful of ice back into the bowl and shook his head. Perhaps it *was* a good time to get up. It would give him a bit of time to get dressed and to plan his revenge for the twins' thwarted prank.

"Rachel, Isaac," said Imorean as he meandered from his bedroom and into the living room. In his arms was the bowl of ice, on its way back to the freezer.

"Yes, Imorean," said Rachel innocently. The twins were sitting on the couch, watching early morning cartoons. They were fraternal twins, but looked quite similar. Rachel seemed to be almost a carbon copy of Amelia, with the exception of her face being more heart shaped, rather than thin. Isaac also had dark brown hair, but his eyes were pale blue, and he had a rounder, chubbier face than his sister. They were the children from Amelia's second marriage.

"So, what was this all about?" asked Imorean rattling the bowl of ice before he dumped it back into the freezer.

"Just trying to wake you up," replied Isaac, the younger of the two.

"Well, that wasn't a very nice way of doing it," said Imorean, folding his arms across his chest and frowning at the two of them. He watched as the twins looked hesitantly at one another.

"We're sorry, Imorean," said Isaac, hopping down off the

couch and looking at the floor. "We won't do it again."

"I should hope not," replied Imorean, crossing the small living room and placing a hand on Isaac's shoulder. The young boy squealed in a mixture of horror and delight as a cold ice cube slithered down his back. Still sitting on the couch, Rachel's eyes widened and she moved to spring down and run to the safety of her and her twin's shared bedroom.

"Not so fast," laughed Imorean, grabbing her collar and giving her the same treatment as her brother.

"That was mean," grouched Isaac as the ice finally tumbled out of his shirt.

"Not as mean as what you planned to do to me, you little imps," replied Imorean, ruffling his younger half-brother's brown hair.

"It would have been funny," protested Rachel, following Imorean into the kitchen.

"Yes, for you two, not for me," said Imorean, smiling over his shoulder at them.

"Is Mom still here?" asked Imorean as he reached up to get a box of cereal down for Isaac and Rachel.

"Yeah, she's in bed," replied Isaac. "She said she didn't work today."

"Okay," said Imorean. "When she gets up, can you let her know that I went out into town?"

"Is that chocolate cereal up there?" asked Rachel, putting her hands behind her back and bouncing up and down on the balls of her feet. Imorean smiled. He knew this game of Rachel's well. He would reach items on high shelves in exchange for favors from her.

"Yes," said Imorean, checking the cereal box. "This is chocolate cereal, so will you let Mom know?"

"Yes, we'll let her know," said Rachel.

Imorean rolled his eyes and shook his head. His twin siblings, Rachel particularly, never missed an opportunity to barter for something.

"I'll see you guys later," said Imorean, grabbing his car keys from the table next to the door and dashing out before his siblings could respond.

Imorean deposited the Saving Grace Scholarship application in the drop box at the post office, sighing in relief as he turned away. In a way, the Saving Grace Scholarship was his last hope at a college career. His mother didn't know, but he was planning to enlist in the armed services if he didn't get any scholarships. He knew that his mother didn't want him to enlist, but he wouldn't financially break his family for the sake of a college education or leave university with a huge loan. His family's financial security was worth far more than going to college.

The teenager pulled his jacket closer as he prepared to exit the post office, not really wanting to brave the cold outside.

"Imorean?" asked someone just as the boy was pushing the door open.

The white-haired boy looked up and furrowed his brow as Gabriel Archer trotted up to him.

"Mr. Archer," said Imorean in surprise. "What are you doing here?"

"Michael and I stayed the night in a hotel not far away. I had to send off a few things to the head administrator of Saving Grace. What are you doing here?"

"Posting my continuation of the application," replied Imorean, stepping back and away from the door.

"You already filled it out?" asked Gabriel, sounding surprised.

"Yes, sir," said Imorean with a nod.

"Well done," replied Gabriel, smiling. "I'll bear that in mind."

"What do you mean, sir?"

"At Saving Grace, we value hard work and dedication. I saw yesterday that you had both, and you dropping the application off today just proved that. I'll put in a good word for you when we're evaluating our candidates."

"You will?"

"Of course."

"Thank you," said Imorean, resisting the urge to shake his head in surprise. What luck this had been.

"You're very welcome," said Gabriel, fiddling with the envelope in his hands. "Well, I'm sure you've got things you need to do, so I'll take my leave of you. Have a great day, Imorean."

"You too, Mr. Archer," replied Imorean. He jumped slightly as Gabriel patted him on the shoulder then disappeared into a small cluster of people. Looking out of the door in the direction he'd gone, Imorean saw no sign of him. When the man's hand touched on his shoulder, Imorean had felt a small, electric shock. Imorean paused for a second. It was probably just static electricity, after all, it *was* cold, and static was always worse in the winter. Imorean frowned and looked again wondering where Gabriel had gone. The teenager furrowed his brow in puzzlement. Gabriel seemed to have vanished into thin air, but how? Imorean was certain he had seen him walk along with a group of people. Imorean shook his head and pushed the door to the post office open. Regardless of the man's unusual disappearance, he was glad to have seen Gabriel again. He suddenly felt far more confident about Saving Grace.

Imorean knew he really should have been getting home. He had a lot of schoolwork that he still needed to do. Instead though, here he was on the side of the Blue Ridge Parkway, looking out over a viewing area. He was glad that his fear of heights didn't seem to rule his head when both feet were firmly planted on the ground.

Despite the fact that it was early spring and the air was still cold, Imorean took little notice of the weather. His mind was elsewhere. He really, truly loved where he lived, here in this exact area of the state. He couldn't imagine anything better than being nestled in the middle of the Blue Ridge Mountains of North Carolina. His dream college, Appalachian State University, was only in the next town over, so he had the possibility of staying very close to his family. Imorean closed his eyes and sighed heavily. What if Saving Grace wasn't valid at Appalachian State? What if he had to go to another state for it to be valid? The teenager frowned and slowly nodded to himself. If Saving Grace wasn't valid at Appalachian State he would follow where the scholarship sent him, and from what Gabriel had said today, he felt more confident that he may have a chance of getting it.

Imorean gazed out over the rolling mountaintops, allowing his thoughts to wander further. In school, he was told to ask permission to go to the bathroom, but away from school he was being asked to make decisions that would affect and potentially alter the rest of his life. Thinking of school reminded him with a jolt, that due to the selectiveness of the scholarship, surely the administrators of Saving Grace could only feasibly choose one recipient from each school, if they chose one at all. He and Roxy had applied for the same one. Imorean thought, with a pang of guilt, that he was more likely to be chosen. His GPA was higher, but on the other hand, Roxy's financial need was greater. He shook his head. Which trait would win out when their applications were evaluated? What would become of their friendship afterward?

Grudgingly, Imorean dragged himself out of his thoughts and checked his watch. It was almost eleven in the morning. He should probably start heading home. The boy returned to the truck and put the key into its ignition, breathing his regular sigh of relief when the vehicle sputtered but started after some hesitation. He really needed a new way of getting around.

"Hey, honey," called Amelia as Imorean walked inside. "Lunch is in the fridge if you want any."

"Thanks, Mom," replied Imorean, still quite deep in thought as he crossed the living room.

"Don't block the TV, Imorean!" cried Rachel as Imorean walked in front of the couch.

"Oh, don't block the TV, huh?" asked Imorean, stopping and folding his arms, making sure he was standing squarely in front of the television.

"Imorean!" chided Isaac, bouncing off the couch and wrapping his arms around his older brother's waist. It was the highest place that the seven-year-old could reach.

"Help! I'm being attacked!" cried Imorean, a smile springing to his face as he fell slowly and dramatically to his knees.

"Rachel!" called Isaac, laughing.

Imorean grinned as Rachel jumped off the couch, coming quickly to the aid of her twin. The girl loosely put her arms around Imorean's shoulders, and the older boy humored them by dropping to the living room floor.

"I'm down," he said in defeat as Rachel sat on his abdomen.

"Okay, you two," said Amelia, standing in the doorway to the living room and drying her hands on a towel. "Stop abusing your older brother and let him get up. He's got a lot of work he needs to do."

"But it's so much fun," said Isaac, still holding onto one of Imorean's legs.

"Up," said Amelia, looking at the twins out of the corners of her eyes. "Now."

"Yes, Mom," said Isaac, doing as their mother said.

"I think that means you too, princess," said Imorean,

patting her on the back and trying to encourage her to get off him.

"Hmm," replied Rachel as she stood up. "I guess you're right."

Imorean grinned as his half-sister trotted back over to the couch and hopped back up onto it. Despite the fact that he and the twins were only related through their mother, he couldn't have loved them more than if they were his full blood siblings. He scrambled to his feet before the twins could launch another attack.

"Imorean," said Amelia as he walked into the kitchen and opened the fridge.

"Yeah?" asked Imorean, pulling out a sandwich.

"Could you take Rachel and Isaac to your grandmother's house in time for dinner tonight? I told her that they'd spend some of the weekend with her."

"Sure," replied Imorean.

"She said she and Papa would love it if you'd stay as well. They never really get to see you anymore."

"I would if I could, but I have all my textbooks here and a project to finish. I can't really stay out anywhere tonight," replied Imorean, sitting down at the table.

"Alright, I'll let her know. Just stay with them until after dinner, would you?"

"I can do that," replied Imorean, nodding.

"Thank you," said Amelia, sighing and sitting down across from him. "I would take them, but I've got the late-night shift at the clinic tonight."

"Mom, don't worry about it," replied Imorean, smiling. "You work hard enough. I'm glad to do anything I can to help you. You know that."

"Thank you," said Amelia, smiling apologetically. "I just wish I didn't have to ask."

"It's not a problem," smiled Imorean.

"Can I turn up the heat?" asked Rachel, leaning over Imorean's shoulder from the backseat.

"Can I change the radio station?" asked Isaac, his fingers already on the controls.

"Why doesn't it feel warm in here yet?"

"What kind of music do you listen to?"

"Do you have any gum?"

"Why are there gym shoes back here?"

"Why does your truck stink?"

"It does *not* stink in here," replied Imorean sharply. "Isaac, get in the backseat. You're too small to be up front, and stop fiddling with my radio. Rachel, sit down and put your seat belt on. No, I don't have any gum. I have gym shoes in here because I need them for track practice. Any more questions?"

"Are you angry?" asked Rachel meekly, meeting Imorean's brown eyes in the rearview mirror.

Imorean rolled his eyes and sighed in exasperation as Isaac scrambled over the center console into the backseat. When his younger brother was settled in the back, Imorean reversed the truck out of the driveway.

"No," he replied, smiling in spite of his irritation. "No, I'm not angry."

"So, *can* I change the radio station?" asked Isaac.

"Fine," replied Imorean, shaking his head and reaching for the dial.

"Can we stop and get food?" asked Rachel as Imorean turned his truck onto the highway.

"We're eating at Grandma's, it will ruin your appetite."

"But I'm hungry *now*," argued Rachel.

"I'm sorry," replied Imorean, smirking at her in the rearview mirror.

"Fine," huffed Rachel, sinking down into her seat and

folding her arms.

"Hey, Imorean," said Isaac, leaning forward and resting his elbows on the center console.

"Yeah?"

"Can you tell us a ghost story on the way to Gramma's?" Rachel joined her brother. "Please?"

"Do the two of you *like* to be scared or something?" asked Imorean, shaking his head and smiling. The twins' love of ghost stories almost equaled his own.

"Love it," replied Rachel, joining her brother leaning on the center console. Both of their seat belts were stretched almost all the way out.

"Fine, which story do you want to hear?"

"The Pink Lady!" cried Rachel immediately.

"No! The floating lights on Brown Mountain," argued Isaac.

"The ghosts in Biltmore House," said Rachel.

"The haunted hot springs," said Isaac, throwing out another suggestion.

"Hmm... how about the demon dogs?" asked Imorean.

"Demon dogs?" asked Rachel. "You haven't told us that one before."

"Because you were never old enough to hear it," replied Imorean, smiling and biting the inside of his cheek.

"What's it about?" asked Rachel, her eyes wide.

"You know my friend Cody?"

"Yeah," replied Isaac, nodding.

"Well, he was the one who told me about the demon dog. It haunts the old church in the town of Valle Crucis. One night, Cody was driving home and he passed the church. Only seconds later, a shadow jumped out in front of his car and he had to slam on his brakes. He stopped in the middle of the road and looked around. That was when he saw it. Standing behind his car was a massive black dog with glowing red eyes. It was as tall as a grown man, and just as wide. Cody told me its eyes seemed to reflect the lights of hell itself. Cody slammed his foot on the gas pedal and drove away as fast as he could, taking sharp turns in the road at sixty, seventy miles an hour. But he wasn't fast enough. This demon dog was gaining on him. It was only yards behind him."

"Did he get away?" asked Rachel, eyes wide, her mouth slightly open.

"Yeah, and that's the weird thing," said Imorean. "He crossed a bridge. The dog seemed to be somehow tied to the town of Valle Crucis and couldn't cross the bridge after Cody. It was sheer luck that he got away that night. He thinks it's still waiting for him though. He hasn't been through Valle Crucis since."

The twins were silent for a moment. Imorean darted a quick glance at them. It seemed that his impromptu story had scared them into being quiet. Rachel and Isaac were still young enough to believe in things like ghosts and demon dogs. Imorean though, while he loved ghost stories, didn't buy a single word of the old legend. Ghosts and demons only existed in stories. The truth was, his friend Cody had never had anything to do with any demon dog. Imorean had read about the demon dog of Valle Crucis several months ago while doing a Halloween project for his North Carolina history teacher. He hadn't had a good opportunity to share it with the twins until now.

"Imorean?" said Isaac, getting his older brother's attention.

"Yeah?"

"Grandma and Papa live near Valle Crucis, don't they?"

"Yeah, they do," replied Imorean. "Her and Papa can probably tell you more about the demon dog than I can. Maybe they've even *seen* it."

Rachel shivered, but Isaac leaned further forward.

"What *is* a demon dog?" he asked.

"Gee, Isaac, everyone knows what a demon dog is," Rachel said, berating her brother.

"Don't be mean," said Imorean. "Isaac, a demon dog, or black dog, is another name for a Hellhound. Supposedly, they're the ones who are sent out to drag the souls of the damned into hell. Once a Hellhound decides it wants to take you, you'll be dragged to the underworld, and... you'll *never* be seen again."

Imorean chuckled as Isaac and Rachel whimpered.

"It's not funny, Imorean!" cried Rachel, leaning forward and hitting him on the shoulder.

"You asked for a scary story, and I delivered," replied Imorean, ignoring her light punch. "I guess it's a good thing you and Isaac sleep in the same bed at Grandma's, otherwise a Hellhound might come and find you."

"Stop it!" cried Rachel. "Isaac will never get to sleep tonight."

"Yes, I will," replied Isaac. "You're the one who gets more scared."

"Am not!"

"Are too! I'm not scared at all," replied Isaac, sticking his chin out.

"Hey, quit arguing," said Imorean. "I'm trying to drive here, and you don't want to be arguing when we drive through Valle Crucis, do you?"

"What?" cried Rachel, wrapping her arms around Isaac. "We're driving through there?"

"It's the quickest way to get to Grandma's. If you're arguing, you might attract the dog," replied Imorean, dropping his voice to a hushed whisper.

"Can't we go another way?" asked Rachel, a slight plea in her voice.

"It'll still be light when we go through town. Don't worry, we won't be in any danger," said Imorean, reassuring her.

"And hey, I'm here, remember. I'll always protect you two."

"If you say so," said Rachel, hugging herself.

"I *do* say so," replied Imorean, smiling at her in the rearview mirror. "I'm your big brother, that's my job."

CHAPTER 4

I morean couldn't help but breathe a small sigh of relief as he pulled the truck into his grandparents' driveway. The last fingers of sunlight were just leaving the sky and he didn't particularly like driving at night. The truck's ancient headlights were hardly the best. The drive through Valle Crucis had been completely uneventful. Although, that did not stop the twins from huddling down in the backseat, refusing to look out the windows.

"Come on," said Imorean, throwing his door open. "I don't know about you two, but I'm starving."

He slammed the truck's door shut and trotted up the front steps of his grandparents' house. He waited for the twins to catch up to him and opened the door, letting himself in.

"Grandma?" called Imorean, stepping into the small foyer.

"Imorean, Rachel, Isaac," said Imorean's grandmother, Leanne, stepping out of the kitchen and drying her hands on a tea towel. "You're just in time for dinner. It's about to be on the table."

"Great," replied Imorean, smiling. "Is Papa around?"

"Yes, I think he's in the living room."

"Thanks," said Imorean.

"Imorean," said Leanne, catching the teenager's attention before he could go and search for his grandfather.

"Yes?"

"You *are* staying for dinner, aren't you?"

"Yes, I am," replied Imorean, smiling at her.

"Lovely."

Imorean patted the twins on their shoulders as he squeezed past them and made his way to the living room.

"Papa," said Imorean as he entered. Imorean's grandfather, William, was in his seventies. Imorean knew William was a war veteran, although he rarely mentioned it. From the small bit he *had* spoken of, Imorean knew he had been a combat medic. William was currently sitting on an old couch, buried in a book. Imorean sneaked a looked at the title as he entered the room. *Angels Among Us* by Dr. R. Hall, PhD. Imorean grinned. Angels were one of his grandfather's favorite subjects, which Imorean had always found unusual. His grandparents weren't particularly religious.

"Imorean," replied William, not looking up. "We expected you a little earlier."

"Sorry, I don't trust that old truck at high speeds."

"As you shouldn't," replied William, smiling at his oldest grandson.

"Grandma says dinner is almost ready," said Imorean, sitting down next to his grandfather.

"Well, almost ready isn't ready, is it," replied the old man.

Imorean smiled at the old man's words.

"You look like you've got a question," said William. "What is it?"

"I told Rachel and Isaac a scary story on the way here," said Imorean, his brown eyes flitting to his grandfather. He knew of the old man's love of spooky stories. In fact, it was from

William that Imorean had learned most of the ones he knew.

"Oh? What was it?" asked William, sounding eager and closing his book.

"The black dog of Valle Crucis."

"Old legend," replied William. "Not one I've heard for a while."

"Any truth in it?" asked Imorean, grinning.

"Imorean, I know you don't really believe in such things, but I'll humor you. The legend has been around for generations, and several people have claimed to have seen a black dog here. I have never seen it myself, but... many years ago, when I was about your age, I could have sworn I heard it."

"What did it sound like?" asked Imorean, watching his grandfather's face.

"Awful. I was driving home late one night. It was a full moon and was around midnight. It was warm out, so I had my car windows down. I was driving by that old church when I heard the sound. It was a horrific, other worldly wail. It sounded as though all the tortured souls of hell were screaming. Needless to say, I pushed my old car to its limits to get out of there. It was truly terrifying."

"Couldn't it have just been some cats fighting?"

"Oh, no, Imorean," said William, smiling. "This was the kind of sound that carried a promise. It was angry and evil. It was not a sound of this world. There was a fear to it that you could feel in your bones."

"But, how would a Hellhound even get here?" asked Imorean, furrowing his brow.

"No one really knows how or why," replied William. "All we know is that some creatures, demons, Hellhounds, spirits, some of them are powerful enough to come to this world and blur the lines between our world and the next."

"But, Grandpa, they aren't real..."

"Why shouldn't they be real?"

Imorean grinned and shook his head. "No one has ever proved that they exist,"

"You can prove that something is real, Imorean, but it is much harder to prove that something is real when people do not wish to see it."

"Then why is it that only some people see them?"

"That's because–" began William, dropping his voice to a conspiratorial whisper.

"Are you two sitting in here swapping old ghost stories again?" asked Leanne, standing in the threshold and cutting off her husband's sentence.

"Yeah," replied Imorean, still wondering what his grandfather had been about to say. "Just getting good and scared for the drive back home."

"Boys. They never change," muttered Leanne, rolling her eyes. "Dinner is ready, if you want to come."

"Your mother told us about the possibility of your scholarship," said Leanne after dinner while they were all still seated around the table.

"Yeah," replied Imorean. "It seems really interesting, and it's come at the best possible time too. A full ride is exactly what I need. I'm sure I'll get more details about it later on."

"What's the name of it?" asked Leanne.

"Saving Grace Scholarship," replied Imorean, placing his knife and fork down on his plate. He jumped slightly as his grandfather fumbled and dropped his spoon on the floor.

"Well," said Leanne, jerking Imorean's attention back to the present as she placed one hand on top of his. "We wish you the best of luck, and we're right behind you. You really do deserve to get a scholarship. We know how hard you've worked."

"Thank you," replied Imorean. He decided not to tell them about the possibility of him going to a different college. It would be best not to worry them until things were more set in stone.

Down the hall, a clock chimed.

"It's getting late," said Imorean. "I should probably get going."

"Be safe on those roads," said Leanne as Imorean stood. "Watch for deer."

"And Hellhounds," said William.

"I will," replied Imorean, grinning. His grin faltered for a moment when he noticed his grandfather's serious expression.

Imorean turned the music on the radio up as he neared the town of Valle Crucis. Perhaps he was a little more scared by his own story than he had realized. He shook his head and rolled his eyes. It was only a story. A silly, urban legend. Nothing more. There was no reason to be scared. He was only a little more on edge because Valle Crucis looked creepier at night. Yes, that was it.

Telling himself that there was no reason to be scared did not stop his skin prickling as he passed the old, wooden church of Valle Crucis. It was the very church where the Hellhound was said to live. The hairs on the back of his neck began to stand up.

"God, this place is creepy," muttered Imorean, shaking his head and focusing on the road. He pressed a little harder on the accelerator, eager to put space between himself and the church. Imorean relaxed more as he put more distance between himself and the creepy building, and finally breathed a sigh of relief as he turned a hairpin bend. He glanced at the clock in his dashboard. It was nearly eleven o'clock. He raised his eyes back to the road and it dimly registered in his mind that the full moon was reflecting in his wing mirror.

Imorean acted on his reflexes and slammed his foot on the brakes when something smashed into the back of his truck. In the back of his mind, he thought he heard glass shatter. The steering wheel was ripped from Imorean's hands, and his head hit the driver's side window hard as the truck lurched violently. There was a flash of bright green. He screamed and could have sworn the truck nearly rolled. The vehicle's brakes squealed loudly as it spun around in a half circle, stopping when Imorean was facing back the way he had come. He could smell burning rubber.

"What did I hit?" asked Imorean aloud. He knew that there had been a lot of accidents caused by deer and bears on this road. For a moment, the teenager sat still, his entire body shaking. Even his breath was hitching.

Imorean's blood turned to ice in his veins as he heard it. A loud, vicious snarl that carried promises of violence and doom. Imorean wanted to move, but he was riveted to his seat. Primeval instinct demanded that he sit still. Trees lined both sides of the road and Imorean scanned them with his eyes, almost completely paralyzed with fear. He could barely breathe. Then something moved in the darkness. Imorean's mouth opened slightly as a huge, black shape stepped out of the woods and into the light cast by his headlights. The teenager didn't know whether to be relieved or terrified as the creature turned to look dazedly in his direction. It was nothing more than a rather large and very confused black bear.

The teenager remained still as the bear ambled into the woods on the opposite side of the road. Then he laughed nervously in relief. He slowly turned his truck around, and began to continue on his way home. The thought that he might have hit the black dog now seemed preposterous. Hellhounds and black dogs only existed in urban legends and Halloween stories. They *weren't* real. For the rest of the drive though, Imorean refused to glance into his rearview mirror, not wanting to know if there was something behind him.

It was Amelia's terrified voice that woke Imorean the next morning.

"Imorean, honey, are you okay?" she asked urgently, shaking his shoulder.

"Hmm?" asked Imorean, opening his eyes blearily. His head was pounding.

"I saw your truck. What happened?"

Imorean sat up, rubbing his eyes as he did so.

"I hit a bear on the way home last night," replied Imorean.

"Are you sure?" asked Amelia, looking confused.

"Yeah, I saw the bear after it ran into the bed of my truck."

"Are you alright? You didn't get hurt, did you?"

"Yeah, I'm fine. I think my truck is a little worse for wear though," replied Imorean, grimacing.

"Don't worry about the truck," said Amelia, putting her hands on Imorean's shoulders. "I'm just relieved you're alright."

"Me, too," replied Imorean. He knew all too well how much damage bears could do.

"Don't drive on that road at night anymore," said Amelia sternly, standing up.

"I wasn't planning on it," replied Imorean, remembering his fear from the night before.

"I'll pick up the twins today. I'll see if Papa can meet me halfway."

"Sounds good," replied Imorean, slowly. "I should probably go have a look at the truck."

Imorean didn't wait for his mother to respond as he hopped out of bed, threw on some clothes, and walked quickly outside to inspect the damage to his vehicle.

The teenager sighed heavily in defeat as he took in the massive dent in the bed of the truck. He shook his head. He had been lucky. Not many people got away from a run in with a bear with such light damage.

"What?" he asked aloud, frowning as he saw something unusual. There was a large patch of black fur stuck just above his back wheel. He reached down and grabbed it. There was more than enough for him to roll between his fingers and get a feel of.

"This isn't bear fur," he said slowly. He knew very well what bear fur felt like, and this wasn't it. This was much more like... dog fur. The teenager breathed in sharply and caught an unusual pungent, burning smell. Odd. Imorean swallowed hard and grimaced. *Had* he hit the demon dog last night? No, that was impossible. He had *seen* the bear with his own eyes, and demon dogs weren't real. They were mythical creatures. Imorean shook his head and dropped the fur on the driveway. It had to be bear fur. He was just being paranoid.

There was something behind him. Approaching fast. Imorean ducked, bobbed, and weaved through the dense undergrowth, trying desperately to outrun his pursuer. He sensed a terrible danger in the presence behind him. As though it had hidden motives. Imorean looked ahead. The light of the moon flickered between branches bare of leaves.... He was nearing the edge of the forest. What lay beyond? Imorean swallowed. He was about to find out.

A horrified gasp was torn from Imorean's chest as he broke free of the woods and skidded to a halt. The ground simply dropped away. Below him, there was nothing but blackness. A nightmarish, bloodthirsty growl rumbled behind him. Imorean turned. Glowing brightly with menace between the trees, drawing ever closer, was a pair of red eyes. It was jump or die. Did he dare face the bearer of those terrible eyes, or did he fling himself from a cliff? Which fate was worse, which end more awful? Imorean swallowed his fear, and took his chance. He launched himself forward into the open air, falling down, down, down.

CHAPTER 5

Imorean was glad that after several weeks the rumors about how he had dented his truck were beginning to die down. Of course, the favorite rumors among students was that he had hit the demon dog of Valle Crucis, but Imorean insisted the truth was that he had only hit a bear. Although she vehemently denied it, Imorean had an inkling Roxy had started the rumor.

"They still won't shut up about it," said Imorean to Roxy one day during lunch. They were the last at their table. The other students who had shared it had since wandered off to meet up with some of their other friends.

"That's because nothing ever happens here. You denting your truck has been the most interesting thing since sliced bread," replied Roxy in between bites of sandwich.

"Sure," replied Imorean.

"You know we get notified today if we received the Saving Grace Scholarship," said Roxy.

"It's *today?*" asked Imorean, grateful for her changing the subject.

"Yes, bonehead," replied Roxy, smiling and elbowing him affectionately. "Have you not been keeping track of the days?"

"Not as well as I should have," replied Imorean. He was slightly shocked. "It's already April tenth?"

"Yep. Do you think they'll come to our houses, or do you think they'll just email us?"

"I'm not sure, Roxy," replied Imorean. "Most scholarship associations would just send a letter or email, but I don't know. Saving Grace seems to be different somehow."

"You're right," said Roxy. "I'm excited... and worried."

"Yeah, me too. I wasn't until you reminded me," said Imorean, elbowing Roxy in the side.

"That's what I'm here for," replied Roxy. She went quiet for a moment and looked thoughtful.

"What's on your mind?" asked Imorean.

"I have to get this scholarship, Imorean," she said. Her voice was serious for a moment. "I don't think I could deal with another day of being at home with my dad. Me and him have been at each other's throats for weeks now."

"What about your mom?" asked Imorean. He knew that Roxy's home life was chaotic at best, and abusive at its very worst. He felt the familiar thorn of guilt in his heart. Only one of them could get the scholarship. In their competition, there could only be one winner. Academic prowess or financial need? It could not be both.

"She's hardly home anymore," replied Roxy. She was quieter now. "You know how she is."

"Hey," said Imorean, the tone of his voice caught Roxy's attention and caused her to look at him. "You'll get it. Like you said when we applied, your GPA isn't much lower than mine, and, if anything, you need it *more* than I do."

Imorean knew as he spoke the words that he didn't entirely mean them. A sudden, sharp tug of selfishness made him think that while Roxy may have needed the scholarship more than him, he deserved it more.

"I guess you're right," replied Roxy, smiling slightly.

"Of course I am," said Imorean, grinning, glad he was able to lift her mood. "I'm always right."

"Get off your high horse, Imorean," said Roxy, shaking her head.

Both students looked up as the bell rang to signal the end of lunch.

"You're off to calculus?" asked Roxy.

"Much as I don't want to go, yes," replied Imorean. "You're going to English?"

"Yeah," nodded Roxy. "I'll see you later. Look, call me as soon as you know about Saving Grace, okay?"

"I will," replied Imorean. "I promise."

"Great, and I'll let you know as soon as I can."

"Sounds like a deal," said Imorean with a smile. Even as he smiled, the gesture felt poisoned somehow.

Imorean ran a worried hand through his white hair as he checked the mailbox at the end of the driveway. There was nothing in it. He could already taste the bitterness of crushing defeat. Surely the administrators at Saving Grace wouldn't give no response at all if a student didn't receive their scholarship after applying for it.

Imorean took a deep breath as he turned and walked back up the short, gravel driveway. His mother would be home soon, and Imorean decided to make a pot of coffee for them both. It might sweeten the sharp taste of his failure to receive Saving Grace. He tried to genuinely hope that Roxy would be the student to get the scholarship now, but he couldn't help knowing that he would feel uncharacteristically jealous.

The water in the coffee pot was almost boiled when Amelia pushed open the door to the small house.

"Hey, you," she said, sounding as happy and chipper as ever.

"Hey," said Imorean glumly, unable to put any happiness into his voice.

"What's got you so upset?" asked Amelia. Imorean could hear the instant concern in her voice.

"Today was the notification date for Saving Grace. I've already checked my email account and the mailbox. Nothing. I'm going to go ahead and assume I didn't get it."

"You *do* know that the mail has just arrived, don't you?" asked Amelia, holding out a thick envelope to Imorean. It was stamped with a large seal, bearing the image of an eagle in flight.

"What?" gasped Imorean, blinking hard. He could barely believe what he was seeing. The packet seemed too big to be a rejection letter. Had he, *he,* got the scholarship? Was it possible?

"If I were you, I'd open this," replied Amelia, wagging the envelope at Imorean.

The white-haired teenager took the envelope from her and quickly ripped into it, unable to conceal a grin as he removed a thick wad of paper. He unfolded it and silently read the words on the page.

Dear Imorean Frayneson,

Congratulations! We are pleased to inform you that your application for the Saving Grace Scholarship has been processed and approved. As you have already learned, Saving Grace is only valid at select colleges. This year, the scholarship is will be credible only at Gracepointe University. Gracepointe University is a college of liberal arts and sciences based in the locality of the town of Gjøvik, Norway. Know that you are in no way obligated to accept this scholarship. If though, you choose to accept it, subsequently, dropping the scholarship is not an option unless you are capable of repaying the tuition fees. Please let us know your decision by April twentieth. All contact information can be found on the second page of this information packet. Your first semester of classes is being constructed based on your chosen major and will be given to you upon your arrival at Gracepointe. All visas, books, tuition, housing, meal plans, uniforms, and transportation fees — including oversize and excess luggage during the flight — are paid for in full. Further travel documents will arrive following your acceptance of this letter. Your scholarship representative will meet you at your assigned airport to escort you to Gracepointe University.

Virginia Representative: Alfred Guardon
North Carolina Representative: Gabriel Archer
South Carolina Representative: Michael Archer

Thank you for your application and we hope that we can look forward to seeing you at the start of the semester.

Sincerely,

U. Ingram
Head of Admissions
Gracepointe University

Imorean sat stock still on the couch, having replaced the papers on the living room table. Norway. Norway... That wasn't what he had been expecting. Not only out of state, but also out of *country*. He was broken out of his daze only when his mother rested a hand on his shoulder.

"What are you thinking?" she asked, sitting down next to him and taking the papers from him.

"I — I don't know," replied Imorean, resting his head in one hand. Both he and Amelia fell silent as she read over the information in the packet.

"What about Appalachian State?" asked Amelia, furrowing her brow. "Norway is a really long way away."

"App State is just a dream if we can't find a way to pay for it."

"We have your financial aid," said Amelia.

"That won't cover it. We both know that," replied Imorean.

"Can't you take out a loan?" asked Amelia. "A lot of students do that."

"I know, but I want to come out of college with as little of a loan as possible. Have you seen the interest rates on those loans? My debt would be sky high. I would *never* be able to pay it back."

"Well, Imorean," said Amelia, running her fingers through his white hair in a comforting way. "It's up to you. I'll support you no matter what you choose. You know that."

"I know," replied Imorean, smiling at her. "Thanks, Mom."

Amelia smiled, but behind her smile, Imorean could see sadness and worry sparkling in her eyes.

"So, who else got it?" asked Amelia.

"I'm not sure. I haven't asked any of my friends yet," replied Imorean. He was almost positive that all the other applicants at his school would have come away empty handed.

"Do you know anything about this... Gracepointe University?"

"I know as much as you do," replied Imorean, frowning slightly. "I'll look it up later."

"I see," replied Amelia, scanning the other papers in the packet.

"I'll be right back," said Imorean, taking his cell phone out of his pocket. "I told Roxy I'd call her as soon as I knew."

"Right," replied Amelia. "I'll pour that coffee now. I think we both need it."

Imorean wandered into his bedroom, mindlessly dialing

Roxy's phone number. He bit the inside of his cheek. He had got the scholarship. Roxy would be suffering the very downfall he thought he had taken earlier. What would the end of this conversation mean for their friendship? Would it be able to withstand one of them having been chosen over the other?

"Imorean!" shouted Roxy, answering on the first ring. "I got it! I got Saving Grace!"

"What?" replied Imorean, the thought of Norway temporarily brushed aside. "That's awesome! Well done."

"What about you?" she asked. "Did you get your answer?"

"Yeah... yeah, I got the scholarship too," replied Imorean. He was confused. Two of them had got the scholarship? Of only one hundred possible slots, two students from the same school had taken them? Was that possible? Had there been a mistake?

"You sound miserable, what's up?" asked Roxy.

"You did read where the college is based, didn't you?" asked Imorean, choosing not to voice his concerns to Roxy yet.

"Yes," replied Roxy. "I think it's a wide-open opportunity and it's not one that I want to waste."

"Good point," replied Imorean, feeling more heartened that Roxy was planning on accepting Saving Grace.

"Are you going to take it?" asked Roxy.

"I'm still thinking," replied Imorean truthfully. "I think I want to do some research on this Gracepointe University before I say anything."

"Already done," said Roxy. "I looked up Saving Grace last night on the internet and saw that they were connected to Gracepointe. Everything checks out, Imorean. Gracepointe University is perfectly legit, and it looks awesome."

"Should I be surprised that you beat me to the research?" asked Imorean, smiling in spite of his worried mood.

"I can do some things on my own," replied Roxy.

"I suppose," said Imorean. A moment later, he furrowed his brow. "Don't you think it's unusual that we both got the same scholarship? Out of a hundred possible recipients, two of them came from the same school."

"Well, yeah, that's weird, but didn't they say during our interviews that they hadn't had much luck with candidates?"

"Well, they didn't say that during mine, but maybe you heard it during yours," replied Imorean, nodding slowly. All of a sudden, the Saving Grace Scholarship was sounding more like an adventure than an undertaking. He felt much more at ease knowing that Roxy would be accepting the scholarship as well. At least he would know someone else on the campus. The thought was like a breath of fresh air.

"Hey, Imorean," said Roxy. "I have to go. Call me when you make a decision."

"I will," replied Imorean. "Bye."

"Bye."

Imorean sighed and ended the call. He looked down at the carpet, considering his options. Saving Grace was a full ride scholarship to a college in Norway. He would know one other person on the campus. On the other hand, he would be incredibly far away from his family. He would probably only see them once or twice a year. Could he deal with that? Imorean looked down and considered. Homesickness would be awful, but perhaps it was time he spent a while away from his family. Maybe going to another country would help him spread his wings a bit and learn to be more independent.

The teenager nodded. This was a huge decision, but he had a feeling it had already been made from the moment that the letter had entered his hand. This could be his last chance at higher education, and he wasn't going to squander it. He couldn't squander it. Imorean smiled. Somehow, choosing Saving Grace felt right. He did want to wait a day or two before he contacted the administrators, just to be sure that he was making the right choice.

Imorean emerged from his bedroom some time later. Rachel and Isaac were sitting quietly on the couch. When they caught sight of him, they looked up with wide eyes. Was that fear Imorean detected?

"Are you going away?" asked Rachel, slithering off the couch and trotting over to him.

"Going away?" asked Imorean, inclining his head.

"Mom said you got a scholarship to go to Norway."

"I'll explain later," said Imorean, smiling at them.

"Okay," said Rachel hesitantly, looking at her older brother.

"It's nothing to worry about, I promise," replied Imorean, patting Rachel on the head and walking into the kitchen. He had realized only a few days ago that maybe he wanted to get away from North Carolina, to see more of the world, and Saving Grace was a golden opportunity to do that. He knew, or somehow felt, that going to Norway was the right decision for him to make.

Imorean was standing on the path. There was no moon above. He was in the woods, and he knew precisely where. This was a place filled with death and blood. A terrible thing had happened here. It was the site of the start of his worst memory. The terrible fear that Imorean felt in this place was all consuming. His heart pounded so hard that he wished it would stop completely. His blood was rushing through his veins. The ancient instinct of a prey animal told Imorean to stay completely still. He was not alone. Leaves rustled and twigs cracked. Something was lumbering through the forest. Imorean swallowed hard. It was something big. He stood still, unsure of what was approaching. Imorean caught the sense that the large creature was searching for something, seeking, hunting. Finally, more sounds, terrible sounds. The monster had caught a scent, and a frightful howl tore from its throat, wailing and wending its way up through the trees toward the distant stars.

CHAPTER
6

I morean felt that graduation had sneaked up on him. Time had passed in a blur. It seemed as though only a few months ago he had applied for Saving Grace, the reality was, and now he had finished taking all of his exams. Tomorrow morning he would be walking across the stage as a graduating senior.

His packet of information from Gracepointe University had come through right on time, along with his plane ticket. In the packet, he found a rule book, a campus map, and a list of all the classes he could select. He and Roxy, along with the other thirty-three North Carolina recipients would be flying out of Raleigh Airport on July thirtieth, just a few weeks after graduation. The only things Imorean had purchased were his passport and a new laptop. His old laptop was a DenTech model, and was one of the few models of computer not allowed on the campus. It was annoying, but it couldn't be helped.

Imorean had wondered for a few days why he and the rest of the recipients were leaving the United States so early, most colleges started in late August after all. He had later realized that it was to ensure that they got adjusted to a new country, oriented themselves to the college, give the homesickness time to subside, and fill out any and all paperwork that could have been left accidentally incomplete. He assumed that it was also due to the fact that the university needed to stagger the arrival of the students so that the representatives escorting them across the Atlantic would not be overwhelmed.

Imorean finally felt as though everything was slowing back down. Rachel and Isaac had already finished school and were spending a few days with their grandparents, so Imorean and his mother had the house to themselves.

"Imorean," said Amelia, walking into the living room.

"Yeah?" asked Imorean, looking up from some last-minute paperwork that had arrived from Gracepointe.

"Are you busy?" she asked.

"Not really, no," replied Imorean. The paperwork could wait for a little while. He only had a matter of weeks left with his mother, and he wanted to make the most of them.

"Let's go out for a bit," she said, picking up her car keys from the hall table.

"Okay," replied Imorean, placing his papers on the coffee table and standing up. He could do with a break from the monotony of paperwork anyway.

"Are you getting excited?" asked Amelia as they walked together out to her car.

"You have no idea," replied Imorean. "I can hardly believe that in just a few weeks I'll be on my way to Norway. It's like I'm living in a dream. Four years of studying abroad. I'll come back fluent in Norwegian. Who knows what else I'll be learning. There's going to be *so* much opportunity."

"I'll miss you," said Amelia. Imorean stopped for a moment. He fought the urge to grimace as he realized just how insensitive he had been.

"I know you will," he replied.

"But I know that this is what's best for you, so that's comforting to me."

"I'll miss you as well, you know I will. I think I'll be home at Thanksgiving or Christmas, or failing that, I'll definitely be home for summer."

"I'm sure you will," replied Amelia, getting into the car and starting it.

"So where are we going?" asked Imorean.

"I just want to spend some time with you before you go, and my work hours have been extended, so I don't know quite how much time we'll be able to spend together."

"Okay," said Imorean, noticing his mother's serious tone. Both of them fell into a silence as Amelia steered the car out of the driveway.

The early evening sun cast a golden glow over the green, tree topped mountains as Amelia drove her small car along the Blue Ridge Parkway. Imorean looked out of the window and smiled. He loved this town, this state, and this country, but now realized it was time to move on. At least for a little while. He knew that at the end of his time at Gracepointe University he would return home.

Amelia stopped the car at a viewing area and got out. Imorean followed her around the front of the vehicle and stood next to her as his mother looked out over the mountainous landscape. Imorean smiled and followed her gaze. He knew this place. A few songbirds flew out of a nearby tree and flitted around in the open sky for a few seconds before diving back down within the safety of its branches. A large buzzard coasted languidly overhead. Or maybe it was an eagle. Imorean wasn't sure from this distance.

"So, what brings us all the way out here?" asked Imorean.

"Do you remember your father?" asked Amelia, looking over at him.

Imorean furrowed his brow. Of course he remembered his

father. Every day for the past nine years, Imorean had worn his father's watch. Christian Frayneson had been a hunting guide, one of the best in the area. His experience, though, had not stopped his untimely death on one of his guided hunts. Imorean's father had been killed in a black bear attack nine years ago. Imorean was still certain that if he hadn't had to look after the other members of his hunt, he would have come home. Two years after Christian's death Amelia had remarried, but went their separate ways after the marriage took a turn for the worse. After Amelia and her second husband had divorced, Imorean had found himself once again the man of the house, but the second time, he was helping his mother look after two much younger children.

"Of course I remember Dad," replied Imorean, shaking himself. His voice was a little colder than he would have liked.

"You're so much like him," said Amelia, her voice quaking slightly.

"Mom," began Imorean. He knew that talking about his father upset Amelia. It upset him as well.

"I want... I need to tell you this," protested Amelia. "The two of you are so alike. You always have been. You both have an adventurer's spirit. He would be so incredibly proud of you and everything you've done."

"I just wish I could tell him," said Imorean, looking down.

"And I wish he could see you now," said Amelia, gazing back over the mountains.

"So why here?" asked Imorean, turning his eyes to the hills.

"This was one of his favorite areas," replied Amelia. "I know how much the two of you love these mountains. It seemed right... When did you say your flight was?"

"July thirtieth. Only a little over a month away now," said Imorean.

"Well, I'm excited for you, Imorean, and I know your

father would be as well. He'll be watching over you, and if not him, I'm sure there will be other angels watching out for you."

"I know," replied Imorean, smiling softly. There was something oddly cathartic about this conversation. It was the first time in many years that talking about his father hadn't hurt. He gently bumped Amelia's shoulder with his own. "I'm sure there will be some watching out for you, too, Mom."

"My little boy is all grown up," said Amelia, sniffling as she stood upright and straightened the collar on Imorean's jacket.

"Mom," chided Imorean good-naturedly.

"Sorry," replied Amelia. "You know that you'll always be my little boy, don't you?"

"Oh, I know," said Imorean. "But right now this little boy needs to get to bed. I have a kind of important graduation tomorrow morning."

"Good Lord," said Amelia. "So you do. I can barely believe it."

Imorean smiled, but all of a sudden, the hair on the back of his neck stood up. They were being watched. It was a feeling he had felt only once before. It was the same, sick feeling that he had gotten as he had passed the stone church in Valle Crucis. Nervously, Imorean looked over his shoulder. Behind him was only the forest and the mountains. Nothing was markedly different.

"Is everything alright?" asked Amelia, jerking Imorean back to the present.

"Yeah," replied Imorean. "It's late. Let's go home."

"Alright," said Amelia, patting Imorean on the shoulder and walking back to the car. Just as his mother opened her car door, Imorean's blood ran cold. Hot, rancid breath was fanned on the back of his neck, accompanied by a horrific, savage snarl. Imorean spun on his heels and looked around. On the ground at his feet, was a single, shiny, black feather.

Imorean looked in the sky for any birds. There was nothing but thin air. Quickly, Imorean walked to the car, his heart racing in his chest. No matter how much he tried to tell himself that it was just his imagination, he knew deep down that there was no way that that snarl hadn't been real. What was happening to him? Was he going mad?

"Are you alright, Imorean?" called Amelia from her side of the car. She didn't seem to be aware of anything out of the ordinary. "You've gone very pale all of a sudden."

"Yeah, yeah, I'm fine," Imorean replied hastily. "Let's just get home."

"Okay. You go straight to bed as soon as we get there."

"Okay," nodded Imorean.

The white-haired teen felt utterly relieved as his mother turned the car around and began the drive home. Imorean couldn't resist just one glance in the wing mirror though. He instantly wished he hadn't. Shining from within the woods was a pair of eyes. They were fiery red and seemed to glow with a light all of their own. There was something about them that seemed to bore into Imorean's very soul, threatening to devour it. All of a sudden, Imorean felt so incredibly worthless and helpless, as though he had been cast adrift into a vast ocean. A single word rose to the forefront of his mind. *Marked.* Imorean blinked and rubbed his eyes, hoping that the eyes would vanish. As he opened his eyes though, Imorean's heart skipped a beat. The vivid, red eyes were gone. Imorean shook his head. Was the creature gone? What had it been? The teenager swallowed hard. He had a horrible feeling that there was something following him.

CHAPTER
7

"Okay, seriously, Imorean?" asked Roxy, as they donned their caps and gowns along with the other graduating seniors. They were standing next to one another, heads close, having a quiet conversation. Imorean was glad of the other seniors talking over them, drowning out most of what he said.

"I'm just telling you what I saw," replied Imorean. "I *know* I saw something weird yesterday. The eyes were exactly like the ones the Hellhound had in the story about Valle Crucis."

"Don't be such a knucklehead. Hellhounds don't exist," said Roxy in a sing-song voice, fiddling with the tassel on her cap.

"You wouldn't be saying that if you had seen what I saw yesterday."

"Imorean, I hope you know just how insane you sound," replied Roxy.

"I know," said Imorean. "Believe me, I know, but I swear that's what I saw."

"Okay," said Roxy, shrugging noncommittally. "So, you

think you saw the eyes of a demon dog. What do you want to do about it?"

"I don't know," said Imorean, shaking his head. "I don't even know if I was seeing it right."

"Well I don't either. Hey, maybe you just saw a ghost or something, or maybe you're just going crazy, either way, I don't think there's anything you really can do about it."

"You're probably right," sighed Imorean, rubbing his eyes. He had barely slept the night before. Nerves and anxiety had kept him awake.

"Look, for now, just put it out of your mind," said Roxy, putting a hand on his shoulder. "Summon all your remaining energy. We are about to be graduates of this prison known as school."

"Got it. Walk now, worry later."

"Exactly," replied Roxy, clapping Imorean on the back.

Imorean smiled at her. She always had a way of distracting him from his problems, and now, in full daylight, Imorean wasn't too sure of what he had seen the previous evening. Maybe it had just been a mirage of some sort. Imorean frowned. No, it couldn't have been. There had been too much detail. Too much... presence about the creature. Imorean placed his graduation cap on his head and cleared the frown from his face. The creature, or whatever it had been, was gone. It was too late to worry about it now. It was best that he put it out of his mind. He had other things to focus on.

"Congratulations to our newest class of graduating seniors!" shouted the principal of Imorean's high school. The roar from the senior students was deafening as they all stood and applauded each other. They had been sitting out on the football field for several hours now, waiting for everyone to finish marching across the stage. Families and parents had packed into the bleachers on either side of the football field, cheering for their respective student.

Imorean couldn't hold back the cheer that leaped from his

mouth at the principal's words. Along with the other students, he hurled his cap into the air, watching as the black square spun in the midday sunlight. At this moment, he couldn't have felt less worried about the eyes in the woods. This was his day, and here he was, finally a graduated senior.

"Imorean!" cried his mother, rushing out onto the football field with the rest of the parents.

Catching his cap, he yelled, "Mom!" jogged over to her. He had to fight to get past a few other parents, but when he was finally standing in front of his mother, grandmother, grandfather, and half siblings, he couldn't wipe the grin off his face. This was one of the proudest moments of his life.

"Well done," said Amelia, pulling him into a tight hug.

"Thanks, Mom," said Imorean, returning it.

"We're all so proud of you," said Leanne, clutching tightly onto William's hand.

"Thank you, Grandma," replied Imorean, unable to stop smiling.

"So, off to Norway in a month or so, isn't it?" asked William, clapping Imorean on the back.

"Yeah," replied Imorean with a nod. "I'm so excited."

"And we're excited for you," said Leanne, moving to embrace her oldest grandchild. "It'll be a fantastic new experience."

"I can't wait," said Imorean.

"I'm sure," replied William, smiling at Imorean. Imorean furrowed his brow for a moment. There was a hidden hesitation lurking in William's eyes. As though there was something he wasn't telling. The shadowed look was gone only seconds later.

"Come on, everyone," said Amelia. "Picture time!"

Imorean exchanged a glance with his grandfather as Amelia pointed the small, digital camera at them. They both knew how carried away Amelia could get with taking pictures.

"Ha!" shouted Imorean, reaching out and grabbing onto the black gown of a fellow senior and pulling them into the picture as well.

"Imorean! What are you doing?" cried Roxy.

The white-haired teenager held onto his struggling friend as his mother quickly snapped a few pictures.

"Just thought you'd want to be in the next family photo," said Imorean, releasing his hold on Roxy when Amelia finally lowered the camera.

"Ah, yes, the unwilling friend desperately trying to escape being photographed will make a lovely portrait."

"Won't it, though?"

"Okay, Imorean, Roxy," called Amelia. "Let's get one of just you two."

Imorean looked at Roxy and widened his grin, holding onto her tightly as she tried again to dash out of the picture. He knew how much she hated being in photographs. Imorean jumped as Rachel squeezed her way in between himself and Roxy, taking a second to grin cheekily up at him.

Just as Amelia snapped the first picture, Imorean felt something land on top of his cap. While his mother was checking the photos she had taken, Imorean ran a hand along the flat surface of his cap and swept off what had landed there. Reaching down, he frowned as he looked at the object he had picked up. It was a simple, green feather. Quickly, Imorean looked up, perhaps a mallard duck had just flown overhead. The teenager's frown deepened when he saw that the skies were clear.

"Imorean!" called Amelia, catching his attention. "Focus, it's picture time!"

"Sorry," replied Imorean, looking back at his mother and allowing the grin to return to his face.

CHAPTER 8

I morean couldn't stop his knee from nervously bobbing up and down. The past few weeks seemed to have gone by in the blink of an eye. He had been very busy sending back and forth last-minute paperwork to Gracepointe, but at last, the departure day had arrived. Amelia sat next to him in the driver's seat, and Roxy sat behind him in the backseat of the car. Her own parents had been unable—or unwilling Imorean thought was more likely—to bring her. Behind Amelia's car, Imorean's grandparents followed, bringing the twins. The day was finally here. Today, he, along with the first section of North Carolina recipients, would take the flight from Raleigh in North Carolina to Oslo in Norway.

Imorean reviewed the details of their trip. He and Roxy would meet Gabriel Archer, their area representative for Saving Grace, at the airport and all would be flying out of North Carolina on a late flight. Imorean thought that their flight was at almost nine o'clock at night. He would have to check the ticket to be sure. They would have a six-hour layover in London to change planes, then proceed on to Norway. The last leg of their journey would be on charter buses.

"Excited?" asked Amelia when they had passed Durham.

"I think that's an understatement," replied Imorean.

"What about you, Roxy?" asked Amelia, looking in the rearview mirror at the girl in the backseat.

"I can't believe it's finally here. I've been waiting for this day since I knew I'd gotten the scholarship."

"Well, I'm excited for both of you. This is going to be an adventure for you two."

"I'll take pictures for you," said Imorean, grinning at his mother.

"You know me too well," smiled Amelia.

Imorean's own smile faltered as he noticed the expression in his mother's eyes. Was that apprehension? Maybe even fear?

"Rachel and Isaac are terrified that you're running away and never coming back," said Amelia, changing the subject. There was something in her voice that made Imorean pause. He remembered what she had said about losing him, and felt a surge of sympathy. Was his mother also worried that he wouldn't come back?

"We'll be back," replied Imorean. "Maybe at Thanksgiving, maybe at Christmas, depending on how long of a break we get, and definitely during the summer."

"Well, I'm glad I can reassure them with that," said Amelia.

"What about you?" asked Imorean. "Does that reassure *you*?"

"A little," replied Amelia, lightly biting her lower lip. "Only fifteen minutes now."

"Mom," said Imorean, resting one hand on his mother's arm. "Don't worry."

"Yeah, Mom," said Roxy, leaning over from the backseat to touch her 'other mother' on the shoulder. "We want this.

This is a golden opportunity for both me and Imorean."

"I know," replied Amelia, smiling at both of them. "I'm just going to miss you. Both of you."

"Well, I'm glad you'll miss me too," said Imorean. "For a moment there, I thought you were just talking to Roxy."

"Oh, I'll miss Roxy more," said Amelia, not taking her eyes off the road as she ruffled Imorean's white hair.

Imorean snickered then swallowed hard as they turned off the highway and onto the road that would lead them the rest of the way to the airport.

After being dropped off in front of the terminal, the pair slipped through two sets of sliding doors, heavy suitcases and backpacks in tow.

"So where did Gabriel say he'd meet us?" asked Imorean, looking around the terminal.

"It says here that..." said Roxy, scanning one of the many pages that they had been sent describing details of their trip. "Hold on, why aren't you doing this? You're the real brains of this outfit."

"I thought I'd let you flex yours for a change," replied Imorean. "Give you something to do."

"Oh, thanks," said Roxy, shaking her head.

"So, where?" prompted Imorean.

"It's that airline's check-in desks," replied Roxy, looking up and pointing across the entrance plaza to their flight's check-in area.

Imorean followed her line of vision and, being several inches taller than Roxy, was able to easily look over the heads of most of the people in the plaza.

"Well," said Imorean. "I don't see him, but let's go check in and get rid of all our baggage."

"Leave it to students to show up as soon as I leave my post for two minutes," said a voice, approaching from behind.

"Mr. Archer," said Imorean, turning and grinning at the

taller man.

"Mr. Frayneson, Ms. Daire, how are you both?" asked Gabriel, stopping next to them.

"We're well, sir," replied Imorean. As he made eye contact with Gabriel, the older man's eyes seemed to shine, and his grin felt somehow contagious. Imorean found himself smiling in return.

"Good, good. Have you checked in yet?"

"No," said Roxy. "We were looking for you."

"My apologies," nodded Gabriel. "I'll help you both get settled. Then we're going to wait here for a couple of hours for the rest of the recipients to show up. Did you two come alone?"

"No," replied Imorean. "My family drove us. They're parking right now."

"Fantastic," said Gabriel. "It's always good to see families helping their students. Well, let's go and get you two checked in."

"Yes, sir," replied Imorean. The white-haired boy looked over at Roxy, and both exchanged a grin as Gabriel led the way across the floor to the desks.

As their guide took Imorean's and Roxy's passports and boarding passes away to the check in desk, Imorean's family approached.

"Well," said William, placing a wrinkled hand on Imorean's shoulder. "The moment's finally here."

"I know," replied Imorean, nodding eagerly. He grinned at his grandfather, but William's eyes were elsewhere. They were riveted to Gabriel's back. There was something like horror in the lines of his face.

"We'll miss you terribly," said Leanne, distracting Imorean as she walked forward and wrapped Imorean in a tight hug. Imorean let go of the look on his grandfather's face. He must have imagined it.

"I'll miss you all, too." Imorean grinned as Leanne let him go and pulled Roxy into a hug as well.

"When are you coming home?" asked Rachel, catching the tail of Imorean's shirt.

"I'm not too sure, Rachel," replied Imorean, leaning down to her height and putting a hand on her head.

"You *are* coming home, aren't you?" asked Isaac, standing next to his twin.

"Of course I am, silly." Imorean used his other hand to ruffle Isaac's hair. "Who knows what kind of trouble you two would get into if I wasn't home from time to time?"

"You're not leaving because of us, are you?" asked Rachel, looking down at the tile floor.

Imorean couldn't stop his brows from rising then furrowing together in a frown.

"No," he said, keeping his voice quiet. "No, of course not. I'm going because this seems like the best thing for me right now. I'm coming home soon, I promise."

"Okay." Rachel launched forward and wrapped her small arms around Imorean's shoulders, burying her face in his neck.

"It's okay, princess," said Imorean, putting a hand on her back. "I'll be home soon. I promise."

Rachel did not respond verbally, instead she retreated and stood behind Leanne, waiting for Isaac to join her.

"Hey, you," said Imorean, resting his hands on Isaac's shoulders. "You're the big man in the house now. What do you say, think you can keep those two safe?"

"I think so," replied Isaac, pulling himself up to his full height.

"Good man." Imorean grinned at his younger brother. "Thanks, Isaac. I know I won't have to worry about them now."

"I'll look out for them," said Isaac seriously, drawing up

his shoulders as he spoke.

"Your sister in particular," teased Imorean, maintaining his smile and knowing that Rachel wouldn't listen to a thing Isaac said.

"I'll try," said Isaac, looking down.

Imorean smiled at him. Saying goodbye was harder than he had expected. Much harder. The reality of the moment was starting to settle in. This was the last time he would see his family for months.

"Be good," Imorean cautioned, pulling Isaac close to his chest. Isaac, in turn, wrapped Imorean in a tight hug. The older boy wasn't sure, but he thought he heard Isaac whimper softly.

A few seconds later, Imorean released his younger brother, not knowing exactly when he would see him again. He hoped it would be soon. The white-haired teenager stood up and looked around for his mother, wondering where she had gotten to.

"Will they be safe?"

Imorean turned and saw Amelia talking to Gabriel. The teenager resisted the urge to shake his head. There was no doubt in Imorean's mind that if his mother weren't so unsettled by his departure, she would have been flirting with their escort.

"Don't worry Mrs. Frayneson," replied Gabriel. "They'll be safe as houses with me."

"It's been a long while since anyone called me Mrs. Frayneson," said Amelia. Imorean saw a light blush color his mother's cheeks and tried not to roll his eyes.

"Oh," replied Gabriel, sounding taken aback.

"I go by my maiden name, Amelia Watson."

"Well, I apologize, Ms. Watson. Yes, they'll be perfectly safe. Believe me, no harm will come to either of them."

"That puts my mind slightly more at ease," replied Amelia,

folding her arms nervously over her chest.

Imorean smiled and caught his mother's eye. She quickly left Gabriel's side and made her way over to his.

"I'm not worried about you, you know." She kept her arms crossed as she spoke.

"I'm sure," replied Imorean, grinning.

"Thank you. I would stay until your plane lifted off, you know I would, but I have the late shift at the clinic again tonight, and–"

"Mom," interrupted Imorean. He knew how much his mother hated long drawn out goodbyes. "It's okay. I understand. Like I said, I'll see you at Thanksgiving or Christmas, and failing that, during the summer."

"Video chat me?" asked Amelia, tears welling in the corners of her eyes.

"As much as I can," replied Imorean, smiling at her.

"Okay. Let me know as soon as you get there," sighed Amelia, her gaze dropping to the floor. All of a sudden, she leapt forward and wrapped her arms around Imorean. The boy was taken aback by her surge of strength and stumbled slightly.

"I'll miss you, too." Imorean smiled, in spite of the sad moment.

"See you soon." Amelia rubbed her eyes clear of tears.

"See you soon," replied Imorean, pulling himself up to his full height.

"Good luck, Imorean," said Leanne, putting a hand on Imorean's shoulder and using her other one to stroke his hair.

"Thank you, Grandma," replied Imorean, nodding slowly. He dimly noticed his mother saying goodbye to Roxy, as well.

"You be good," said William, bringing up the rear. "Watch out for Roxy, write to us, and keep your grades up."

"I will," said Imorean, nodding.

"And keep your wits about you," said William quietly so

only Imorean could hear. "Not everyone at that new school is going to be your friend."

Imorean furrowed his brow and frowned as his grandfather joined the rest of Imorean's family near the door. It was strange advice to have been given. Imorean watched his grandfather for a moment. Why did he get the feeling that the old man knew more than he was saying?

After a short wave between the two parties, William nodded at Imorean then followed his wife, the twins, and Amelia out of the automatic, sliding doors. Imorean blinked back bittersweet tears, and in the blur, he could have sworn he saw a strange mutation of his grandfather's shadow. He blinked hard, and the image was gone. A trick of tears.

"So, when is the rest of our group supposed to be here?" asked Imorean, turning to Gabriel, feeling suddenly desperate for something new to talk about. Anything at all to focus on.

"Very soon. A couple of hours at the most We chose Raleigh because it's more or less in the middle of the state. Have either of you ever flown before?"

"I have, I flew with my family to Florida once," replied Roxy.

"Good. What did you think?" asked Gabriel, moving across the wide, open entrance plaza to a bench. Imorean adjusted his backpack and followed their guide.

"I liked it. Flying is fun," replied Roxy, depositing her luggage on the tiled floor and rolling her shoulders.

"Well, at least I've got one good flier. And you, Imorean?" asked Gabriel, sitting down and stretching out his long legs.

"I've never flown before," replied Imorean, sitting down next to Gabriel. "And heights actually scare me a little bit. Actually, they scare me a lot. I'm terrified of heights."

"Really?" asked Gabriel, frowning. "But you live in the mountains. I don't understand."

"I'm fine when I've got both feet firmly on the ground, and I love looking out over the mountains. I just don't know how I'll be when I'm thousands of feet up in the air flying in a pressurized, metal tube."

A sick feeling rose in Imorean's mouth as he spoke. He had been trying to quell this feeling of horrible anxiety all day.

"Well," replied Gabriel, smiling in a comforting way. "You won't even feel like you're moving. I promise."

"What time is it in Gjovik?" asked Roxy.

"Gjøvik," said Gabriel, gently correcting her pronunciation. "Gjøvik is six hours ahead of us. We'll be traveling for seventeen hours. This is no short trip."

"Wow," sighed Imorean, shaking his head. A seventeen-hour trip? How would he survive? Perhaps the trip was going to be more of a nightmare than he had originally thought.

"Stay here, please," said Gabriel. "There's another one of the recipients."

CHAPTER 9

I morean looked up as Gabriel trotted away into the crowds. The airport was starting to empty with people now. How many of them would be on the same flight as him, he wondered.

Gabriel reappeared a moment later with a boy whose auburn hair was cut short. Imorean studied the newcomer that Gabriel had brought. The teenager was equally as tall as himself, if not slightly taller, but very lanky, as though he had grown tall very suddenly. His face was angular, like an upside-down triangle. His hazel eyes were wide and bright, as though they caught all the light around him.

Gabriel motioned between the three students. "Imorean, Roxy. This is Toddy Davis. Toddy, these two young people are Imorean Frayneson and Roxy Daire."

"Hey there," said Imorean standing up and extending a hand for the other boy to shake. He barely noticed as Gabriel slipped away into the crowds once again, probably to flag down another scholarship recipient.

"Hiya," replied Toddy, instantly taking Imorean's hand in

his own and giving it a vigorous shake. Imorean smiled, holding back a chuckle, feeling somewhat bemused by Toddy's energy.

"So where are you from?" asked Imorean, smiling at the newcomer as Roxy tentatively shook his hand as well. While she was perfectly confident around people she knew well, she had a tendency to be shyer around new people.

"I'm from a tiny little place in the east of the state, you've probably never heard of it," said Toddy, adjusting the pack on his back.

"Try us," said Imorean with a grin.

"It's called Bayboro. Pop of only about twelve hundred."

"Well, you're right. Never heard of it," replied Imorean, shaking his head and smiling slightly. "That's interesting, though. Our town is called Blowing Rock and the population is about the same."

"That's a relief."

"Why do you say that?"

"You're small town folk, like me," said Toddy, shrugging off his backpack and flopping down on the bench where Imorean had been sitting. "I was so worried all the scholarship recipients would be from Raleigh or Charlotte or Asheville and I would be the only one from a tiny town in the middle of nowhere."

"Well, you're certainly not alone," said Roxy, resting her elbows on her knees. "What's your major, Toddy?"

"I'm a chemistry major, what about y'all?"

"Biology," replied Imorean.

"Art," said Roxy, twirling a piece of her newly dyed hair between her fingers. This time there were green tips in her dark hair. Imorean wondered how he hadn't noticed before. Perhaps because Roxy's habit of dyeing her hair was now so commonplace.

It wasn't long before all the first wave recipients had

gathered together. Imorean, Roxy, Toddy, and a girl called Mandy chatted with one another in a group. They quickly found out that they were all from small towns, Mandy's being from a small town near the Virginia border. Mandy wore rectangular glasses, which, Imorean thought, framed her narrow face quite well. Her long, blonde hair was the color of straw and her eyes, an opaque blue, were the color of ice. She was thin without being entirely athletic, and was only taller than Roxy by a few inches. Imorean liked her immediately.

The other students, from large cities, seemed to have banded together and were chatting amicably with one another. There was an atmosphere of anticipation over the group. Imorean knew that all of them were waiting. He looked over at Roxy and Mandy for a moment. Both girls had become quite quiet. They seemed nervous.

Imorean turned back to the other students nearby. For the life of him, he couldn't remember many of the other students' names, despite the fact that they had all been introduced. He was sure that when they got to Gracepointe they would become more familiar with one another. Hopefully then, he would be able to refresh his memory.

"Okay, guys." Gabriel stood in front of the two separate, yet together, groups and clapped his hands together.

Imorean watched in quiet entertainment as conversations quickly trailed off and everyone turned their eyes onto Gabriel Archer. There was a strange mixture of tension, anxiety and excitement in the air.

"I have helped everyone check in, haven't I? Speak now if I haven't."

There was a quiet pause, and none of the students spoke.

"Good," said Gabriel. "Well, who's ready to get this show on the road and start heading to Norway? It's going to be one heck of a long trip."

"I am, for sure," said Toddy, standing up quickly.

"We've got one outspoken person," said Gabriel, grinning.

"Come on, guys. Let's get moving."

Imorean fidgeted anxiously, tightening and loosening his seatbelt, as he sat in his seat next to Roxy on the plane. They had been at the airport since four o'clock this afternoon. It was now almost eight, and their flight was finally taxiing to the runway. Imorean felt nauseous, as though he was going to be sick.

The white-haired teen looked around. He was horribly nervous that they had been given a window seat. But would he rather be at the window or wedged in the middle of the plane? Would seeing make it worse, or better? Would he be able to see exactly how high they were?

Toddy was directly behind them, and Mandy was sitting in front of them. Gabriel was sitting next to Roxy, but was across the aisle in the middle section of seats. He seemed to be doing his best to keep his eyes on all twelve of the students at the same time. Imorean had a feeling that Gabriel must be grateful that the students were arriving in smaller groups, rather than all at once.

"So how long was your flight to Florida when you went?" Imorean asked, trying to distract himself from his growing feeling of nausea. His knee was bobbing up and down. His heart was racing.

"It wasn't that long. Maybe two or three hours," replied Roxy, ducking her head a little to look out of the window. Imorean didn't follow her line of sight. He was already begging himself to remain calm.

"How long is this one supposed to be?" Imorean asked, wishing he could consult the ticket, but that was safely stashed in his bag in the overhead luggage compartment, and there was no way that he was moving now. If he got up, he had a feeling he would try to run straight off the plane.

"I think Mr. Archer said this flight would be around seven hours. Total travel time seventeen hours."

Imorean, swallowed hard. "We're going to be in the air for

seven hours?"

He didn't like the sound of that. Seven hours, thousands of feet above the ground. Seven hours in a pressurized tube that truly shouldn't be able to fly. Seven hours spent trying not to fall out of the sky. Imorean himself wasn't entirely sure if it was the idea of flying itself, or the idea of possibly falling from tens of thousands of feet to a terrible death. Either way, he knew that he was afraid.

"It'll be fine," replied Roxy, smiling and shoving his shoulder. "Stop stressing. You sound like an old woman."

"Thanks," said Imorean, rolling his eyes. He knew Roxy was trying to make him feel better, but it wasn't working. All he felt was afraid.

"You're welcome," nodded Roxy.

"What's that?" Imorean looked around nervously as he heard a thump. He was fighting to keep his voice steady.

"It's fine," said Gabriel. "They're just letting the flaps go. Testing everything before we take off."

"Are you sure?" asked Imorean, his brow furrowed in concern.

"It's nothing to worry about, I promise," said Gabriel flashing a broad smile. "I've been commuting from here to Norway and back for several months now. I'm quite well versed in flying."

"Okay," replied Imorean, sighing heavily. Gabriel's and Roxy's words had helped to relax him a tiny bit. Not much, but just a little.

"Hey," said Toddy, tapping the top of Imorean's head.

"Yeah?"

"You as nervous as I am?"

"I think so. Probably more so."

"Don't feel alone," Toddy said, "I've never flown before either."

"Mr. Davis," said Gabriel sharply. "Sit down. We're

getting ready for takeoff."

"Yes, sir, sorry, Mr. Archer."

As the engines of the plane whirred and whined, Imorean gripped the armrests of his seat. It sounded as though a great beast was snarling and growling under the plane. The entire machine vibrated. It felt as though it was going to rattle apart.

"We're on the runway now," said Roxy.

"Are we doing modeling or something?" asked Imorean, making a weak attempt at humor. His voice was shaky. His mouth was dry, and there was an odd sick feeling in it.

"I hardly think this plane would win any beauty contests."

Imorean inhaled sharply and tightened his grip on the armrests as the engines screamed. His knuckles went white as the plane seemed to suddenly lurch forward. Imorean felt as though he had been launched out of a slingshot. He shut his eyes tightly as his stomach seemed to drop. He was reminded of being on a roller coaster.

"Hey," said Roxy, elbowing him in the ribs.

"What?" asked Imorean, grudgingly opening his eyes.

"Look out the window."

Imorean turned his head and looked out of the window next to him. His mouth opened slightly. He felt woozy and sick again, and he shuddered. The ground had dropped away. The airport and the runway below looked like little more than a child's toys. Imorean shoved his terror aside for a moment, and craned his neck to try to get a last glimpse of the Appalachian Mountains. His brows furrowed in sadness as he caught sight of rolling piedmont foothills, but anything further was obscured by a soft, blue haze.

"Whoa!" said Imorean softly as the plane's wings tilted. His knuckles were white on the armrests. It felt as though they were going to roll over. "What's happening?"

"Relax," said Gabriel, smiling. "They're just tilting the wings to even out the air flow beneath them."

Imorean looked back out of the window. The ground looked so distant now. A highway was little more than a thin ribbon of gray. A forest seemed to be splotch of green. A lake was no more than a droplet of water. Quickly, Imorean tried to search for the mountains one last time before the dark, evening clouds above enveloped the plane and all its passengers. His second search revealed no more, if not less, than his first.

"Bye, Mom," whispered Imorean as thick, dark clouds swept past the windows, obscuring all view.

Imorean shook his head as Roxy slept heavily next to him. She could sleep anywhere and through anything. Imorean knew he should try and rest, but he was too nervous. He felt too sick. He couldn't relax all the way up here, thousands of feet above the ground. The cabin was dimmed for nighttime, but not all the passengers were sleeping. Some left their overhead lights on, making it feel too bright. The white-haired teen looked around at the other students. Most of them were sleeping. How could they sleep in such a place, Imorean wondered? A few were watching the in-flight entertainment. One or two were talking with one another. Imorean was baffled as to how they could hear one another over the roar of the engines and the pressure blocking their ears. Imorean sighed and looked out of the window again. There wasn't really anything to see, except the distant stars above them and the silvery clouds below. The clouds made him feel as though he was closer to the ground than he really was. They helped him feel less terrified. In the distance, there was something strange. Imorean narrowed his eyes and strained to see what it was. Surely, it couldn't be. It looked like... daylight. Imorean checked his watch. In North Carolina, it was one o'clock in the morning.

"You're right. That's sunlight," said Gabriel.

Imorean jumped and turned around. Gabriel was standing in the aisle, leaning on Roxy's seat and looking out of the window. Somehow, despite the pressure on his ears, Imorean could hear Gabriel quite clearly. Maybe it wasn't as hard to hear as he had thought.

"How?" asked Imorean.

"We're very far north at the moment, following the curvature of the Earth. Right now, we're relatively close to the arctic circle," replied Gabriel. "Surely you've learned in school what happens in the arctic during the summer?"

Imorean thought for a moment. "The sun never sets."

"Exactly," nodded Gabriel.

"Wow," said Imorean, looking back out of the window. He admitted it, seeing even a glimpse of the midnight sun was pretty cool.

"You should try and get some sleep."

"I can't. I can't relax. I don't like having this much space between me and the ground. I feel sick."

"I see." Gabriel rested a hand on Imorean's shoulder. "Well, just put your head down for a few minutes or something then."

"Yes, sir."

"That wasn't a command, Imorean. You don't *have* to. I just don't want you feeling exhausted when we land."

"Okay. I'll try."

Imorean reached down and picked up the complimentary pillow and blanket. He rested the pillow on the side of the plane, near the window, and placed his head on it, feeling very suddenly tired. His fear was ebbing away. After a few seconds, he sighed and closed his eyes.

CHAPTER 10

I morean rubbed his eyes and tried to stay awake. He was shocked at how drained he felt from all the traveling. Vaguely, he recalled landing at Heathrow airport in London, England. The six-hour layover had passed by in a haze of boredom, frustration, and exhaustion. Even cruising the departure terminal hadn't helped to pass the time. The jet lag had been murderous. Imorean could barely remember boarding their second plane and landing in Oslo. After they had landed in Norway, he and the rest of the North Carolina scholarship recipients were guided onto a charter bus, driven by one of the employees of Gracepointe. The bus had felt far too big to be driving on a highway, but now on winding, tree-lined backroads, it felt massive.

It was early evening in Norway. Dark brown eyes looked dazedly out of the bus's windows, watching the Norwegian countryside pass by. It was so different to North Carolina. Imorean noted that it was greener, yet somehow darker than his home. Even the pine trees themselves were different. Through gaps in the trees, he could see undulating, rolling countryside. They were well out of city limits, and the hour and a half bus ride must be almost over.

"We're getting close to Gracepointe University now. Start waking up your neighbors if they're sleeping," said Gabriel, standing up.

Imorean looked up at their guide. Gabriel didn't even seem fazed by the long trip. He was still bright eyed and lively. Imorean supposed that it was from making the trip so many times before.

"You awake?" asked Roxy blearily, looking over at Imorean.

"I think so," replied Imorean, returning her gaze. Her eyes were bloodshot and her dyed hair was greasy. He supposed he didn't look much better.

"I don't know how I'm still alive."

"Me either."

"Did you stay awake for the whole of both flights?" asked Toddy, leaning out into the aisle.

"No," replied Imorean, shaking his head. "I did for most of the first one, and I tried to stay awake during the second, but I couldn't manage it."

"Same here. I was just too exhausted."

"I know what you mean," yawned in Roxy.

"Hey," said Imorean, glancing out of the window. "I think we're here."

The bus had turned off the main road and down onto a smaller driveway. Thick, pine forests lined either side of the drive.

Imorean momentarily forgot his tiredness. 'Everything here is so different. I feel as if I'm in another world.'

A smile spread across Imorean's face as the bus passed through a high, wrought iron gate and turned into a circular driveway. A huge, red brick building stood impressively nearby. Above the high threshold were written the words *Gracepointe University.*

"Welcome to Gracepointe," said Gabriel, still standing at the front of the bus. "The building you see to our right is the entrance hall. Beyond that is the rest of the campus. All of your luggage is being unloaded and will be taken to your respective rooms by Gracepointe's staff. Are you ready to see your dorms?"

Imorean nodded enthusiastically with the rest of the students. He felt dirty, exhausted, and couldn't wait to slip into a proper bed. It seemed like so long since he had slept in a bed. He wanted to stretch out and work the cramps out of his muscles.

"Come on, everyone off the bus," said Gabriel, making his way down the steps.

There was a flurry of tired yet hurried movement as all the students grabbed their hand luggage, and made their way to the narrow door. Imorean was glad to finally be able to stand and properly stretch his cramped, stiff knees. He felt as though he had been sitting down for an eternity.

Once outside the bus, Imorean shivered slightly. Despite the fact that it was midsummer, it was still quite chilly and the cool, evening air bit straight through his tee shirt. Roxy stood nervously next to him. He knew how uneasy she was about meeting new people and being in unfamiliar places. Imorean frowned in surprise. Standing on the bottom step of the Entrance Hall, just next to Gabriel, was a young, slender woman.

"Males will follow me," said Gabriel. "Females, please follow Seraphina. She will guide you to the female dormitory."

"Gendered dorms, I see," muttered Roxy, frowning.

"Well, it does make sense," replied Imorean.

"Come on," said Gabriel, waving a hand and motioning for the male students to follow him.

"If we don't see each other again today I'm sure we will tomorrow," said Imorean as he walked forward following the other males in the group. He spotted Mandy in the back of the crowd with the other girls. He hoped she and Roxy would have a room together.

"Okay," replied Roxy, frowning anxiously. "I'll see you later."

Imorean was slightly relieved to find himself standing next to Toddy as they made their way up the steps of the entrance hall.

"I hope we're roommates," said Toddy. "It would be nice to have someone I know."

"I agree," replied Imorean.

"We only have one dorm building for each gender, and the rooms are quite small but hopefully you'll find them comfortable enough," said Gabriel as they walked into the welcome hall.

Imorean barely heard the man's words as he looked around in awe. The welcome hall was beautiful. It had high ceilings, supported by wide, wooden beams, a stone floor, which was worn and slightly uneven. Long, narrow windows allowed in thin beams of light. Staircases led up to a second floor, and fantastic, old paintings and tapestries hung all over the walls.

"This was part of the old college. It was renovated just a few years ago," commented Gabriel. "But we can tour the college later, I'm sure you're all exhausted and want to get to your rooms."

There were several quiet murmurs of agreement and Gabriel stepped off again, leading them through the building.

Imorean found his feet working automatically as he followed Gabriel up another set of stairs and through a door that took them back outside.

"This is the main campus," said Gabriel. "Across campus are our main lecture halls. Behind them is the dining hall where we serve all our meals. The girls' dorm is on the other half of the campus, close to the sports center."

Imorean looked tiredly around. The lecture halls were across a large expanse of grass which was dotted with tall, broad branched trees. He thought that the trees would be very easy to climb and sit in. As Imorean gazed across the campus, he thought he could see a few lights on in the buildings. The signs of life were oddly comforting.

"Here we are," said Gabriel a few moments later.

Imorean looked up at the building. Like the welcome hall, it was built of red brick. It was two stories tall and had a large, canopied portico at the front, supported by white, wooden pillars. Imorean found himself smiling. This building was going to be his home for the next year.

"And this is your room. Room 244," said Gabriel, passing Imorean and Toddy a key each. "I saw that you two hit it off as soon as you met, so I figured I would be safe to adjust some plans and put you as roommates."

"Thank you, sir," replied Imorean, taking his key and smiling at their guide. Toddy remained silent. He seemed too tired to talk.

"You're welcome. Well, I'll leave you boys to get settled. Dinner will be at seven o'clock, but don't worry if you miss it. I doubt there will be many students there anyway. There's a fully stocked kitchen downstairs if you get really hungry. Breakfast starts at six tomorrow morning and lasts until ten. Times will adjust as more students arrive and get over their jet lag. Any items you need will be on sale at the student store from now until nine o'clock. It reopens tomorrow at eight."

"Thank you."

Gabriel returned his nod and stepped away, walking briskly back down the hall toward the stairwell.

"Well, I don't know about you, Imorean," said Toddy as Imorean closed the door. His energetic demeanor had vanished, and he seemed drained. Even his bright eyes were dull. "But I'm exhausted."

"I wholeheartedly agree," replied Imorean, his gaze

landing on the beds. There was a large window at the end of the room and one bed on each side of it.

"Which bed do you want?"

Imorean tossed his backpack onto the bed on the right side of the window. "I'll take that one."

"Okay." Toddy dumped his bag on the floor and flopped down heavily on top of the bed, not bothering to so much as take off his shoes.

Imorean smiled tiredly and sat down a bit more gracefully before taking off his shoes. He looked at the end of Toddy's bed and saw that all of the other boy's bags were already in the room. Quickly, he glanced at the end of his own bed and was surprised to see his bags. Imorean shook his head. He would unpack later. He was just too tired now. The white-haired teen kicked his backpack onto the floor and pulled back the covers on his bed. He thankfully laid down under the thick blankets and rested his head on the fluffy pillow. Briefly, he wondered how Roxy was doing with her roommate. After a sigh, Imorean decided he wouldn't worry about it right now, he was just too tired. Sleep was beckoning him. Imorean slowly closed his brown eyes and within moments, the waking world seemed to drop away.

In games of tag, Imorean had never enjoyed pursuing his friends, preferring instead to be the one chased. It provided him with a thrill that was otherwise difficult to find. Imorean had become very good at knowing when a chaser was closing in on him, and had learned well how to outrun and out-maneuver them.

This new game, though, was different. There was a desperation that coursed through every breath he took, and a terror that pounded in his blood. If he was caught here, he would be killed. Imorean could barely see. The forest around him was pitch dark. All he knew was that he had to escape his pursuer. A few thorny branches whipped across his face, leaving bloody scratches in their wake, but Imorean did not even check his stride. His desperation to escape outweighed the pain that came with the scratches.

A long, loud howl to his rear told Imorean that his chaser was closing in on him. Imorean would have whined aloud, had his breath not been tearing in his throat. Suddenly, Imorean broke free of the thick forest, and began to race across a wide, open field. His legs, though, seemed to not want to work anymore and no matter how hard he tried, he could barely run forward. Then, there was silence. Utter, dead silence.

Imorean tripped over a rut and fell flat on his chest, panting heavily. He was surely caught. The boy squeezed his eyes tightly shut, waiting for his fearsome pursuer to close the final gap between them.

"Well, well, well," drawled a low, slow voice just feet in front of Imorean.

The teenager jerked his head up, looking for the speaker. His breath caught in his throat as his eyes locked with a pair of glowing, fiery gray ones.

"This is truly a shocking turn of events," said the voice sardonically, the speaker stepping closer to Imorean. In the dim light, Imorean could just see the newcomer's figure. It was a man, tall and slender, almost feline in his features. Despite the darkness, Imorean could tell already that this man was somehow absolutely perfect.

"I can barely see you," muttered the speaker, snapping his fingers.

Imorean looked around in confusion as a full moon was suddenly revealed and cast down silvery light, illuminating both himself and the speaker. Imorean swallowed hard. He had never been instinctively afraid of anyone before, but this man was different. There was something that reared up in stark contrast to his beauty, and was strikingly dreadful about him. All Imorean could feel was sheer terror. The man's hair was raven black, his skin was so pale that it seemed to be ivory in color. His cheekbones were high, and his face thin. There was a delicateness about him, yet it was tempered by an atmosphere that was colder than ice and harder than steel. It was the man's eyes that truly caused Imorean's blood to freeze in his veins. They were the color of dampened, gray stone and seemed to be glowing with a light all of their own.

"My, oh, my, you do look similar," the man murmured, his eyes dragging over Imorean.

"Who are you?" asked Imorean, his voice barely above a whisper. He scrambled backwards, trying to put distance between them. The teenager swallowed hard as the black-haired man inclined his head and smiled slowly. A set of perfect teeth was revealed, the only exception being the canines which were longer and sharper than they should have been.

"If I were you, Imorean Frayneson, I would be less worried about who I am, as opposed to what I am."

"You know my name?" asked Imorean. He was panting, though whether it was from fear or from running, he wasn't sure. It could have been both.

A second beautiful, perfect smile was flashed at Imorean.

"Of course I do. I wouldn't be much good if I didn't," replied the man. Slowly, he lifted his gaze and glared into the woods at Imorean's back. The perfect smile twisted into a snarl. There was an ancient hate in the expression, something that transcended time and Imorean's very life.

Imorean's hand flew to his chest as his heart seemed to stutter between his ribs. The man uttered a single, slow word.

"Fetch."

The sound of frenzied barking and howling urged Imorean to leap back to his feet and continue his panicked flight, but a set of sharp, strong teeth sank into the fabric of his shirt and hurled him effortlessly into the air.

Imorean cried out as he tumbled off his bed and landed in a heap on the floor. For a moment, Imorean didn't know where he was, then he remembered. Gracepointe University, Gjøvik, Norway.

"Ow," muttered Imorean, reaching up and rubbing the back of his head.

"Are you okay?" murmured Toddy, sitting up in his bed and blinking at Imorean in confusion.

"Yeah, I think so."

"Okay," said Toddy blearily, rolling over to face the wall.

Imorean took a deep breath and realized that he was drenched in cold sweat. His shirt was stuck to his skin. His heart was pounding in his chest. His hands also seemed to be shaking. But why? Imorean frowned as he tried to think of anything that could have caused him to wake up like this.

"Whatever," muttered Imorean, shaking his head and smiling slightly. He supposed it was just waking up in a new place. It couldn't have been anything too important.

"Toddy. I'm going to go get breakfast. Do you want to come?"

Imorean snickered when he received little more than a tired groan in response. For a moment, the white-haired teen considered waiting for Toddy to get up. Then his stomach growled insistently, and Imorean decided that breakfast was far more imperative.

CHAPTER 11

I morean frowned as he walked across the campus in one of his hooded sweaters. Norway, even in the height of late summer, was colder than he had anticipated. It didn't even come close to the North Carolina heat that he was used to. Maybe he should have brought some warmer clothes with him. Imorean wondered what the winter temperatures would bring.

The boy looked around as he walked, enjoying the pristine, scenic campus. Imorean sighed as he walked. The campus didn't seem very large and was rather compact. All the lecture halls seemed to be built quite close together. He supposed that since he hadn't seen much of the campus it seemed smaller than it actually was.

Imorean looked up. Coming from the other direction was a girl that he didn't recognize. She must not have been in the same group as him. He quickened his step slightly, drawing closer to her.

"Excuse me," he said when the girl was in hearing range.

"Oh, good morning," she said, looking up. Imorean's

thoughts skidded to a halt for a moment. Quite pretty, sporting short, blond hair and pale, blue eyes, her face was oval, and her skin clear. She had the body and grace of an athlete, and a presence about her that held Imorean captive somehow. She was one of the prettiest girls he had seen for some time.

"Good morning," said Imorean, grinning at her. *This* was someone he would gladly make friends with. "Are you heading to the dining hall?"

"Yeah, if I can find it," replied the girl with a grin, looking around and tucking her hands deeper into the pockets of her jacket.

"I'm looking for it as well. Do you want to see if we can find it together?"

"Being lost together is better than being lost alone, I suppose." She gave him another broad smile. "By the way, nice job on the dye, or bleach, or whatever you used to color your hair."

Imorean self-consciously reached up and brushed his fingertips over his white hair. It was always the first thing people noticed about him.

He offered her a half-smile. "It's not bleached or dyed."

"That's natural?" asked the girl, furrowing her brow for a second. "Albinism?"

"Nope. My hair went gray around the time I became a teenager, and a couple of years ago, it went completely white."

"Huh. Well, cool."

"I'm Imorean Frayneson, from Blowing Rock, North Carolina."

"Bethany. Bethany Voran, from Columbia, South Carolina," she replied, shaking his hand. He smiled in confusion as she gripped his hand tightly. Her fingernails were perfectly manicured, and the palms of her hands were soft. Something about it struck him as odd, but he couldn't quite pin down what.

"Nice to meet you, Bethany," said Imorean, falling into step next to her, brushing aside his suspicion. It wasn't important.

"And you. So, who was your guide on the way here?"

"I came with Gabriel Archer. You?"

"The South Carolina guide was Michael Archer. Gabriel's older brother, right?" asked Bethany.

"Yeah. I think so," nodded Imorean.

"So, who's your roommate?"

"He's another boy from North Carolina called Toddy Davis. Yours?"

"I got a couple of girls from North Carolina. They seem nice enough, but I didn't get the chance to catch their names last night. You guys were lucky. I heard Gabriel's group got here first."

"I think we did. I didn't see any other students. What do the girls from North Carolina look like? You might be roommates with two of my friends."

"One of them looks short and stout. Pretty sure she's dark-haired. The other girl is really skinny, almost shrimpy. I'd say blond hair. I couldn't really tell. It was dark. Those of us in Michael's group got here really late last night," said Bethany. "I tell you, I wanted nothing more than to slide into bed. I was dead on my feet."

"Me too," agreed Imorean. He felt a twinge of irritation about Bethany's description of Mandy, but was glad that their conversation was flowing quite naturally. That was always a good sign. He didn't want to make conflicts with the first person he had met here. "Your roommates sound like my friends, but I can't be sure until I ask them. So how was the trip with Michael? When I met him for my interview he seemed...."

"Standoffish?" asked Bethany.

"You took the words right out of my mouth."

"The trip was quiet. Almost as though we were scared to talk to each other. Michael has this weird presence about him. Like, he'll step into a room and you'll know he's there."

"That was the vibe I got from him," said Imorean, nodding. Quickly, he looked around, trying to orient himself to the campus again. Everything looked different in the daylight.

"I think that's the building we're looking for," said Bethany, pointing across a large expanse of grassy space to a large, rectangular building with big windows. Imorean narrowed his eyes and saw a few other students going into it.

"I guess it must be." He was realizing again how hungry he was. He thought the last time he had eaten a proper meal was the morning he had left home. Was that two days ago now? It certainly felt like it.

"Want to sit together?" asked Bethany.

"That would be great," replied Imorean, a feeling of self-satisfaction welling up in his chest. "I don't know anyone outside of the North Carolina group."

"You guys were the smallest group, weren't you?"

"Yeah. We only had twelve students total."

"I think we had nineteen or twenty. I can't really remember. It was pretty big. I've heard that the other students will be arriving over the next few days. They should all be here at the end of the week."

"I guess that's why Michael was the one to bring your group. He's pretty rigid and I guess that helps him keep control over a bigger group. You think they'll send different staff to get the rest of the students?" asked Imorean as they ascended the few steps at the front of the building. He could smell food now, and his stomach growled.

"I guess."

Imorean quickened his steps a bit and pulled one of the double, glass doors open for her.

"Thanks."

"No problem."

Imorean stopped as the door closed behind him. There were large, circular tables set out about the open room, and a buffet lined two walls. At the head of the cafeteria was a long table, where there were a few members of staff. Or at least that's what Imorean supposed they were. They looked too old to be students. He wondered if they were maybe graduates or interns.

"So, where do you want to sit?" asked Bethany.

"I'm not sure," said Imorean, looking around. A few of the tables were already full. Clusters of students sat around them, talking quietly with each other. Then something caught Imorean's eye and he frowned. Sitting at one of the corner tables, under a large window was a very small, blond boy sitting all on his own. Something stirred in Imorean, and for some reason, he was reminded of Isaac.

"There," said Imorean without thinking.

"Okay. I'll meet you there," shrugged Bethany, moving toward the buffet table.

Imorean's gaze lingered on the lone boy for a few minutes more before he stepped off after Bethany.

Imorean found his mouth watering as he looked at the food on display, suddenly feeling hungrier than he had realized. He was certain the staff at Gracepointe knew that the new students were American southerners. There was bacon, sausage, pancakes, biscuits, gravy, and a variety of other breakfast foods. Imorean barely knew what to put on his plate first. He looked up to where Bethany stood at the far end of the buffet. She seemed more focused on the cereal, bagels, and cream cheese.

"Can we sit here?" asked Imorean as he and Bethany approached the small boy's table. The boy looked up, giving them both a wide, blue eyed stare from behind a thick set of glass lenses. His face was rosy and boyish, framed with badly cut, dark blond hair.

"Oh, sure," replied the boy.

Imorean was taken aback. In addition to the boyishness of the boy's face, his voice was very high, lacking the depth that came with age and maturity. Imorean noted that this student was markedly younger than himself and his friends.

"Thanks," said Bethany, plopping down into a chair.

The boy nodded and returned his gaze to the thick textbook that lay open on the table next to his tray of food.

Imorean furrowed his brow and took note of what the boy was reading. Were those advanced calculus equations? He looked back up at Bethany, who shrugged and rolled her eyes. Imorean copied her shrugging motion and began to eat the food on his plate. The quality of the food was fantastic. It tasted almost exactly like the food his mother would make on Saturday and Sunday mornings. The taste made him feel a little less homesick.

"Imorean!" called a voice from near the door. The volume in the cafeteria dropped slightly then rose again, obviously disturbed by the interruption.

Imorean looked up, spotting Roxy making her way across the cafeteria toward him. Toddy and Mandy were a few paces behind her. He smiled at the sight of his friends.

"Rox! Toddy, Mandy," said Imorean, standing up.

"Hey," said Roxy as soon as she reached him. "How's the food?"

"Incredible," replied Imorean.

"Great," said Roxy, turning away and trotting off toward the buffet bar.

"Why didn't you tell me you were coming to breakfast?" asked Toddy, sounding scandalized.

"I did. You rolled over and went back to sleep."

"Oh," replied Toddy, looking down before walking away after Roxy.

"You asked who my roomies were," said Bethany, elbowing Imorean lightly. "That's them."

"Yeah, you've got Roxy and Mandy. I've known Roxy forever, and Mandy seems like a nice girl. I'm sure y'all will get along just fine."

"I hope you're right," said Bethany, her gaze lingering on Mandy and Roxy as the two other girls walked away.

"So, what's your name?" Imorean turned his attention back to the small boy who had been at the table first.

"Colton," replied the boy, looking up from his textbook. His voice was thin and almost watery.

"I'm Imorean," he replied, flashing the boy a smile.

"And I'm Bethany."

"Nice to meet you." The boy returned Imorean's smile with a more timid one.

"Where are you from?" asked Imorean, noticing Colton's unease and trying to entice him into a conversation.

"Washington D.C.," replied Colton, dropping his gaze to the tabletop.

"I'm from Blowing Rock, North Carolina."

"That's nice," muttered Colton, his voice growing even quieter so that Imorean had to strain to hear him.

"What's your major?"

"....Mathematics."

"Do you mind me asking how old you are?"

"I'm fifteen," replied Colton, glancing back up in Imorean's direction.

"Wait. You're only fifteen? But Saving Grace was only available to high school seniors."

"I know," said Colton.

"So how did you get it?" asked Bethany, chiming into the conversation. "Not to be rude, but you don't look much like a senior, and at fifteen there's no way you could be one."

"At the end of my sophomore year I had taken enough classes to be considered a senior and I was able to graduate early."

"Wow." Imorean was taken aback. He smiled at Mandy as she sat down, then turned his attention back to Colton. "That's impressive."

"Hold on," said Roxy, returning to the table with a large tray of food. Toddy was a few paces behind her. "Did you say you were considered a senior at the end of your sophomore year?"

"Yes," nodded Colton.

"Didn't you have any friends? I mean, didn't you have any fun while you were in high school? Or were you one of those people with no social life?" Roxy plopped down into a seat beside Imorean.

"Oh... friends weren't really something I had a lot of." Colton picked up his book and stood. "It was nice to meet you, but I think I have some things I need to have a look at back in my dorm."

Imorean frowned at Roxy and kicked her lightly under the table.

"What was that for?" she hissed, scowling at him.

"You just had to ask, didn't you?" said Imorean as Colton scurried away.

"What? I wanted to know how someone juggles a social life and a school life with so much of a workload."

"Most of the time, they don't." Bethany put her spoon down and frowned at Roxy. "Since you fell asleep last night without bothering to introduce yourself, would you care to do it now, Roomie?"

"Oh," replied Roxy, narrowing her eyes at Bethany. "I'm Roxy. Imorean's *best* friend. We went to the same high school."

"What?" cried Toddy, sitting down on Imorean's other side. "Imorean, I thought I was your best friend. After all we've been through."

"Sorry to disappoint you, Toddy," replied Imorean with a chuckle. In reality, Imorean was grateful to Toddy for breaking the tense atmosphere between Roxy and Bethany. He had a sudden, awful feeling that Roxy and Bethany were not going to get along well. He met Mandy's eyes across the table, and the younger girl sighed in resignation.

"So, ah, what's going on today? Does anyone know?" asked Imorean, changing the subject.

"I think we have an assembly at eleven," said Mandy. "I checked my email this morning, and I think that was what I read."

Imorean looked down and checked his watch. Suddenly, he felt confused. His watch told him it was four o'clock in the morning.

"Does anyone know how many hours ahead of North Carolina we are here?" he asked.

"Five hours," said Roxy.

"No," snapped Bethany. "We're six hours ahead."

"Five."

"I'm telling you it's six. Michael told us last night."

"I'm not asking you to argue about it." Imorean resisted the urge to rub his temples. "I'm just asking the time."

"Six hours ahead, so it's ten o'clock," said Toddy as he checked his own watch. "I set mine last night."

"Thank you," sighed Imorean.

"Told you." Bethany smirked in a self-satisfied way.

"Whatever," replied Roxy, waving a hand in the other girl's direction.

"Well, it's ten o'clock now," said Imorean, after he had set his watch correctly. "If you guys hurry up and eat we can go and have a look around campus before we go to the assembly."

"Don't rush me," said Toddy. "Eating is very important."

CHAPTER 12

I morean and his group of friends were quiet as they walked along one of the concrete paths from the cafeteria to the auditorium. Imorean was already starting to figure out the layout of the campus. It was built in a massive, oval-like shape. The four main lecture halls, student store, and gymnasium took up a majority of the main campus. Near the entrance hall were two administrative buildings. The female dormitory was close to the gym, entrance hall, library, and administrative buildings. The male dormitory was on the opposite side of campus, close to the auditorium and the professor offices. Away from the main campus were the student health center, and the billing, counseling, and transport offices. Somewhere beyond them were the sports fields.

Imorean was eager to get more familiar with the rest of the campus, but now wasn't the time. The assembly in the auditorium was starting in a few minutes. As they walked, Imorean couldn't help but notice the unusually high brick wall running along the perimeter of the campus. What was its point? Something about it struck him as odd. Why did the administrators feel a need to hem in a group of college students?

"So, what do you think this assembly is about?" asked Toddy, stumbling on the top step.

"Probably all the regular spew that every school gives students every year." Roxy rolled her eyes as she spoke. "Don't do drugs, don't get drunk, don't assault people, and don't bully people. All that stuff."

"Yeah, you're probably right."

"Well, I don't know about the rest of you," said Bethany, reaching the top of the carpeted steps inside the foyer of the large building. "But I'm feeling tired again, so they'd better make this quick or I'm going to fall asleep."

"You probably shouldn't do that, Bethany," said Mandy quietly.

"Yeah, you'd probably miss something," replied Imorean, furrowing his brow as he walked more slowly up the stairs.

"That's what I've got you guys for," replied Bethany, grinning before trotting ahead into the auditorium.

Imorean glanced at Roxy, Mandy, and Toddy and frowned.

"Did she really just say that to us?" asked Roxy. "What are we? Dogs? Servants? Handmaids? I can't believe we have to share a room with her."

"She's gonna be a challenge," sighed Mandy, shaking her head. "Living with her is gonna be a big challenge…"

"She's an odd one," shrugged Toddy. "Maybe she's just nervous?"

"Come on. I think that may just be her mannerisms. You've got to admit, she's not unlikable," replied Imorean, proceeding up the stairs, his three friends a few paces behind him. He liked Bethany and was willing to give her the benefit of the doubt.

"You're right, Imorean," said Roxy. "She's not unlikable.

She's hateful."

"Do we really have to sit with her?" asked Mandy. "Roxy and I already have to live with her."

"It would be rude to leave her," replied Imorean. "We're all in pretty much the same boat here. None of us really know anyone else."

"Fine, fine." Roxy waved a hand at him. "But you'll be the one sitting next to her."

"Okay, that's fine," nodded Imorean. Inwardly, he smiled. He wanted nothing more than to sit next to Bethany. Partly so that he could try and keep the peace between her, Mandy and Roxy, but partly also to enjoy more of her company.

As Imorean entered the auditorium, he spotted Bethany in the middle of a row of seats. He took a deep breath and made his way toward her. As he walked, he wondered briefly why everyone couldn't just get along with each other.

Only about a quarter of the seats were already filled. Students were waiting for the assembly to start. Imorean quickly counted the students in the room. There were perhaps thirty or forty of them already seated. Imorean narrowed his eyes. There were only about fifty scholarship students from this section. Almost all of them must be here by now.

Imorean sat down next to Bethany, Roxy on his other side, Toddy next to her, and Mandy right on the end. The white-haired teenager looked toward the front of the auditorium, up at the stage. On it were two fold-out chairs and a podium. Imorean wondered who would be speaking to them, and about what. A few more students trickled in and when the lights of the auditorium dimmed Imorean assumed that they were the last ones.

"Are we watching a movie or something?" muttered Roxy, rubbing her head.

"I don't see a screen set up, so I don't think we are," said Imorean, yawning. His body still wasn't used to being six hours ahead, and now in the semi-darkness he was feeling tired again. The teenager perked up slightly though when he saw three people make their way down the aisles of the auditorium. Two walked together down one aisle, and the third walked alone on the opposite side.

Imorean inclined his head when the trio of people ascended the few steps to stand on the stage, then turned to face the seated students. Imorean furrowed his brow in confusion. Standing before them were Gabriel, Michael, and a third man he hadn't seen before. Imorean supposed that he must have been the representative who brought the Virginia students.

"Good morning." Michael had taken up the position behind the podium. As the man spoke, Gabriel and the third man sat down on their chairs.

Imorean almost flinched at the volume of his voice, then he noticed a small, black microphone attached to Michael's shirt.

"Good morning," chorused Imorean with the rest of the students.

"Welcome to Gracepointe University, home of the Gracepointe Eagles. I hope that you have all had a good trip. I am Michael Archer, Chief Administrator of Gracepointe, and I would like to take this opportunity to introduce the other two Saving Grace Scholarship Representatives. Gabriel Archer and Alfred Guardon."

"Good morning." Gabriel stood and faced the crowd. He flashed them a quick grin then returned to his seat.

"I look forward to getting to know each of you." Alfred rose more gracefully to his feet and nodded at the seated students. He was a small, fine man. Tiny by comparison to Michael and Gabriel.

Imorean felt an immediate liking to Alfred. After examining him for a moment, Imorean's eyes though turned almost instantly back to Michael. There was something about the man that demanded full attention.

"Now." Michael continued. "Gracepointe, aside from its

location and very small size, is just like any other college. We have many sports teams that you can join, and we have a variety of majors that you can choose from. Many of you have already done so. In addition to my position as one of the administrators, I am also head of the sports department. I am standing here to tell you about some of the various teams and clubs you can partake in. To name a few, we have a fencing team, sparring team, an archery team, a track team, a swimming team, and, my pride and joy, a skydiving team which I am the coach of. There is no experience necessary to join any of the teams, just a desire to do well on them."

A large, burly student near Imorean raised his hand.

"Question?" asked Michael.

"Yes, sir," replied the student, standing up. "There's no football team?"

"Indeed not. You are more than welcome to start a football club if you want."

"Oh," said the student, sinking back into his seat.

Imorean furrowed his brow. No football team? That was unusual. What kind of a college didn't have a football team? Then again, it was only the United States that prided itself so much on football. Most European countries played soccer, and sports had less bearing on school life. Imorean looked over as he heard the student mutter something just barely audible.

"Excuse me," snapped Michael.

Imorean raised his brows in surprise. How on Earth had Michael heard the small murmur from his position at the head of the room, when Imorean could barely hear it himself?

"Stand up, student," ordered Michael.

The burly boy looked around nervously and stood up again.

"What is your name?"

"Anderson, sir. Baxter Anderson."

"Well then, Baxter Anderson," glared Michael, while leaning forward on the podium. "Perhaps next time you have a comment you would like to share, say the words aloud as opposed to muttering them beneath your breath."

Imorean saw Baxter's gaze drop to the floor and he sat down heavily in his seat, clearly embarrassed. Imorean felt sorry for him, remembering Michael's sharp tongue from his interview for Saving Grace.

"It may come as a shock to some of you, but while Gracepointe does provide various sports, it does not emphasize any particular need for them. Instead, we value academics and independent thinking much more highly. Most sports tryouts will be tomorrow in the gymnasium. All are welcome, and encouraged, to come. We will hold another session of tryouts when the second group of students arrive."

With that, Michael stepped back from the podium and Gabriel stood up.

"Thank you, Michael," said Gabriel, making his way up to the podium.

Imorean smiled upon seeing the man who had guided himself and the other North Carolina students over the Atlantic Ocean. He was the kinder of the two brothers.

"Well." Gabriel rested his elbows on the podium and looked completely at ease. "I hope your first night in the dorm was good, and that you are starting to adjust to being six hours ahead of home. I apologize to the many of you who arrived late, but I hope you're able to get a proper night's sleep tonight. Now, in addition to my job as a representative, I am chief of all academic activities at Gracepointe. Gracepointe, as Michael said, prides itself on academic success. Our curriculum may move a bit faster than what you are used to. If you find yourself in trouble with your classwork, I will help you to find a tutor. We have many upperclassmen who would be more than happy to help. I am also the man who will be everybody's academic advisor for this year. I look forward to getting to know each and every one of you on an academic level."

Imorean smiled as Gabriel beamed at the students seated in the audience. The man had a strange, endearing smile. It seemed old somehow, yet Imorean had a feeling that Gabriel couldn't have been any older than thirty.

"Good morning, students," said the third man, stepping to the podium. "As Michael said a moment ago, I am Alfred Guardon. I am the head of the counseling department. If you are having any sort of problem outside of the classroom, please schedule an appointment with me, and I will do everything in my power to help you. My department also arranges all trips home. If you want or need to leave the college for any reason, please let me know and I will try to arrange something for you. Visits to the town of Gjøvik are permitted in groups of four to six, but will not be permitted until all students have arrived and settled. That being said, we will not be offering off-campus trips until October."

"Thank you, Alfred." Michael rose to his feet and made his way back toward the podium. "Now, students, there are a few ground rules that may not have been addressed in the student handbook. Perhaps some of you have noticed that Gracepointe is surrounded by a high, brick wall. The wall's purpose is *not* to keep you in, but rather to keep animals out. Norway does have wolves, not very many, but they are out there. Gracepointe is also surrounded primarily by forest, and is considerable distance from Gjøvik. The last thing we need is having wolves or any other kind of wildlife on the campus, or worse, for one of our students to wander off into the woods and get lost. The first major rule of Gracepointe is that in order to leave campus you must have a pass signed preferably by a professor, a counselor, or a sports coach. West campus and the sports fields are not considered off campus, so no pass is necessary to go to either of these places. Please understand that this rule is in place solely for the purpose of your protection. I ask that you honor all rules and exercise caution.

You are in a foreign country, of foreign tongue, and foreign culture. It would be in your best interests to listen to and obey the rules we have laid out.

"The second major rule of Gracepointe is that students must report to the student health center on West Campus once a month during autumn and winter. The temperatures here in Norway are much colder than what you are used to and we want to try and ensure we keep you all in good health. When the seasons change, we will be selling heavier coats in the student store if any of you need them. If none are to your liking, you may always go into Gjøvik and shop there."

"The third rule is that uniforms are mandatory during the week. When you go back to your dorm rooms later, you will find six sets of uniforms already hanging up in your closet. Your regular attire is acceptable on the weekends and outside of class.

"Now, remember, sports tryouts are tomorrow all day. Schedules for the tryouts will be posted in the common rooms of your dorms, the student center, and in the dining hall. Classes start next Monday. On your way out, please be sure to collect a campus map from the staff members at the doors. Schedules will be handed out at lunchtime tomorrow. Return here to collect them. Thank you for your attentiveness."

The lights overhead came back on, and Imorean blinked hard. Everything seemed far too bright. He wished that they had left the lights off.

"Can we leave?" asked Roxy, looking around.

"I think so," replied Imorean, noticing other students beginning to get up. "Come on."

Imorean nudged Bethany gently, as the girl seemed to have dozed off during the assembly.

"I'm awake," she said, her eyes opening quickly.

Imorean furrowed his brow. Surely, he must have imagined it, but for a split second, he thought that he had seen a flicker of vivid, sharp red in Bethany's eyes.

"Come on." Imorean shook his head, clearing his vision. "Roxy, Toddy, Mandy, and I are going to explore the rest of the campus. Do you want to come?"

"Nah." Bethany shook her head. "I'm feeling tired, I'm going to go back to my dorm and go to sleep. I'll see y'all at dinner."

"Suit yourself," said Imorean, turning and making his way toward Roxy and Toddy who were standing at one of the doorways waiting for him.

"Imorean," called a voice from behind the teenager as he was walking up the aisle. Imorean turned and smiled when he spotted Gabriel. The man was quite a lot taller than most of the students, but seemed to somehow blend in with them.

"Good morning, Mr. Archer," said Imorean.

"How are you finding Gracepointe?" asked Gabriel, falling into step next to Imorean.

"So far, I like it. But then again, I've only been here a matter of hours."

"I'm sure you'll settle in."

"I'm sure I will, sir."

"So, what are you going to do today?"

"My friends and I were planning on exploring the rest of the campus."

"A good idea, indeed. It's good to get familiar with your surroundings. Maps are brilliant, but there's nothing quite like going out and actually walking around a new place."

"Mr. Archer." Imorean furrowed his brow. "Where are all the other upperclassmen? This is supposed to be a four-year college, isn't it?"

"Ah. They come later, but they also don't attend Gracepointe. The university campus here is for first year students only. It is a transitional campus of sorts. We have another campus a bit further north that the other students go to."

"I see," replied Imorean, biting the inside of his cheek in confusion.

"Gabriel," said Michael, coming up alongside his twin brother.

"Yes?"

"We have a meeting with the faculty, do you not remember?"

"Good Lord." Gabriel checked his watch. "So we do! Imorean, I'd like to stay and chat, but I've really got to go. I'm sure I'll be seeing you soon."

"Yes, sir." Imorean slowed as he approached his friends. His brown eyes stayed riveted to Michael and Gabriel for a moment longer though. There was an aura about the twins that he couldn't quite put his finger on.

"Hey." Roxy waved a hand in front of his face. "Earth to Imorean. Are you coming with us, or are you going to ogle the reps all day?"

"Very funny."

"Well, we're ready. Just waiting on you."

"I'm ready, let's go," said Imorean, stepping out in front of his friends and leading the way out of the auditorium.

CHAPTER 13

"I think I'm in love," sighed Imorean, as a gentle breeze rippled through his white hair. After leaving the auditorium, he, Roxy, Mandy, and Toddy had walked onto the sports fields to try and get some idea of their surroundings. This was the only part of Gracepointe that was bordered by a rolling, green field and not immediately by forest. The tops of trees were visible in the distance.

"I know what you mean," said Roxy.

Imorean gazed out away from the college, taking in the scenery. There was something about it that reminded him vividly of home. The rolling hills shrouded by a blue haze in the distance looked so much like the ones he had just come from. These though, were somehow different. They felt older in a way. Imorean was suddenly filled with a sense of being home. Somehow it was as though he was supposed to be here. Something felt *right*.

"I could be at App State right now and I would barely know the difference," said Imorean, smiling.

"Only difference between here and home is that we

wouldn't need jackets during summer at home," replied Toddy, leaning on the fence next to Imorean. The boy's bright face sobered slightly. "And our families."

Imorean noticed that the brick wall surrounding main campus did not extend to the sports field, and he was glad that the fields were hemmed in by only a low, chain link fence. He felt slightly freer here.

"So, do you guys think you'll join any of the teams?" asked Imorean, wanting to lighten the atmosphere.

"That skydiving team sounds pretty interesting," replied Roxy. "I've never heard of a school having one before."

"Well, Michael did say it was quite new," said Toddy. "I'm thinking about that sparring team. What about you, Imorean? Skydiving?"

"No way," replied Imorean, smiling and shaking his head. "I don't do very well with heights, as you could probably tell from the plane ride. I like to have both feet on the ground. I might join the track team or the swim team."

"You've got no sense of adventure," said Toddy, shoving Imorean in the shoulder and knocking him off balance.

"I've got enough of a sense of adventure, thank you." Imorean folded his arms in mock irritation. "I'm *here,* aren't I?"

"Fair enough. What about you, Mandy?"

"Not skydiving for me." Mandy rubbed her arms as though the idea made her nervous. "I would like to check out the fencing team though."

"I think you'd be good at it." Toddy flashed a bright grin at her.

"You know what I'm excited about," said Roxy.

"What's that?" Imorean asked.

"Seeing the auroras. Apparently, Norway is one of the best places in the world to see them."

"Mom would love that," mused Imorean, taking a brief

glance upward at the sky.

"Wouldn't she, though. We've got to take some pictures for her."

"Wait," said Toddy. "Are you two brother and sister? I thought you were just friends."

"We are just friends," replied Imorean. "But I've known Roxy since we were both very young, and my mom has pretty much adopted her."

"I call her Mom, and she answers to it," grinned Roxy.

"Right," nodded Toddy. "She seems nice. I'd like to meet her someday."

"She'd love you," said Roxy. "Both of you."

"I wonder what it was that that boy said today in the auditorium," frowned Mandy. Imorean looked at her, glad he wasn't the only one to have heard Baxter muttering.

"I don't know, but Michael sure didn't seem to like it," replied Roxy. "I would *not* like to be on the receiving end of his temper."

"I wouldn't either," agreed Toddy. "When I first met Michael, he seemed like he was pretty easy to get angry."

Imorean nodded a few times. He was starting to get the feeling that everyone noticed that about Michael.

"I wonder why they want to keep us on campus," said Roxy, sitting down on the grass, and shivering slightly as another cool breeze cut across the fields.

Imorean sat down with her, his back resting on the chain link fence behind them.

"I think it's so we don't get lost," replied Imorean. "I mean, we've just got here, we don't know where anything is, and none of us speak Norwegian. If one of us were to wander off, imagine the trouble all the staff would have to go to in order to find us."

"That's true," nodded Roxy.

"You didn't sound too sure of your answer, Imorean," said

Toddy, plopping down on the grass as well.

"I don't know." Imorean rested his chin in one hand. "I have no idea what the staff are actually thinking, so I can't exactly say with any certainty what their intentions are. All I can do is guess."

"How wise," chuckled Toddy.

"Oh, he's always like this." Roxy ruffled Imorean's white hair. "Of the two of us, he's the scholar, I just eat everything."

"Roxy," scolded Imorean.

"Well it's true," said Roxy, leaning back on the grass so that she was only propped half up.

Imorean shook his head and rolled his eyes. "No, it's not."

"Well, I do tell the occasional joke as well," shrugged Roxy.

"I'm looking forward to going off campus every now and again," said Toddy. "I've heard Norway has some of the most breathtaking scenery in all of Europe, if not the world."

"I hope they let us off campus," said Imorean.

"I'm sure they will," said Roxy. "This is probably just a temporary system to ensure no one does anything stupid. After all, Guardon said that they would start getting off-campus trips ready in October."

"You're probably right. Roxy, Toddy, Mandy, I need to go and video call my mom. I told her I would when we arrived, but we got in so late last night I decided not to. Do you want to come with me?"

"Sure. That would be nice," smiled Toddy.

"Yeah," replied Roxy. Mandy nodded her own agreement.

"Alright," said Imorean, rising to his feet. "I'm sure they have computers in the library we can use."

"Can't we just go into your dorm room? You brought your laptop, didn't you?" asked Roxy, getting up a little more slowly.

"Of course, I did. But I don't want to go up to the second floor to get it, and I don't even know if girls can go into the male dormitory. I don't want to get into trouble on our first day here."

"Good point," replied Roxy, shrugging.

"Okay," said Imorean, leaning back in the library chair. He gazed anxiously at the screen, waiting for the computer's video call to connect to his mother's one. Quickly, he glanced at his watch. It was already two o'clock here, which meant it should be around eight in the morning in North Carolina. She should be home.

"Come on, Mom. Pick up. Pick up."

"Nervous much?" asked Roxy, elbowing him.

"Shut up," replied Imorean, jabbing her right back with his own elbow. He looked up and a grin sprang to his face as the computer's dark screen lit up, revealing the slightly blurred image of Imorean's mother and two siblings.

"Imorean!" she cried, beaming at him.

"Imorean!" chorused the twins, pushing to the front of the picture. Their noses were almost against the computer's webcam.

"Hey," said Imorean, grinning. "Back up you two, I can barely see you. You're so close."

"How's it going?" asked Amelia, pulling the twins back and allowing Imorean to see all of them.

"Great. I'm sorry I didn't let you know we got here last night. We were so late getting in."

"How long was the journey?"

"Seventeen hours. Mom, these are my friends, Toddy and Mandy. We met them at the airport. They're from North Carolina, too."

"Hello, Toddy, Mandy," grinned Amelia. "Nice to see you."

"And you, ma'am."

"Nice to meet you," smiled Mandy.

"Don't be formal with her," said Roxy, leaning into the

picture. "Just call her Mom. That's what everyone else does."

"I was wondering where you had got to," said Amelia, catching Roxy's attention.

"Oh, I'm never far away," replied Roxy.

"I've noticed. Good to see you, hon."

"Imorean," said Rachel, reaching toward the screen. "When are you coming home?"

"I don't know yet, Rach. Hopefully soon."

"Did they say whether or not you got Thanksgiving off?" asked Amelia.

"No. They haven't said anything about breaks yet. I can check the calendar when I get back to my room."

"You need to come home," said Isaac, looking at Imorean forlornly.

"I miss you too, Isaac." Seeing his family when there was so much space between them all was alien to Imorean. All of a sudden, he was ridden with a horrible, homesick feeling and felt a strong pull to go back to them. Imorean covered his mouth as his lower lip trembled.

"Hey, Toddy, Mandy, let's go have a look around the library." Roxy stood up quickly. "See you later, Mom!"

"Bye bye, Roxy. Nice to meet you, Toddy. You too, Mandy," replied Amelia, glancing in Roxy, Mandy, and Toddy's direction. "Imorean, are you alright?"

"I'm fine," said Imorean, his voice feeling thick in his throat. "This is weird, though. You're all so far away, and I'm here. If it weren't for Roxy I'd be all alone. I can talk to you like this, but it's not the same."

"Imorean, you can drop the scholarship if you want, can't you?"

"I don't know… but I do like it here, so far. I don't think I want to drop it."

"Aside from Toddy and Mandy, have you met anyone nice?"

"Yeah," replied Imorean, taking a deep breath and turning his thoughts away from how much he missed his family. "There's a girl called Bethany that I met this morning who seems pretty nice. She's a little stuck up though."

"Is she pretty?" asked Amelia, smiling.

"Kind of."

"Do you like her?" Rachel had launched back to the front of the screen.

"I don't know, Rach," smiled Imorean, looking away. "She's just a nice girl."

"How many of you are there at the school right now?" asked Amelia.

"So far it's just fifty of us. I don't know when we'll meet our upperclassmen, and we're still waiting for the second group of students to get here."

"Oh, crap!" cried Amelia as she glanced upward. Imorean knew she was looking at the clock on the mantelpiece. "I'm sorry, Imorean, I've got to go. I'll be late for work otherwise."

"Oh," replied Imorean, feeling disheartened. "Okay, I'll talk to you later."

"Love you, sweetheart." Amelia, kissed her hand and pressed it to the webcam.

"Love you, too," said Imorean, forcing a smile.

"Bye, Imorean!" called the twins, waving at the screen. Imorean returned their wave.

The call screen winked black and the computer's background reappeared in view. Imorean sat at the computer desk for a moment, his head in his hands. He had hoped that the call would have lasted longer. Seeing his family had been a treat. With a heavier heart than he had expected, Imorean signed out of his face to face calling account and got up from the chair at the desk. As he stood up, Imorean wondered where his friends had got to. The library was one of the biggest buildings on campus, so he might have quite a long search ahead of him.

Imorean walked through the building, idly scanning the bookshelves as he looked for his friends. He was certain that this was the second time he had passed this area while on the ground floor. Suddenly, he caught sight of a set of stairs. Perhaps they went up to the second or third floor. As Imorean moved onward to ascend the stairs, he noticed that they went down as well. The library had a basement? He wrinkled his nose and frowned. He didn't particularly like the idea of being in the basement on his own and decided that he would check down there after searching the remaining two floors. Just as Imorean moved to make his way up the stairs, he heard voices coming from the basement. They were too far away to make out with any certainty, but Imorean decided to wait just in case it was his friends. The voices drew more and more clear. They were both quite distinctly male.

Imorean leaned forward to make his way up the stairs, but stopped himself once more. He recognized Gabriel's voice, and he thought he heard Michael's as well. Their voices were raised slightly and the tones were aggressive. Were they arguing?

"Thanksgiving is an important break for these students. It's a big American holiday," said one of the voices. Imorean felt almost certain that it was Gabriel. The white-haired teen pressed against the wall on the other side of the staircase, hopefully stepping out of Michael's and Gabriel's line of sight. Something about the conversation had piqued his interest, yet he felt slightly guilty for being nosy.

"Their meaningless holidays do not matter to me," snapped another voice. That was almost certainly Michael. Imorean narrowed his eyes. Now he was definitely interested.

"That's your problem, Mikey, you've got not empathy," replied Gabriel.

"Do not call me Mikey. It is not my job to be empathetic,"

growled Michael. "It is my job to make sure that our students are brought to a safe location, which I have achieved. It is also my job to ensure that they *remain* safe, and if that means banning a few vacations, I will not hesitate to do so."

"Michael. They're going to want time with their families."

"What is your point?"

"I just think we should wait before we do anything. Let them have at least one break at home with their families before the curriculum… gets harder."

"Warm thermals work the best for new fliers, and we need to use the long days that we have right now for training purposes."

Imorean frowned. Was Michael really that worried about the skydiving team? Why was he even concerned? The skydiving simulator was inside. And why would they need to ban the Thanksgiving vacation on behalf of the skydiving team? It didn't make any sense. Even though the two brothers were ascending the stairs, Imorean decided to stay for a moment more to see if he could find out anything else.

"I know that," replied Gabriel. "But I really think we should wait before we decide anything yet."

"And I do not. Listen to me, little brother, for the last two years, we have waited too late to work with the students. We cannot afford to do it a third time. We must act now, before it becomes too late," said Michael. "To sate you though, you and I will consult this evening with Mr. Guardon, Dr. Ingram, and Dr. Hall, and we will come to a decision between the five of us."

"If you say so. It still feels odd calling them that," replied Gabriel, sounding put out.

"Indeed… I think you would like to know, Gabriel," said Michael. From where he stood, Imorean saw the top of Michael's head now, and shuffled slowly and quietly up a few more of the stairs. It would definitely not be good at all if he were caught eavesdropping, particularly not on, seemingly, so tender and suspicious a conversation.

"What?" sighed Gabriel.

"Our conversation is no longer private."

Imorean raced up the stairs, taking them two at a time, moving quickly toward the second floor. Surely Michael hadn't seen him. He had kept hidden from the brothers during their conversation. How had they possibly known he was there?

Imorean flung open the door at the top of the stairs and kept moving, paying no mind to the rows and rows of bookshelves on the second floor of the library.

"Imorean?" called Roxy's voice from between two shelves.

The white-haired teenager barely heard her and dashed between two bookshelves, praying silently that Michael and Gabriel hadn't spotted him.

CHAPTER 14

I morean laid on his back and stared at the ceiling in his and Toddy's dorm room. After the event in the library he gone straight back to the dorm room and stayed put, feeling too anxious to leave it again.

'What's going on here?' thought Imorean, twiddling his thumbs. 'The plan to ban an entire break on behalf of the skydiving team? That doesn't make any sense. And what was all that about keeping us safe? We're safe here and at our homes, aren't we?'

"Imorean," said Toddy, entering the dorm room, Roxy in tow. Neither Mandy nor Bethany were with them. "Where have you been?"

"Huh?" asked Imorean, sitting up and jerking himself out of his thoughts. "Roxy, are you allowed to be in here?"

"Yes, I am," nodded Roxy. "I asked the woman in charge of all the females. I just can't spend the night with you boys. Now, are you going to tell us what's going on?"

"...I overheard a conversation in the library."

"That's a shock. Were you sitting too close to some

people?" asked Roxy. "I mean, actually hearing a *conversation* in a library is something. Imagine that, other people in a school library."

"Stop being facetious. I was looking for you both, and I kind of heard it by mistake."

"Well spill," said Roxy, commandeering the wheeled swivel chair in front of Imorean's desk.

"Yeah. We wanna hear." Toddy sprawled on his bed and rolled so that he could face Imorean.

"Shut the door, would you, Rox?" asked Imorean.

"Ooh, secretive, are we?" Roxy kicked away from the desk, rolled to the door, and pushed it closed, then rolled back.

"Kind of. I was on the stairs, wondering where the two of you were when I heard Gabriel and Michael coming up from the basement. They were arguing."

"The library has a basement?" asked Toddy.

"What were they arguing about?" asked Roxy.

"Yes," nodded Imorean. "They were talking about banning all the students from going home for Thanksgiving. Something about thermals being best for new fliers, and something about training purposes. I don't understand why they would take away our vacation just for a sports team. And training? This isn't a military college... I mean, Michael said earlier that Gracepointe didn't place much value on sports. He also said something about keeping all of the students here safe, and I don't quite know what he meant by that. After that, he said that he and Gabriel had waited too late for something. Twice in a row they had waited too late, and he didn't want it to happen again... I feel like there's something going on here that we're not being told."

"You don't say?" Roxy raised an eyebrow.

"I'm being serious, Roxy. It's really weird. It sounded as though it was a pretty heated argument as well. Gabriel was in favor of us going home."

"And Michael thought we shouldn't be allowed to leave?" asked Toddy.

Imorean nodded.

"I don't get it," said Roxy. "Keep us safe?"

"I don't understand, either," replied Imorean. "But I want to know exactly what's going on around here."

"Me too," said Roxy.

"Me three," agreed Toddy.

"But how are we supposed to find out?" asked Roxy, turning her gaze on Imorean.

Imorean looked up and met her eyes. He frowned for a minute then looked at the floor. A horrible plan was forming in his head. A horrible, terrifying plan.

"Michael is the skydiving team coach. I'm going to join the skydiving team," sighed Imorean. The words came as a surprise to even himself. "I think if I'm around Michael enough, I can find out why the team is so important, then we can hopefully discover a bit more."

"You hate heights, though," said Roxy. "I'm surprised you didn't have to change your underwear during the flight over here."

"It's not that bad."

"It kind of is," replied Roxy. "I watched you practically wet your pants during takeoff."

"I'm going to do this, and see what I can find out." Imorean plowed on stubbornly, disregarding Roxy's words. "Besides, Michael said that there's a simulator inside, so I won't be going any great height."

"You know skydivers jump out of planes, right?" asked Roxy.

"I am aware of that," replied Imorean, narrowing his eyes at her.

"I'll join with you." Toddy sat up as he spoke. "I want to know what's happening just as much as the two of you."

"Well, I suppose I'll join as well," sighed Roxy.

"Roxy, I'm not sure if that's a good idea," said Imorean.

"Excuse me?" asked Roxy.

Imorean paused, wondering how to phrase his next sentence.

"You and I both know that you've never been the most athletic person."

Imorean felt guilty as he saw Roxy glance self-consciously down at her stomach. "You're probably right." The girl's voice was quiet. "All my fat would probably cause trouble."

"Roxy, you know I didn't mean it like that," said Imorean, his feeling of guilt deepening. He hadn't meant to point out to Roxy what she through was her biggest flaw.

"It's whatever," shrugged Roxy.

Imorean sighed quietly.

"I suppose spectating wouldn't be too bad," said Roxy, looking up. Imorean saw mischief in her smirk. "I'll get to watch Imorean pee himself."

"Very funny." Imorean narrowed his eyes but smiled at her.

"I'm hilarious," replied Roxy. "But who knows, maybe I'd hear something that the two of you might miss."

"When did Michael say tryouts were?" asked Toddy.

"Tomorrow, and they'll be posting a schedule of tryouts in our dorm common rooms," said Imorean. "Now I just need to try and stay off Michael's and Gabriel's radars for the next week."

"Oh, that should be simple," said Roxy confidently.

"Do you have a plan?" Imorean looked up in surprise.

"No, I was being sarcastic."

"Thanks," sighed Imorean, rolling his brown eyes.

"You're welcome," nodded Roxy.

"Imorean, do you think they even saw you?" asked Toddy.

"I'm not sure. That's something else that's bothering me. I was well out of Michael's sight. I was on the set of stairs above them, so I was directly over their heads. There was no way they could have seen me. I didn't make any noise, nothing to give myself away, yet Michael seemed to *know* I was there."

"Creepy." Roxy pointed a finger at Imorean. "Creepy stuff always happens to you."

"Maybe Michael is psychic," smirked Toddy.

"Yeah, right," scoffed Roxy. "And Imorean saw a Hellhound before we came here."

"I never said I saw one," replied Imorean. "I just said that I saw something strange."

"Wait," said Toddy. "What? I want to hear this story."

"This stupid, urban legend near where we live. There's supposedly a black dog that haunts a nearby town," said Roxy. "And Imorean thinks it ran out of the woods one night and hit his truck."

"I never said that," sighed Imorean. "And I know I hit a bear, not a dog."

"That's kinda scary." Toddy's eyes flicked between Imorean and Roxy. "Anything else weird?"

"Do you really want to know?" asked Roxy. "Imorean always has weird things happening to him."

"Really?" asked Toddy. "Tell."

"She's being stupid." Imorean rolled his eyes. He was embarrassed.

"He's self-conscious talking about this stuff. Like I said, there's always something weird happening with him, like how he always manages to walk into a conversation at exactly the right time."

"That's just coincidence," protested Imorean, a slight blush rising to his cheeks. He wished Roxy didn't enjoy telling these stories so much. He was certain that the things that happened to him were just normal occurrences.

"Yeah, right? So, you walking in on your first girlfriend talking to her friends at the exact moment she said she had been cheating on you was coincidence? I don't think so. Especially when it happens not once, not twice, but three times."

"You have awful luck in relationships," said Toddy.

"Yeah, tell me about it," muttered Imorean, turning his gaze to the carpeted floor. Roxy went on.

"He crashes into a bear in the middle of the night and gets away completely unharmed with only a dent in his truck. Bears normally total cars. We all know that."

"Luck," insisted Imorean firmly.

"That time you and I were out riding my aunt's horses and yours bolted. You fell off and landed on your feet?"

"Quick reflexes," frowned Imorean, rolling his eyes. There were perfectly logical explanations for all the stories Roxy was telling.

"He also talks in his sleep and has nightmares," said Roxy nonchalantly.

"So?" Imorean couldn't help feeling annoyed now. "A lot of people do."

"Keep telling yourself that. His mom told me a really cool story about him," said Roxy, looking at Imorean then at Toddy. "She told me that when Imorean was still a baby she found him one morning with a green bird's feather in his crib. All the windows were closed and they had no pet birds, so it was a complete mystery as to how it got there."

"It was from a stuffed animal. There's nowhere else it could have come from," said Imorean.

"A stuffed animal with real bird's feathers?" asked Roxy. "And that feather at our graduation?"

"How did you know about that?" asked Imorean, looking up at her.

"I was standing right next to you, you goober. I saw you

pull it off the top of your graduation cap. You and I both know there were no birds in the sky that day, except for the occasional buzzard, and don't even get me started on that weird birthmark on your chest."

"Roxy, that's enough," snapped Imorean. She was one of the few people who knew about the pale brown, vertical mark in the center of his chest. It was his only birthmark, and something only his family and Roxy knew about.

Roxy grinned and held her hands up in surrender. "Okay, okay, sorry."

"Dude," said Toddy, grinning at Imorean. "I think you're thinking too little of all the stuff that's happening to you. It sounds like you've got an angel watching over you."

Imorean flopped back down on his bed. "Maybe I do. But for now, I hope that angel can help me stay out of Michael and Gabriel's way until skydiving tryouts tomorrow."

"Imorean," said Roxy. "They probably never even saw you. It'll be fine."

Suddenly, Imorean felt worried. "What if I lose my scholarship for this?"

"For accidentally overhearing a conversation?" asked Roxy. "They can't do that. I don't know what the criteria are for taking away our scholarships, but that can't possibly be one of them. Stop worrying like an old woman, you know it's irritating."

"Sorry to interrupt," said Toddy, his stomach growling. "But I think it's about time we went to get dinner."

"I wholeheartedly agree," replied Roxy. "Are you coming, Imorean? Or are you going to confine yourself to your dorm room for the next week?"

Imorean narrowed his eyes slightly at her, genuinely annoyed. The effect of his glare, though, was ruined when his stomach grumbled insistently.

"I'll come," he huffed.

"Oh, smile, you party-pooper," said Roxy, standing and pushing Imorean's chair back under its desk. "You'll get wrinkles if you keep glaring like that."

In spite of his irritation, Imorean smiled. Roxy's permanent good humor never failed to wash away his bad tempers, even if she was sometimes the root cause of them.

CHAPTER 15

I morean stood between Roxy and Toddy as they entered the cafeteria that evening. Most of the students were already grouping together. Across the room, Imorean caught sight of Bethany and Mandy sitting at the same table they had been at that morning. He grinned, glad to see the two blonde girls.

"Oh, lovely," grumbled Roxy. "She's already here."

Imorean elbowed Roxy. "Don't be mean."

He glanced over at the girls once more and this time caught sight of a smaller student sitting just across from Bethany. He narrowed his eyes slightly, straining to see who it was. Imorean smiled when he noticed that it was the same boy from the morning. Colton, that was his name. The small boy was once again buried in a book.

"Roxy," said Imorean. "Can you grab me a plate of food? I'm going to go and get us a seat."

"Alright," replied Roxy, walking quickly along with Toddy.

Imorean picked his way across the cafeteria to Colton and

stopped next to the boy's table.

"Hey, you," said Bethany brightly, turning in her seat and beaming up at Imorean.

"Hey, Bethany," smiled Imorean.

"Where's everyone else?" asked Mandy, looking over Imorean's shoulder.

"They're getting food. Excuse me," said Imorean, catching the boy's attention. Colton looked up from his book, his glasses askew on his face.

"Can me and my friends sit here?" asked Imorean.

"Oh, sure." Colton gathered his items to leave the table.

"No, no. I didn't mean you had to move, I meant to ask if you minded us sitting with you."

"Oh..." replied Colton, sounding surprised. "Sure, I don't mind. That would actually be nice."

Imorean smiled and sat down across from Colton.

"You know you didn't have to ask," hissed Bethany, leaning toward him.

"It's polite." Imorean made sure that his voice was equally as quiet. He turned his attention back to Colton, feeling oddly reminded of Isaac. "I couldn't help but notice that you were alone this morning, and you're alone now. Haven't you made any friends?"

"Not really." Colton shuffled, seeming uncomfortable. "I don't make friends very easily."

"What about your roommate?" asked Mandy with a smile. "Isn't he making an effort to be your friend?"

"I feel I may end up being more his tutor than his friend," replied Colton, looking down.

"Oh? Who is it?"

"Baxter Anderson."

Imorean frowned. Baxter Anderson. The name rang a bell. A moment later, Imorean realized who it was.

"The football player from this morning?" asked Imorean.

"The very same," replied Colton.

"Well, my friends and I will gladly be friends with you," said Imorean with a friendly smile.

"Is that girl with the dyed hair one of your friends?" asked Colton hesitantly.

Imorean grimaced, remembering how Roxy had greeted Colton earlier that morning.

"Yes, she is," nodded Imorean. "She has a tendency to speak without thinking. Everything she says has to be taken with a grain of salt…. or a whole shaker of salt."

"You can say that again," said Bethany, rolling her eyes.

Imorean brushed aside her comment.

"I see." Colton sounded slightly more relaxed. "Well, thank you. I really appreciate it."

"You're welcome," said Imorean with a nod. "You said your name was Colton?"

"That's right," replied Colton. "I'm very sorry, but I can't remember yours."

"I get that a lot. My name is Imorean."

"And this is your dinner," said Roxy, putting a plate of fried chicken, mashed potatoes, and gravy on the table in front of Imorean.

"You're amazing. Do you know that?"

"Well, I have my moments," smiled Roxy.

"Roxy, Toddy, this is Colton. Colton, these two are Roxy and Toddy. I'm assuming you, Bethany and Mandy already know each other."

"Nice to meet you," replied Roxy, sitting down next to Imorean.

"Hey there." Toddy's words were nearly unintelligible around a mouthful of food.

"Nice to meet you properly," said Colton quietly.

"And, yes, we already introduced ourselves," said Bethany, frowning.

Turning his attention back to Colton, Imorean could tell in the boy's voice that he was grateful to have people sitting with him. White hair drifted across Imorean's forehead as he cocked his head at Bethany. She looked as though she had just eaten something sour. Imorean wondered what was wrong. He turned and looked at Mandy. She was smiling at Colton. He suddenly had a feeling that she too had younger siblings. He felt oddly grateful that she was there.

"So, you mentioned you graduated as a sophomore?" asked Imorean, turning his attention back to Colton as he ate.

"Yes," said Colton.

"How?"

Colton smiled, pushing his glasses up his nose. "A lot of work."

"I can imagine." Imorean cringed. He remembered how overloaded with work he had felt, and he had completed high school in the typical four years.

"I have a question," said Colton, inclining his head.

"Yeah?" asked Imorean.

"What kind of bleach did you use on your hair?"

"None. It's naturally this way."

"I asked him the same question when I first saw him," said Bethany. Imorean smiled a tiny bit when Bethany took him by the shoulder and shook him slightly. He felt his face warm just a tiny bit.

"How unusual," said Colton, his baby blue eyes widening in interest. When he spoke again, his voice was higher in pitch and sounded matter of fact. "A lack of naturally occurring melanin and an overproduction of hydrogen peroxide."

"What?"

"The reason your hair is white. Does it run in your family?"

"N—no, I don't think so," replied Imorean, surprised at Colton's quick diagnosis. It was exactly the same one that doctors had given him when his hair went completely white.

"Incredible," said Colton. "Most premature graying runs in families, but not always."

"Where did you learn that?" asked Imorean, grinning and inclining his head. He pushed his empty plate of food away and turned his full attention to Colton.

"Oh, I read a lot of books."

"We can tell. You were reading about calculus problems this morning, right?" asked Mandy.

"I love mathematics and sciences," said Colton, smiling.

"Yeah, he's a smarty pants," said a large, burly boy, sitting down next to Colton, who frowned slightly.

Imorean recognized the new boy as being Baxter Anderson, the one who Michael had reprimanded earlier that day.

"I'm sorry," said Imorean, feeling defensive of Colton. "I don't think anyone invited you into the conversation."

"Oh? And who are you?" asked Baxter, glaring at Imorean.

"Imorean Frayneson. No need to ask who *you* are. Michael made sure everyone recognized you during the assembly this morning."

"Imorean? What kind of a name is that?" asked Baxter, sounding amused.

"It's *my* name," replied Imorean, raising his chin slightly. Despite Baxter's outward cockiness, Imorean couldn't help but feel a wary liking to him.

From the corners of his eyes, Imorean noticed Roxy giving him a sidelong glance, wondering how the conversation was going to go. He knew she hated being put anywhere near awkward situations.

"Fair enough, albino boy. What have you been doing today, bud?" replied Baxter, clapping Colton so hard on the back that it knocked his glasses askew and almost sent him forward onto the table.

"Easy, Baxter." Mandy sounded annoyed as she spoke.

"He's half your size."

"Sorry, Colton," said Baxter nonchalantly. "So, who are the rest of you?" asked Baxter, looking around the table at Roxy, Mandy, Bethany, and Toddy.

"I'm Roxy," she said sweetly. Overly sweetly. Imorean knew that tone. He could tell Roxy had already taken a disliking to Baxter.

"And I'm Toddy," said the boy, not looking up from his food.

"Mandy."

"I'm Bethany," she said, tucking some of her short, blond hair behind one ear. Imorean frowned very slightly as Bethany batted her eyes at Baxter. So much for her liking him. Then again, it was probably for the best. He had never done well in the dating sphere.

"Do you play any sports?" asked Baxter.

"No," replied Imorean. His good mood had been successfully soured.

"Oh, I do," said Bethany. "I was on the soccer team at my high school."

"It pissed me off that they don't have a football team here," said Baxter glumly.

"Maybe you could start one," suggested Imorean, resting his elbows on the table. While annoyed, he wasn't going to be rude.

"Yeah, I could, but I mean I thought college was all about the sports."

"Then you seem to have been misinformed," said a voice from behind Imorean.

The white-haired teen's blood chilled in his veins, and his mouth went dry. Slowly, he turned and raised his brown eyed gaze to Gabriel. The man was looking down at him with vague interest. To his right, Imorean saw Roxy, Mandy, and Toddy glance at him in concern.

"Imorean," said Gabriel.

Imorean turned all the way around in his seat, his heart pounding. "Yes, sir?"

"I need to see you in my office."

"Yes, sir." He had only been at Gracepointe for a matter of hours. What if he lost his scholarship just for overhearing that conversation? What would his mother say? Would he have to pay back any money? He could only imagine the disappointment in his mother's and grandparents' eyes. Classes hadn't even started yet.

"Imorean?" asked Gabriel. "Follow me, please?"

Imorean had hardly noticed that Gabriel had turned and was leading the way to the glass doors of the cafeteria.

"Yes, sir." Imorean got up from the table. His legs were shaking slightly. He felt uncomfortably sick.

"Good luck, Imorean!" called Toddy.

Imorean barely heard him, and swallowed hard as he fell into step next to Gabriel.

"How do you like the campus?" asked Gabriel as they entered his small office. It had been quite a long, silent walk from the cafeteria, through main campus, and finally to the staff offices on west campus. Imorean had not spoken a word throughout the entire walk.

"It's nice, sir," replied Imorean, trying to keep his voice steady. He couldn't help but feel like a trapped animal when the door closed behind himself and Gabriel.

"That's all?" asked Gabriel, grinning at him and crossing the room to sit down in a chair behind a huge, wooden desk. On Imorean's side there were two chairs. He didn't know whether he should sit down or not.

"I like it." Imorean glanced nervously at Gabriel.

"Sit down. Is there something wrong?" asked Gabriel, inclining his head. "You look very nervous about something."

"Am I in trouble, sir?" asked Imorean, frowning and biting

the inside of his cheek as he sunk into one of the chairs across from Gabriel.

"No? Why would you be?" Gabriel raised one eyebrow. "*Should* you be?"

"I..." began Imorean. He debated for a second, wondering if he should continue.

"You?" prompted Gabriel.

"I heard you and your brother arguing in the library earlier. I'm sorry, I didn't mean to hear you. I'm not going to lose my scholarship, am I?"

"Going to–" began Gabriel, sounding shocked. A moment later, he dissolved into snickers.

"Sir?"

"I'm sorry, Imorean," said Gabriel, getting a hold of himself. He draped one arm over the back of his chair and slouched in it. "That's just too funny."

"What do you mean, sir?"

"I called you in here to let you know that we're missing one of your immunizations. I had no idea that you had heard that little altercation between myself and Michael earlier today."

"Oh..."

"But put your fears to rest," said Gabriel, smirking. Imorean furrowed his brow. "You won't be losing your scholarship. We want you here at Gracepointe. That's why we gave you the scholarship. We wouldn't take it from you just for you overhearing a conversation. That's ridiculous."

"Sir, if you don't mind my asking, are you going to cancel our Thanksgiving break?"

"I'm afraid that's up to Michael and the transportation department. It's not my call. When we have a certain answer, we will let you and the rest of the student body know. It's nothing to worry about."

"What did Michael mean by keeping us safe?" Imorean plowed on, wondering if Gabriel would let anything slip.

"Imorean, I am really not at liberty to tell you these things," said Gabriel, shaking his head. "It's highly unprofessional."

"Sorry, sir."

"It's fine. Curiosity is natural. Now, the immunization we are missing can be administered at our health center here. All you need to do is take this paper down to the student health center at some point this week and they will give it to you. I recommend going tomorrow. They probably won't be too busy."

"What is it?" asked Imorean, taking the paper Gabriel was holding out.

"It's a childhood one you apparently missed. I'm afraid I wouldn't be able to tell you what it is. I'm no doctor. Just be sure you get it done in a timely manner."

"Yes, sir." He folded the paper in half and slipped it into his pocket.

"Well, I'm sorry for pulling you from dinner. I've been looking for you all day, and the dining hall was the only place I felt sure that I would be able to find you. You should probably go ahead and go to bed. It's getting late."

"Yes, sir," replied Imorean, standing shakily.

"Relax. It takes a lot to be made to leave Gracepointe. You're in no danger of losing your scholarship."

"Yes, sir. Thank you, sir."

As Imorean stepped out of Gabriel's small office, he frowned. Something hadn't been right. Something in Gabriel's tone was wrong. There was something that he wasn't saying. Something that he was guarding. Imorean tucked his hands into his pockets as he walked and allowed his thoughts to wander. His curiosity about what was actually going on at Gracepointe was by no mean sated. If anything, it had grown. And now, he knew what he was going to do.

Imorean's eyes opened as the alarm he had set on his

phone went off. He turned it off quickly, hoping it hadn't woken up Toddy. The other boy shuffled in his sleep and rolled over, his breathing still even. Imorean breathed a sigh of relief. This was something he needed to do on his own. He dressed quickly in dark clothes, pulled a black baseball cap on over his head, grabbed his keys, and made his way quietly out of his room. He already knew Toddy wouldn't wake up as the door slammed. He seemed to be a very heavy sleeper.

Imorean breathed a sigh of relief as he passed through the lobby on the ground floor of the dorm, and found it empty. No one to ask him what he was doing. It was colder outside than Imorean had thought it would be, and he shivered slightly even in a long-sleeved tee shirt. The cool though, did not distract him from his self-assigned mission. He paused as he stepped off the portico at the front of his dorm. It wasn't against campus rules to be out of the dorms at night, but still it felt odd. The campus itself was deserted. Only a breath of wind rustled the leaves on the trees. Maybe it was the silence that was making Imorean feel nervous. He swallowed and followed the path he had taken earlier that day down to the sports field. He kept off the pavement as much as he could, and stayed close to the shadows. He didn't want any of the staff to see him and ask what he was doing.

The white-haired teenager looked up a few minutes later as the wrought iron gates to the sports field loomed up in the darkness. They seemed imposing now in the darkness. Imorean stopped in front of them. The gates were closed. That on its own didn't mean anything though. Imorean rested a hand on the latch and pushed. The gates rattled but didn't budge. Locked. Imorean looked up at them. Why were they locked? There was no reason to lock them. Imorean took a deep breath and turned on his heel, heading for the opposite end of campus. There was one more place he wanted to check.

Imorean arrived at the entrance hall, slightly out of breath. Nervousness had gotten the best of him, and he had ended up jogging the length of the campus. He ascended the steps to the wide, wooden double doors of the entrance hall. This was where he had gotten his first look at Gracepointe. He rested his hand on the latch of one of the doors and pressed, pushing inward as he did so. The door didn't swing inward. It, like the gates to the sports fields, was locked. Imorean looked up at them. He felt forlorn. Why were he and his friends locked inside? Imorean stood before the locked doors and stared at them hard. Were he and his classmates prisoners here? Imorean narrowed his eyes, and barely noticed the flash of green in his peripheral vision. There was one way to find out, but it would have to wait for another night. Were these gates locked solely for their protection?

CHAPTER
16

Imorean groaned as he woke up. He was exhausted, and hadn't got much sleep the night before. A consequence of waking up every hour or so. His nerves were still rattled from what he had found out the night before. The boy sat up in bed. It was already light outside. Surely it wasn't as late in the day as he thought it was. He glanced at the clock on the dresser between his bed and Toddy's. It was seven o'clock in the morning. Imorean felt surprised as he ran a hand through his white hair. It looked too bright outside to be so early. He supposed he should get up. He knew going back to sleep would be futile. Everything felt... wrong. Just twenty-four hours ago the world had been right, and now it was wrong. Just wrong.

As Imorean got dressed, he thought back on everything that had happened the day before. The conversation he'd overheard between Michael and Gabriel was still concerning him. The locked gates concerned him even more. It just didn't make sense.

"Toddy," said Imorean, when he was fully dressed. "Breakfast?"

"I don't like monkeys," mumbled Toddy, shuffling in his sleep.

"And *I'm* the one that sleep talks?" muttered Imorean, shaking his head. He tried again, raising his voice. "Toddy, I'm going to get breakfast. Do you want to come?"

"Bring me the spaceship."

Imorean shrugged and left the room with a quiet laugh, feeling slightly concerned for his friend's mental health. His laugh quickly died quickly his chest, crushed down by the weight of his worries.

The smell of food hit Imorean like a brick wall as he entered the dining hall. His stomach turned, and he didn't feel hungry anymore. Worry pushed his appetite away. The food felt like a betrayal somehow.

He raised his gaze and looked around the dining hall, wondering if there were any students who might welcome someone sitting with them. Naturally, there weren't many students awake at this time of the morning, so Imorean didn't have many people to choose from.

"Imorean," said a small voice from the corner table where Imorean and his friends had sat the night before.

The white-haired teenager looked up. Colton.

"You're already awake?" asked Imorean, smiling as he sat down across from the small boy. He thought vaguely about going to get breakfast, but again, as he thought about everything that had already happened, his appetite deserted him.

"I'm an early riser."

"So am I." Imorean studied the boy in front of him for a moment, wondering whether or not he should trust him. He seemed genuine enough. "Have you eaten?"

"Yes," nodded Colton.

"Let's go on a walk. I have something I want your opinion on, and I don't really want to talk about it here."

"Alright," replied Colton, stuffing the book he was reading back into a shoulder bag and standing up.

"So, what's so secret?" asked Colton.

"I'm not sure," replied Imorean, holding the door open for the smaller, younger boy. They exited the dining hall, and were both bathed in the crisp air of early morning.

"What?" asked Colton, sounding confused.

Imorean slowed his steps slightly to allow for Colton's smaller ones.

"I heard the two Archer brothers talking yesterday," said Imorean, tucking his hands into his jacket pockets. It was probably easier to talk about the Archer twins now, and the locked gates later.

"And?" probed Colton.

"I'm getting to it. They said something about banning our Thanksgiving vacation on behalf of the skydiving team, or at least that was what I got out of it. They also said that our safety was their first priority. What confuses me the most was something Michael said. He said that the warm days we have now were needed for 'training purposes,' and that he and Gabriel had waited too late twice to do something with the students and they couldn't afford to wait too late again."

"That's odd," said Colton, adjusting the way his bag set on his shoulder.

"Do you want to sit down?" asked Imorean, noticing Colton's awkward struggle.

"This bag is just heavy," replied the boy.

Imorean nodded and veered immediately off the brick path to make his way onto one of the green commons. The white-haired teenager stopped at the base of a large, green leafed tree and sat down on the manicured grass. Colton joined him after a second of hesitation.

"So, what's got you so worried about what you heard?" asked Colton.

"It was something in their tone," said Imorean, frowning. He debated for a moment. Should he mention the gates? No, probably not. Not yet. "It was urgent, and... I don't know. I just get the feeling that they didn't want anyone to know what they were talking about."

"I see."

"You don't think I'm nuts, do you?"

"Not really. I mean, this entire situation is unusual. A group of one hundred American, college students attending an English-speaking college in Norway, and all of us being here on full ride scholarships."

"Hmm," hummed Imorean, resting his chin in a hand and furrowing his brow.

"Though, I suppose something like this is not unheard of."

"I'm more concerned about what information is being kept from the students."

"What did your other friends say?"

"They agree that there is something quite unusual going on here. I'm determined to find out what it is."

Colton pushed his glasses further up his nose. "So how do you plan to do that?"

"I'm going to join Michael's skydiving team."

"Well, tryouts are in an hour in the student recreation center."

"How did you know that?" asked Imorean.

"I read the schedule that they posted this morning. Why did you choose to ask me my thoughts about what's going on?"

"Because I can tell that you're clever, and I want to try and get as many people's opinion on this as I can."

"I understand."

Imorean saw him smile slightly.

"Why did Gabriel pull you from dinner last night?" asked Colton.

"I have an immunization that's missing from my record. Gabriel said that they could administer it here, so I suppose I should go and get that done. I should have some time between now and the tryouts."

"I'll come with you," said Colton, standing and picking up his bag. "It's not like I've really got much I need to do today."

"Alright," said Imorean with a nod. A second later, he furrowed his brow. "Are you sleeping alright? You've got dark marks under your eyes."

"I would be sleeping just fine if Baxter didn't snore," sighed Colton. "Oh well, I suppose it can't be helped, can it? Do you think they sell ear plugs at the student store?"

"It can't hurt to look," replied Imorean, grimacing.

"Imorean Frayneson," said Imorean, passing the sheet of paper Gabriel had given him the night before to one of the nurses behind a desk in the student health center. He had put the issue of the locked gates to the back of his mind. He had a lot more to focus on right now. Solving the mystery of the gates would have to sit on the backburner for a little while.

"Ah," she replied, taking the paper. "Yes. Mr. Archer called and told us to expect you this morning. We'll have a look at what needs doing. If you'll take a seat, we'll be back with you shortly."

"Thank you," replied Imorean, turning away from the desk and walking back to Colton. The white-haired boy sat down next to his friend and folded his arms. If there was one thing he was more terrified of than heights, it was getting injections. He swallowed hard and shuffled uncomfortably. Next to him, Colton was buried in a book once more. Imorean couldn't quite figure the boy out. He was perfectly friendly one minute, then quiet and reserved the next. It didn't make much sense to him.

"Mr. Frayneson," called a nurse, opening a door that divided the lobby from the rest of the student health center.

Imorean's head jerked up. It had been many years since he

had heard anyone call for Mr. Frayneson. 'Mr. Frayneson' had always been his father. It was a name Imorean had only recently started hearing himself as he got older. He stood and walked toward the nurse in the doorway. Colton gave no indication that he had noticed Imorean leaving. The older teenager shrugged his shoulders and tried to smile at the nurse holding the door open for him.

"Thank you," he said, falling into step next to the nurse as she led the way down the wide, carpeted hallways of the health center.

"Oh, you're polite," she beamed. "That's a welcome surprise. How are you this morning?"

"Nervous."

"Oh? Why is that?"

"I don't particularly like doctors." Imorean knew that his nerves were showing through his voice. "Or needles."

"We hear that a lot," replied the nurse. "You've got nothing to worry about. Dr. Hall and the rest of our nurse staff are exceptional."

"I hope you're right." Imorean's nervous smile fell from his face.

"Come right in here. Dr. Hall will be with you shortly."

"Thank you." Imorean stepped past her and entered the room she had opened the door to.

"You're very welcome," she replied, shutting the door behind him.

Imorean sat down on one of the seats in the office and gazed idly around the room for a moment.

'Nervous and bored. What a lovely combination,' he thought. Imorean huffed and blew some of his white hair out of his face. He would need a haircut before long. The teenager's eyes wandered and he caught sight of a small stack of books on one of the counters in the office. Most of them looked like medical books, but there was one close to the bottom of the stack that caught Imorean's attention. *Endowment of Divinity.* Imorean inclined his head. What on Earth was a book with a title like that doing in a doctor's office? He was getting ready to stand up and reach for it when there was a sharp rap on the door.

"Good morning, Mr. Frayneson," said a man in a white coat, stepping into the exam room.

Imorean jumped. He felt for a split second that he had seen this man before in some long-forgotten dream, but the eyes were wrong somehow, and the features seemed too strong. Imorean calmed himself as he realized that this man, while tall, fine featured, and black haired had clear, blue eyes—not the gray ones that the man in his dream had. A pair of wire rimmed glasses were perched on his nose. This must be Dr. Hall.

"Good morning, sir," replied Imorean, standing up.

"Raphael Hall," said the doctor, extending his hand for Imorean to shake.

"Imorean Frayneson."

As soon as Imorean took Dr. Hall's hand, a strange jolt of energy ran through him. As Imorean released the doctor's hand, he shook his head in confusion. That had never happened before when he had shaken someone's hand.

"Sit down, Imorean," said Dr. Hall, smiling at him. "Now, according to your file, it appears that you are missing one of your immunizations."

"I can't imagine how that would happen, sir. My mother was always very careful to make sure that my siblings and I received all our vaccines."

"Well, here it is," replied Dr. Hall, extending the sheet for Imorean to look at. "Plain as day. It's missing."

"Right." Imorean glanced over the paper. To him, the words on the page made little to no sense. After all, he was no doctor. His eyes flitted down to the blank space on the paper. The injection he needed was something called the EDE. He furrowed his brow. He didn't remember ever seeing this on any other medical form. He shook his head. Surely, he had just never noticed it.

"Now, it's nothing to be concerned about," said Dr. Hall, taking the paper away from Imorean's line of sight before the boy could read any more of it. "A lot of people, actually most all of you, are missing this, so I imagine the clinic will be quite busy for the next few days."

"Why are so many people missing it? And what exactly is the immunization that I'm missing?"

"We aren't sure," replied Dr. Hall. "It's not an issue we have ever run into before. It could simply be that it was not administered at the time in your tristate area. The immunization is EDE. It helps to strengthen your body's endocrine system. Now, I'm sure you have quite a busy day ahead of you, so I'll send in one of my nurses and she'll give you the vaccine, then send you on your way."

"A—alright," replied Imorean, stuttering slightly and feeling taken aback by the doctor's suddenly brisk tone. Imorean returned the smile that Dr. Hall offered him, but dropped it as soon as the door to the room closed again. Almost all of the admitted students were missing the same injection? It hadn't been administered in their area? Imorean frowned. He wondered if refusing it would jeopardize his scholarship. Probably. He didn't see much choice other than grinning and bearing what was to come.

"Mr. Frayneson," said the nurse Imorean had seen earlier, pushing the door open.

"Yes," replied Imorean, furrowing his brow in concern.

"I'm sorry, dear," she said, laying a needle, syringe, and bottle of opaque fluid down on one of the office's counters. "I know you mentioned earlier that you didn't like doctors or needles."

"Not at all," replied Imorean, not bothering to grimace.

"I'm afraid that this one has an oilier makeup than other

injections."

"Meaning?"

"It's going to hurt."

"More than a tetanus shot?" asked Imorean, furrowing his brow.

"Afraid so," replied the nurse, shaking her head.

Imorean's blood chilled, and he swallowed hard as he watched her prepare the injection. For a brief second, he forgot his apprehension when he saw the fluid. The nurse had been right, it looked very thick, but that was not what caught Imorean's attention. The EDE liquid was somewhere between white and silver in color and seemed to be swirling in the syringe. Imorean furrowed his brow. He had never seen any other injected fluid look like that.

"Do you want to lie down for this?" asked the nurse. Her voice jerked Imorean out of his thoughts and he nodded nervously.

The teenager panted slightly as he crossed the room to the small bed in the corner. The sound of sanitary paper crinkling beneath him on the exam table rang in his ears like an alarm bell and Imorean swallowed hard.

"Relax," she said, swiping an alcohol pad over Imorean's upper arm. "On three. One. Two."

Imorean nearly jumped off the bed as the needle jabbed into his arm. He screwed his eyes shut and turned his head away, feeling betrayed. That had not been on three. All of a sudden, a strange, alien feeling washed over him. It was a chilling, intoxicating energy. He opened his mouth and tilted his head back, basking in the sensation, his entire body limp, pliant, and somehow cold. It sounded as though water was rushing in his ears, filling his head with cotton and blocking out all other noises. The only sound was the even, steady beat of his own heart. He felt blank. Content. As though he was being lifted out of the room. There was a soft happiness in the moment, and for a heartbeat, Imorean felt as though he was home.

"Imorean," said the nurse, her voice breaking foggily through Imorean's daze.

He opened his eyes slowly, and looked at her, as the world returned quickly to reality. His body felt as though it was returning to its normal temperature, and he could hear properly again. As the nurse placed a Band-Aid over the place where the needle had entered, Imorean's arm started throbbing painfully.

"I—is the pain normal?" asked Imorean, looking up at her.

"Oh, yes. We've seen many students react that way during the administration of this injection. We aren't sure what it is about EDE that causes that reaction though."

"Am I free to go?" asked Imorean.

"You may want to stay sitting down for a moment more. In the past, I've seen a few students fall over after receiving that injection. Sometimes they even vomit."

"I'm pretty sure I won't fall," said Imorean, swinging his legs off the bed and standing up. His legs were slightly shaky underneath him, but he thought that was just due to anxiety before he had received the jab.

"That's quite impressive," said the nurse, raising her eyebrows.

Imorean gave her a shaky smile and rubbed his arm.

"I'll show you out," said the nurse. "I'm sure you can't wait to get away from here, can you?"

"Not to be rude, you're right, but I can't," replied Imorean, rubbing his arm again.

Imorean was relieved to step out of the student health center and into the fresh air. The rush of energy he had felt after receiving the EDE shot had faded and all he felt now was tired. Somehow the conversation he had overheard, and what he had found out about the gates didn't seem like an issue anymore. All he wanted to do was sleep. Sleep would solve everything.

"Are you sure you're alright to go to a sports tryout?" asked Colton, trotting next to Imorean and trying to keep up.

"I'm sure," replied Imorean, sighing and rubbing his eyes. He yawned widely, and as he glanced sideways, he noticed Colton looking up at him in concern.

"I'm fine. Really."

"I hope so." Colton did not sound convinced.

Imorean lengthened his stride a bit, trying to make sure he wouldn't be late for the skydiving tryouts.

"Imorean." Colton fell behind slightly. "I'll see you later. There's something I want to research in the library."

"Alright," replied Imorean, stopping and nodding at the smaller boy. "I'll see you at dinner tonight?"

"Yes," nodded Colton. "I'll see you later."

CHAPTER 17

I morean slipped into the gym as quietly as he could and glanced around, looking for Toddy or Michael. Surely the surly, irritable head of the sports department would understand that Imorean had been late to the tryout because of a medical appointment, wouldn't he?

The white-haired boy spotted a cluster of people of about twelve people standing at the far end of the gymnasium and made his way quickly across the floor to them. He saw Michael standing in front of them all, talking animatedly.

"*You* are late," snapped Michael, when Imorean approached the group.

"I'm sorry, sir," replied Imorean, spotting Toddy near the back and coming to stand next to him. "I had to go to the student health center. It won't happen again."

"I should hope not. Someone please brief him on what I said before he arrived," said Michael.

"I got you, bud," said Toddy, elbowing Imorean.

"As I was saying. This is only an indoor simulator. Inside it, you will not find any of the real-world elements or situations that you will have to face when we eventually do go out on a plane jump. It is very good practice for getting ready though. Is anyone here afraid of heights?" asked Michael, looking around.

Imorean didn't dare raise his hand. Michael's question sounded like a challenge.

"Fantastic," said Michael. Imorean's felt the man's pale, green gaze linger on him for a few seconds. "First flier, please."

"Me," said a voice near Imorean. The white-haired boy looked over to see Bethany step up. He found himself pleasantly surprised to see her here. She hadn't mentioned that she planned on joining the team.

"Hey," said Toddy, catching Imorean's attention. "Mr. Archer said that when we get in the wind tunnel, he'll help us get airborne, then all we have to do is keep ourselves in the spread-eagle position. He did say that part of being on the team involves jumping out of planes, and if we get really good he'll send us up in a helicopter."

"What? I thought this was indoor skydiving."

"It is. But he wants us to get our certifications as well. He said earlier that if we didn't want to do this we were to step away and not waste his time."

"I'm staying," said Imorean, not hesitating. Something deep in his heart wanted to prove to both himself, and to Michael, that he could do this.

"Are you sure? I mean from what I've heard, I know you're not too comfortable with heights."

"I'll be fine." Imorean felt guilty about the tone of annoyance in his voice.

"Okay," shrugged Toddy. "It's up to you."

Imorean looked away from Toddy to watch Michael and Bethany. As she approached the tall man, it looked for a second as though the two of them were squaring up to fight.

Then they gave each other what seemed like forced smiles, and Michael passed Bethany a pair of goggles and motioned to the open door of the flight tunnel.

"Don't I need any special equipment? You know, maybe a helmet?" asked Bethany, hesitating.

"Not for this wind tunnel," replied Michael curtly. "It is specially designed."

"I really don't need a helmet?"

"Not necessary."

Imorean's jaw dropped as he saw Michael rest one hand on Bethany's shoulder, then lightly push her through the door into the wind tunnel. He stepped in behind her and helped to balance her in the rush of air.

"Surely, he's not going to do that to every student," said Imorean to Toddy.

"I hope not," replied Toddy.

Imorean watched as Bethany hovered about six feet off the ground, supported by the artificial wind within the tunnel. When he was assured that she was balanced, Michael stepped back into the threshold of the entry door and faced the remaining students.

"Allow your core to stay rigid, while the rest of your body remains relaxed," he said. "See how she is holding her hands, just out in front of her? For now, that is how I want you to hold yourselves."

He turned back to Bethany and rested one hand on her back, guiding her back to the door to exit, and helping her to stand upright.

"Very good."

Imorean couldn't help but notice that Michael displayed no emotion when he spoke. The words were empty.

"Thank you," said Bethany, running a hand through her short, blond hair.

"When each of you has finished your dive, please exit the

gymnasium. I will let you know by tomorrow if you are qualified enough to join the team or not."

"Yes, sir," said Bethany, passing the goggles back to Michael and walking quickly away.

Imorean smiled at her as she passed him. She returned his smile with a broad, bright grin of her own. Imorean hoped that Michael would think she was good enough to join the team. He wanted as many of his friends on the team as he could get.

"You, latecomer," said Michael, pointing to Imorean. "I hope your friend has briefed you successfully, because you are up next in the tunnel."

"Me?" asked Imorean, moving hesitantly forward through the other students.

"You were the only one who came late," smirked Michael.

"Yes, sir." Imorean swallowed hard as he ascended the few steps and stopped next to Michael.

"Goggles," said Michael, passing Imorean a clean pair.

"Thank you," said Imorean, slipping them over his head and blinking a few times, adjusting to the strange feeling of having to look through plastic lenses.

"Go for it," said Michael, shoving Imorean forward through the entrance door.

Imorean stifled a cry as he stumbled forward into the wind tunnel. Immediately, his legs were swept out from underneath him and he felt his body caught up by the wind from the fans. Imorean froze, not knowing quite what to do. His body hovered in the center of the tunnel, spinning quite quickly around in circles. He couldn't make a single move to control himself. His limbs felt as though they were not his own. Imorean didn't dare move an inch for fear of what might happen. He looked up at Michael in the doorway of the tunnel, searching for any sign of help. Instead, the man simply leaned on the doorway and watched, his pale eyes narrow and disdainful.

Imorean clenched his teeth and tried not to whimper. He didn't like this. He wanted more than anything to put his feet back on the ground. This was awful. Why had he decided to do this? Then he remembered. The vacation that was threatening to be taken from them. The locked gates. The odd behavior of the staff at the school. As Imorean studied the skydiving coach, he felt certain that it all linked back to him. Imorean steadied his breathing and allowed his body to be buoyed up by the rushing air. A moment later, he relaxed. Maybe this really wasn't too bad, provided this was as high as he was going to go. As though he had heard Imorean's thoughts, Michael stepped forward and placed one hand on Imorean's back and the other on his shoulder, guiding him back to the door and out.

Imorean couldn't help but feel immensely relieved when he could touch his feet to the floor once again. He felt that he could breathe again.

"Well done," said Michael quietly.

"Thank you, sir," replied Imorean, sweeping the goggles off his head and looking at the coach. He noticed that there was a slight wrinkle between the man's eyes. Michael's pale gaze was more piercing than normal and Imorean felt for one ridiculous second that the man was seeing not just his body, face, and physical appearance, but also his heart and soul. There was a strange, ethereal push at the back of his neck, and Imorean shook his head. When he looked back at Michael, the intense look in the coach's eyes had vanished.

"You should go. Your class schedule will surely be ready for pickup."

"Yes, sir," replied Imorean, shaking his head and passing the goggles back to Michael. The white-haired teenager walked away, looking back only when he heard the coach call for Toddy. Imorean gave his friend a confident thumbs up as he passed.

When Imorean finally reached the entrance doors to the

gym he paused. The idea of Michael being able to see his soul was ridiculous, so why had he felt like an insect under a microscope when the man had looked at him? Perhaps it was just the expression in Michael's eyes. Imorean rubbed his arms, clearing the gooseflesh that had gathered on them. There was an uneasy feeling in his stomach, but perhaps that was just from having been in a skydiving simulator. He shuddered and shook his head again, trying to clear his thoughts. He wanted to talk to Roxy, Toddy, and Colton together and see what they thought about all of this. He would go and collect his schedule now, and worry about everything else later.

"Imorean!" cried Roxy.

Imorean looked up at the sound of her voice and saw her almost instantly. She was sitting on the steps of the auditorium, holding a slip of paper in her hand.

"Roxy." Imorean broke into a jog to close the gap between them.

"Take a look at this," said Roxy, jumping up and waving the piece of paper under his nose.

"I will if you stop waving it around," replied Imorean, snatching at the paper unsuccessfully.

"Here." Roxy thrust it into his hand. She certainly seemed to be either excited or upset about something.

"What is this?" asked Imorean, looking at the paper in his hand.

"Honestly, for someone with as high of a GPA as you had, you can be so stupid sometimes, Imorean. It's my class schedule."

"What about it?" asked Imorean, scanning the words on the paper.

"Since when does studying mythology fall under getting an art degree?" asked Roxy, narrowing her eyes.

"Studying mythology?" Imorean passed Roxy's schedule

back to her.

"Didn't you read it?" asked Roxy, in exasperation.

"Not really," replied Imorean, dodging her punch and as he made his way up the steps to the auditorium.

"Whose group are you in?" asked one of the staff members at the door.

"Gabriel Archer's. North Carolina," said Imorean, looking around. He noticed three tables, each with four large folders on them.

"Right over there," replied the staff member, pointing to the furthest table.

"Thank you," nodded Imorean.

"You wouldn't happen to be Imorean Frayneson, would you?" asked the young, female staff member behind the table.

"I am," replied Imorean, smiling slightly. "Why?"

"A young lady was in here earlier asking if she could take your schedule, as well as her own."

"I know her." Imorean resisted the urge to roll his eyes.

"Biology major, huh?" asked the staff member as she passed his schedule to him.

"I am. Thank you."

"You're very welcome."

As Imorean made his way out of the auditorium, schedule in hand, he frowned. He had mythology on his schedule as well. What on earth did that have to do with a biology degree? The two were hardly related. Imorean shook his head and shrugged. It must just be a foundations class.

"Do you have it as well?" asked Roxy sharply, as Imorean descended the steps toward her.

"Yes," replied Imorean, looking up at her. "I suppose that since Gracepointe is based in a country other than the United States they want us to know as much about other countries as we can, you know, get a little culture. I guess they think that by studying myths and legends is a good way to do this."

"Well, I certainly don't want to take it," said Roxy, folding her arms as she waited for him at the bottom of the steps.

"Do you think we can drop the class?" asked Imorean.

"I'm not sure. Maybe you should go and ask Gabriel."

"Why me?" asked Imorean.

"He seems to like you."

"That's ridiculous. I think he acts that way with all his students," replied Imorean, rolling his eyes slightly. "Besides, it might even be too late. After all, classes start next week. I guess the rest of the students will be here over the next few days."

"They do!" cried Roxy, her hands landing in her hair. "Oh, that means we'll have to wear the putrid uniforms they gave us."

"Putrid?" asked Imorean in amusement.

"Imorean," said Roxy, grabbing the front of his shirt tightly. "I have to wear a skirt. A *skirt!*"

"I'm sorry," replied Imorean, trying to hide his smile.

"I can't wear a skirt, Imorean. I've never worn a skirt in my life." Roxy wailed and ran a hand through her dyed hair.

"You haven't seen the male uniforms yet. You'll get a good laugh out of seeing me in a sweater vest, I'm sure."

"I hope I will. I could do with a good joke."

"You weren't supposed to say that," said Imorean, ruffling her black hair. The green highlights in it were starting to fade away.

"I can't leave my hair loose either," cried Roxy, sighing in defeat. "I have to either braid it, bun it, or ponytail it."

"Wow, you get three choices," said Imorean, raising his eyebrows.

"I never tie up my hair, Imorean," said Roxy. "Name once in all the time you've known me that my hair has been up."

Imorean frowned for a moment, thinking. In all honesty, Roxy was right. She always wore her hair loose, down around her shoulders.

"This stinks," said Roxy, folding her arms and shaking her head.

"I'm sorry."

"What are you going to do for the rest of the day?"

"I need to go and get ready for track tryouts. I'll want to see you and all the gang soon though. I think I'll be busy with sports things for the rest of the day."

"Oh..." said Roxy, sounding disappointed. "I'll see you later then."

Imorean looked after her as she quickly walked away. He wondered what he had said to upset her, then shook his head. She was probably annoyed that he was leaving her alone with Mandy and Bethany. He had pressing things of his own to do. He would have to worry about Roxy later.

Imorean changed into the running gear he had brought with him and made his way from the dormitory to the track on the sports field. He adjusted his small gym bag on his shoulder and approached the growing crowd of students on the tarmac of the track.

"Is this the track and field tryout group?" he asked, looking at a boy he thought had been in the skydiving tryout. He was a tall boy, with shiny brown hair and brown eyes. He had a bright face, and one that Imorean immediately felt himself warming to. For a split second, Imorean wondered if he would look like this student if his own hair hadn't gone white.

"Yes," nodded the boy. "You're in the right place. I'm Dustin. You?"

"Imorean," he replied, extending his hand.

"Good to meet you," said Dustin, smiling and shaking Imorean's hand. "Where are you from?"

"North Carolina. You?"

"Eastern Virginia," grinned Dustin.

"Were you on the track team during high school?" asked

Imorean.

"I was a sprinter. You?"

"Distance runner," replied Imorean. "I did cross country and track."

"Nice."

"Do you know who the coach is for this?"

"I think they said it was someone called…. Coach Miller. I think that was the name."

"Thanks," said Imorean, nodding.

"No problem," replied Dustin. "I think that's him coming now."

Imorean followed Dustin's gaze and spotted a short figure making its way quickly toward them from the direction of the main campus.

"Good luck," said Imorean.

"And you," replied Dustin.

Imorean began to stretch out the muscles in his legs as the figure closed the distance between itself and the rest of the track team. He was looking forward to running again. Running was something he had always been good at, and it was something that he enjoyed.

Imorean found himself sitting between Roxy and Toddy later that evening during dinner, glad he had decided not to attend the fencing tryouts. According to Mandy though, not very many students had shown up for them. Imorean's entire body was sore after the workout that Coach Miller had given them for track. Every muscle in his body hurt, and he felt slightly nauseous. He had forgotten just how much energy track took out of him. Skipping breakfast didn't help him feel less tired either.

"Imorean," said Roxy, jerking him out of his daze.

"Hmm?" he grunted, looking up.

"Are you going to eat your food, or use it as a pillow?"

"I don't think I'm that hungry," replied Imorean, pushing

the plate a few inches further away.

"Are you feeling okay?" asked Bethany from across the table.

"Yeah. I had to get a shot this morning, and I think that's messing with me a little."

"You're pretty pale," said Toddy, inclining his head.

"No," disagreed Roxy. "I think he's a nice shade of green actually."

"Well, when you agree on a color let me know," sighed Imorean, resting his elbows on the table. He wanted to tell them about the gates, but for some reason, he didn't want to mention them until he had some more information.

"Do you want to go back to the dorm room?" asked Colton. "I'll walk with you if you do."

"...Actually, yeah. That would be really good of you," said Imorean, standing up.

"Something is really wrong with him," said Roxy as Colton tucked his book into his bag.

"I'm standing right next to you, Roxy. So, don't talk about me like I'm not here."

"Imorean never skips dinner. He's a healthy, young individual."

Imorean shook his head as Roxy brushed aside his reprimand.

"Are you ready?" Imorean asked as Colton closed his book bag and stood up. The younger boy nodded as Imorean led the way to the door.

Imorean breathed a sigh of relief as he and Colton stepped out into the cool, evening air. Being outside was soothing his nausea slightly.

"Do you want to go back to the student health center?" asked Colton.

"No," said Imorean, almost immediately. "I'll just sleep this off. I'm sure it's just something I ate, or all the chaos catching up to me, it could also be the shot."

"Are you sure you don't want to go to the health center? You might be experiencing a negative side effect."

"If I still feel awful in the morning I'll pay the doctors a visit, but tonight I'd really rather not."

"If you say so."

"You're making your way to the dorms awfully early yourself."

"I need to get into the room before Baxter does," said Colton, his voice becoming quieter.

"Why is that? I mean, you've told me he snores, but surely he can't snore so loudly that it wakes you up."

"No, it's not that. He plays music and online games very loudly until all hours of the night. He's not exactly quiet about it either. It's worse when Ryan's there."

"Do you think you should go and see the counseling department? They might arrange for you to switch roommates."

"It'll be fine. I don't want to cause a stir," murmured Colton.

Imorean frowned and gave Colton a concerned glance, but didn't press the subject any further. He was determined he would keep a closer eye on both Baxter and Colton, and if anything, odd happened he would drag Colton to the counseling department.

Imorean laid awake in bed that night, his clothes for the next day were folded neatly on his trunk at the end of the bed. The teenager's eyes were riveted to the ceiling. He felt almost too nauseous to sleep, and all the unusual events of the day were doing nothing to put his mind at ease.

He was a biology student. How on Earth was studying mythology relevant to his degree? It wasn't a class he had signed up for. There were so many questions racing around his head. Michael and Gabriel's conversation. The gates. The injection he had been almost forced to accept. Michael's unusual behavior earlier that day during the skydiving tryouts. None of it made any sense. He wished he could ask someone what was happening, but there was no one he really could ask. The only one he could think of was Gabriel, but he already knew what the man would say. Imorean rolled onto his side, facing the wall. He hoped that the new position would help to settle his stomach a bit more. Finally feeling more tired and more comfortable, the teenager yawned, closing his brown eyes. He would talk with his friends in the morning and maybe, just maybe, after some time and a team effort, they would be able to get to the bottom of what was going on.

Imorean closed his eyes and began to drift into sleep, then his heart skipped a beat and his eyes shot open. In the darkness of his and Toddy's room, he heard a deep, dark, feral snarl. He had heard that sound before. All of a sudden, there was hot breath on the back of his neck. Imorean rolled over quickly, his chest heaving and his stomach churning, just in time to see a pair of red eyes vanish into thin air. The teenager swallowed hard. He had been fully awake. He had *not* imagined that. There was no possible way this had been a trick of his imagination. Imorean ran one hand through his hair. Had the demon dog of Valle Crucis followed him here? Did it actually exist? Imorean was starting to believe that it did. He laid his head back on his pillow, but kept his eyes wide open.

"Fetch," whispered a quiet voice.

Imorean looked over at Toddy, wondering if his roommate was talking in his sleep again. Toddy lay dormant, his mouth closed. Imorean rolled onto his back and stared fearfully at the ceiling. There was no way that he would get to sleep now.

The night air was chilly, but Imorean barely felt it as he stood again before the gates leading to the sports field.

Imorean inclined his head. Bethany was sitting on the

ground, arguing with her laptop's black screen. She was spitting vehemently at it, in a voice that wasn't quite human. Mandy was sitting on a beanbag near the wall, but the beanbag wasn't fabric. It was made of feathers. Roxy and Toddy were arguing over a silvery staff, but the staff turned into a snake, which dropped from their hands and slithered away from them.

The snake approached Imorean, and everyone around him fell silent.

"Leave," hissed the snake.

"Leave here?" asked Imorean, stooping and picking up the snake.

"Leave Gracepointe."

"Why?"

"Go over the wall, and you will know."

Imorean slung the snake around his shoulders, and shoved his hands into his jacket pockets, then looked over his shoulder. He had heard voices floating across campus from the direction of the entrance hall earlier, and guessed that the next group of arriving students must have just gotten in. That meant that almost all the staff's attention would be focused on the entrance hall. Imorean looked at his friends, who stared back at him. He placed one foot on the lowest bar of the gates, and pushed up, climbing awkwardly toward the top. The gates were strong, and very hard to climb. There were very few handholds on the vertical bars, and Imorean constantly felt himself in danger of slipping. The snake whispered encouragement to him in a language that Imorean couldn't understand, and one that he wasn't entirely sure that he liked. Something about it sent shivers down his spine. At last though, he was high enough to place on hand on the flat top of the brick wall. Imorean pulled himself up onto it and looked around. The gates were locked from the inside, keeping with the staffs' position that they were there for the protection of the students. Imorean frowned. So, why did he have such a strong, gut feeling that they were there to keep them in, rather than keep other creatures out? He looked at the snake, and it flicked its tongue in satisfaction.

Imorean leaned forward and dropped to the ground on the other side of the brick wall. It was eerily quiet here, as though he had left the entirety of the campus behind. He felt isolated. The snake had vanished, leaving him alone in the darkness. Imorean stood up and looked around. He was the only soul here. He stepped forward, moving toward the woods, toward the world beyond the gates, but before his foot trod even one pace on the forest floor, Imorean was flung harshly backwards, a bright flash of green setting rings around his darkening vision.

CHAPTER
18

A cold shower was what finally washed away Imorean's lingering feeling of fear and apprehension from the night before. After he had dried himself and got dressed, he glanced in the mirror. There were dark shadows under his eyes, clashing terribly with his white hair. He looked like a corpse. This would be the first impression that any of the newly arrived students got of him. His dream from the night before had been right and the second wave of students had indeed arrived. He had no idea what the rest of the dream meant, if anything at all.

"Charming," muttered Imorean.

"Hey," said Toddy, sticking his head into the bathroom. "Are you coming to breakfast or are you still feeling bad?"

"I'm coming," replied Imorean, standing up straight and exiting the bathroom.

"Do you think you made it onto Michael's skydiving team?" Toddy asked as they walked down the stairs.

"I'm not sure. In a way I hope not, but in a different way, I really hope I did," replied Imorean, reaching the bottom of the stairs first and holding the door open at the bottom for Toddy.

"I think it would be really cool. But then again, I'm not afraid of heights."

"There's the list," said Imorean, following Toddy into the common room and spotting a sheet of paper posted on one of the cork boards near the main door. Toddy quickly trotted over to it with Imorean following behind, a bit more slowly. He wished he had more energy this morning. Reality and dream felt oddly blurred and he felt as though he really had returned to the gates the night before. In his heart though, Imorean knew he hadn't left the dorm.

"Imorean!" Toddy was waving him over.

"What is it?"

"We both made it!"

"Awesome," said Imorean, scanning the list for himself. Sure enough, his and Toddy's names were written on the sheet of paper.

"What's the plan now, mastermind?"

"I'm not entirely sure," replied Imorean, rubbing his side. He had already decided to keep his suspicion about the locked gates to himself for now. "I suppose we'll just try to keep an eye on Michael. That's the only thing I can think of. Perhaps we'll find out something else."

"Sounds good."

"Breakfast?" asked Imorean, tossing his head. The moment he did so, he regretted it. His vision swam and the feeling of nausea returned for a few seconds. A pair of gates appeared in the far corners of his vision. They were gone a fraction of a second later. Toddy didn't seem to notice.

"Sure thing," replied the other boy.

"Can I walk with you?" asked a small voice from behind Toddy. Imorean leaned over and spotted Colton.

"Of course," he replied. "Is everything alright?"

"I suppose," said Colton as the three boys exited the dormitory.

"What do you mean?" asked Toddy.

"Hey, roomie," called Baxter, coming up the steps at the front of the dormitory. Baxter was standing next to an even larger boy. The larger boy was very tall, several inches taller than Imorean, had dark, red hair and brown eyes. His shoulders were huge and seemed to dwarf the rest of his body somehow. His face was square and seemed set in aggression. Imorean remembered him from the flight over and had taken a dislike to him then. The boy's name was Ryan.

"Do you want to join the football club? We'll let you be the ball boy," snickered Ryan, glaring disdainfully at Colton.

"They're what's wrong," murmured Colton. "Baxter's made friends."

Imorean barely heard the small boy. He narrowed his eyes at Baxter and his friend and descended the steps, approaching the other teenagers. Imorean's blood was boiling in his veins. He hated seeing people being talked down to. His big brother instinct had raced to the surface.

"You wanna join the team, albino boy?" asked Baxter.

"I do not," snapped Imorean. "What I do want is for you to leave Colton alone."

"Easy, man, I was just messing with him."

"Didn't look much like messing to me."

"Fine, fine, whatever," said Baxter, raising his hands in surrender and shaking his head. "I don't wanna start anything."

"What's your problem anyway?" asked Ryan, stepping forward. Imorean was struck now by the difference in their heights.

Imorean held his ground. "I don't like the way you're talking to my friend."

"And I don't like the way you're talking to me," sneered

Ryan.

"Imorean, just leave it," said Colton.

Imorean looked down at the younger boy. He saw something in Colton's eyes that he had seen several times before in Roxy's. A pleading desperation, as though he was begging Imorean to back down.

"Come on, Imorean," said Toddy. "We're meeting the girls for breakfast."

"Fine," replied Imorean, glaring one more time at Ryan and Baxter before turning around.

"That's what I thought," called Ryan.

A sudden flare of anger rose in Imorean and he whirled around. It was only Toddy's tight grip on his shoulder that forced him to stop. Imorean quelled his temper and allowed Toddy to turn him away, but looked over his shoulder as they walked. Baxter had already turned and was talking to some other boys, but Ryan was still glaring after him. Imorean glared back. He couldn't help but sense trouble on the horizon.

"So," said Bethany at breakfast. "Did you two boys make the team? I did. I'm psyched. I used to do a lot of skydiving at home."

"Yeah, me and Imorean both made it," said Toddy. "I'm pumped. What about you Imorean?"

Imorean didn't respond. He had barely paid any attention to what Toddy had said. He frowned. Odd. Something odd. Something he couldn't place. Something about Bethany, but what?

Imorean closed his brown eyes in disgust. He didn't want his food. His stomach was suddenly feeling upset again. Maybe he *should* go to the health center. Then again, they would probably just jab more needles in him and he didn't particularly want that. Imorean sighed and gazed out of the window. The cafeteria easily had the best view on campus. Through the window, Imorean could see over the brick wall surrounding the main campus. Some distance away he saw rolling hills, hidden slightly by a blue haze. He smiled slightly, feeling closer to home.

Brown eyes flashed open and Imorean jumped in surprise as someone snapped their fingers in front of his face, jerking him out of his thoughts.

"Imorean!" Roxy placed both hands on his cheeks and shook his head back and forth. "Are you with us?"

Imorean frowned at Roxy and removed her hands from his face, placing them back on the table.

"We've been talking to you for the past few minutes," said Mandy.

"He looks green again," said Roxy.

"I do not look green," insisted Imorean. "What were you saying? Sorry, I was daydreaming."

"We could tell. Your eyes went all glazed and you looked like a zombie." Roxy made a face as she spoke, distorting her own features.

"Thanks, Rox," said Imorean, rolling his eyes.

"That's what I'm here for."

"Are you excited about starting on the skydiving team?" asked Mandy, smiling.

"Oh, yeah, sure. I mean, I guess so," replied Imorean, quirking a smile back at her.

"I can't wait until we start doing proper jumps. Do you think they'll teach us to BASE jump as well?" said Bethany.

"BASE jump?" asked Imorean.

"It's like skydiving," said Bethany. "But you don't go up in a plane, you jump from a stationary object, and as opposed to pulling the parachute cord in midair and coming down quite slowly, you fall for most of the dive. Then when you're close to the ground you pull the parachute cord."

"Sounds dangerous," mused Imorean.

"Oh, it is. There have been a lot of accidents," said Bethany.

"And a lot of deaths."

"You sound awfully eager."

"I love extreme sports."

"So far I like the skydiving we're doing," said Toddy, continuing to eat breakfast.

"I don't do sports," said Roxy, pushing her empty plate away from herself. "I make art and I provide moral support."

Imorean smiled. It was true. The more effort something required, the less likely Roxy was to do it.

"Hey, you." Roxy waved her hand in front of Imorean's face. "What's wrong? You're zoning out on us again."

"Oh, I just didn't sleep very well last night," said Imorean, repressing a shudder. He tried to turn his thoughts away from the menacing growl he had heard in his room and the haunting nature of the locked gates from the night before. Out of the corners of his eyes he saw Roxy give him a concerned glance. He quirked a small smile in response before going back to pushing his breakfast around the plate.

"So, Imorean," said Toddy.

"Yeah?"

"Do you know if you made any of the other teams?"

"Well, I only tried out for track and skydiving, but I'm hopeful about the track team."

Imorean was grateful for the lull in their conversation that followed Toddy's question. It gave him a few minutes of quiet to relax. He frowned as his stomach gave an uncomfortable lurch.

"I'm going to go and get some fresh air," he said, turning to Roxy.

"Do you want me to come with you?" asked Roxy.

Imorean looked down at her half-eaten meal and debated for a moment. He didn't have the heart to pull her away from it, and shook his head.

"No. It's fine. I'll meet up with you guys later."

"We have skydiving practice tonight in the gym at seven," called Bethany as Imorean stood.

"I'll be there," he nodded, making his way toward the cafeteria's glass doors.

Imorean breathed a sigh of relief when he finally stood outside. It was nice to be out of the stifling cafeteria. He turned away from the dining hall and started walking. He didn't really know where he was going, but that didn't really matter.

"So, what's wrong?" asked Roxy, falling into step next to him.

Imorean smiled as he heard her voice. He should have known she would follow him.

"Nothing really. At least I don't think so."

"You haven't been yourself for the past couple of days."

"I know."

"You didn't sleep well last night. Why not?"

Imorean hesitated. Roxy already knew the story about Valle Crucis, and she had been his best friend since grade school. Would she understand what was going through his head?

"I... it's about the demon dog of Valle Crucis," said Imorean in a quiet voice.

"Oh? Again? It's just a silly legend, Imorean," said Roxy, sounding surprised.

"Roxy... after I hit that bear back in the spring there's been something weird going on. I found fur on my truck the next morning, but it wasn't bear fur. The texture wasn't right. Ever since that night I've been hearing things. I keep hearing these growls... and I'm seeing eyes. Glowing, red eyes."

"Maybe you're just dreaming them."

"While I'm wide awake? I can't be. I must be going mad."

"No," said Roxy, shaking her head and waving a hand nonchalantly in his direction. "I'm surprised at you, Imorean.

You're usually so rational and levelheaded. I'm sure there's a perfectly reasonable explanation behind what you think you're hearing. And if you are going mad, I'll still be your friend."

"Thanks, Roxy. I'm glad you'll stay friends with me even if I end up cuckoo for Cocoa Puffs."

"That's what I'm here for. I'll pay you visits in the insane asylum. Honestly though, I'm more concerned about your new eating habits. Well, lack of eating habits. I've seen you eat, like, half your own weight in food before. What's happened?"

"I don't know, Rox. I guess it's the change in diet or something. I just don't have an appetite anymore. I'm worried and I'm not hungry."

"It's been since you got that shot a couple of days ago."

"Has it?"

"Mmm-hmm," nodded Roxy. "Are you sure you don't want to go and see one of the doctors here?"

"Yes. I don't think they can really do anything. I'm sure it's just the medicine cycling through me. If it persists I might go."

"You will go, okay?"

"I will go. Now will you stop fretting over me?"

"Well your mother isn't here to do it, so someone has to. and I know how bad you are about taking care of yourself," replied Roxy, reaching up and ruffling Imorean's white hair.

"Fine, mother hen," said Imorean, running his fingers through his hair in a vain attempt to straighten it. In a quieter voice, he added, "Thank you."

"It's the least I can do," said Roxy, smiling at him.

CHAPTER
19

After nearly a month into their stay, Imorean was glad for the start of classes. They were a good distraction. He found himself surprised at how quickly the time here at Gracepointe was passing. It was already August. Class would provide a welcome break from the sports practices he found himself caught up in. Track in the morning, skydiving in the evening. Each day, Michael was having the members of the skydiving team spend longer and longer in the simulator.

The previous night, Imorean and Toddy had returned to their dorm room feeling exhausted. Michael had had them working on negotiating air fluctuations, something Imorean found he was awful at. He wasn't particularly keen on the sensation of being weightless either. He still found it to be very disconcerting.

Something that Imorean was happy about though, was that his sleepless nights had more or less ceased. Between Michael terrifying him in the simulator and the track coach almost literally running him into the ground, Imorean was asleep as soon as his head hit the pillow each night.

"Come on Imorean," said Toddy, shaking his shoulder. "You're about to go face down in your cereal."

"Sorry," mumbled Imorean, fighting to keep his eyes open. He had had a particularly exhausting workout the day before. The track coach had sent him and some of the other distance runners on a six-mile run around the perimeter of the campus and Imorean was still tired from it.

"Don't be sorry," said Toddy. "I just don't want you to ruin your uniform before we even start."

"Why don't you actually eat something?" suggested Roxy. "That might help you to perk up a bit."

"Hmm," grunted Imorean. "You might be right. Do any of you have the class on mythology on your schedule?"

"Yes," replied Toddy and Colton together. Bethany looked up from her bagel and nodded her head.

"I'm a mathematics major," said Colton. "Learning about mythology is not necessary for me to earn my degree. I've tried to drop the class, but I wasn't allowed to."

"Me too," said Toddy. "I'm a chemistry major. That's going to be hard enough without having to study another irrelevant class."

"And me," said Bethany. "I'm here for sports medicine."

"I can't really complain," said Mandy. "I'm here for English. I don't have it until Tuesday though."

"We all have the class then," said Imorean, laying his schedule on the table. "But what for? I don't understand it."

"I don't either," huffed Roxy, picking at her gray skirt. "Maybe just another odd quirk of Gracepointe? A mandatory humanity class or something?"

"Could be. I mean, this is Norway, after all," shrugged Imorean, watching her from the corners of his eyes and smirking. He and all his friends were wearing the uniforms of Gracepointe. The males wore gray trousers, black shoes, and a white collared shirt covered by a khaki vest with the school colors of pale blue and pale yellow around the collar. Both males and females were expected to wear ties that also bore the college colors. The school's mascot, a soaring eagle, was embroidered on the right sleeve of all the university's shirts and jackets. Imorean found it all to be a bit unusual, but he was realizing more so all the time that Gracepointe was a rather unusual college. He reasoned that since they were at college in Norway, maybe they were adhering to rules that Norwegian colleges and schools instilled. Then again, he could be wrong. After all, he had never been to college before, let alone in Norway.

"Imorean," said Colton, looking up from his book.

"Yes?" asked Imorean. He was starting to feel more awake. Colton opened his mouth to say something, but was cut off by the harsh gong of the nine o'clock bell. The first class of the day was getting ready to start.

"Sorry, Colton," said Imorean. "We'll talk about it later, okay?"

"Sure," replied the smaller boy, sounding disheartened.

"Come on, Toddy," said Imorean. The two boys had compared their schedules the night before and had found out they had their first class of the day together.

"See you guys later!" called Roxy.

"See you in mythology!" returned Imorean, waving over his shoulder.

"Well," said Imorean, rolling his eyes as he walked out of his and Toddy's first class. "*That* was a complete waste of my time."

"And mine," huffed Toddy. "Honestly, I'm a chemistry major. How in the world does appreciation of Norwegian literature tie into my degree?"

"Search me," replied Imorean. "I've got an hour before mythology. What do you want to do?"

"I guess we could go to the library for a while or something."

"I might need to get a couple of books on Nordic Lit. I know nothing about the stuff."

"Me neither," replied Toddy. The boy glanced at his watch and covered his mouth. "Crap! I've got to go, Imorean. I'll see you in the mythology class."

"Where are you going? We have an hour."

"I've got to go to the health center. Something about a shot," replied Toddy, already jogging away from Imorean.

The white-haired teenager glared in confusion at Toddy's retreating form. Another person with a missing injection? Imorean found himself wishing he had been able to talk properly to his friends that morning. It wasn't right that he hadn't been able to have a good opportunity yet. He adjusted his bag on his shoulder and continued toward the library.

Imorean was on the second floor of the library, skimming over some of the spines of the books. So far, he had not found anything that he needed and his thoughts were starting to wander. The teenager spotted a table and chairs near one of the windows and made his way over to it, sitting down heavily. His tired mind was churning. So far, all the students he and his friends had talked to were registered for mythology. Imorean had seen several clusters of students making their way to the health center again today. Surely not all of them could be missing the same jab, but Dr. Hall had said earlier that many of the students from his area were missing that particular injection. Imorean wondered why. It just didn't seem to make sense. Michael and Gabriel's conversation in the library several days prior was still weighing heavily on his mind. He shook his head and wished that he could have heard the beginning of the conversation.

The white-haired teenager glanced at his watch. His next class wasn't starting for a while. He still had some time to relax.

"Hey, you," said Bethany, appearing from between some of the bookshelves.

"Hey," Imorean looked up and smiled at her. "What are you doing here?"

Grinning, Bethany tossed her bag down under the table and sat across from Imorean. "What? Is it illegal for me to be in the library?"

"Depends what you're here for." Imorean felt his smile widen.

"Just to relax, probably the same as you."

"Oh, yeah?" Imorean raised one eyebrow. "How's your day going?"

"Pretty good, I suppose. Yours?"

"It's been alright. I'm curious what's going on with all these students missing injections."

"Missing injections?" asked Bethany.

"Yeah. A lot of students are missing something called EDE. Didn't you know?"

"No," said Bethany, shaking her head. Her short hair just barely brushed her shoulders. "I already had that injection. Dad made sure I got it."

"So, let me get this straight," said Imorean, smirking. "You and your dad did extreme sports together and he made sure you got a shot that no one else here seems to have?"

"Yeah."

"Your dad got you awfully well prepared for this place."

"He made sure I was well prepared for anything and everything."

"He seems like a good guy," said Imorean. Again. Something odd. What was it though?

"You should meet him sometime," said Bethany.

"Is that an offer?"

"Yeah, I think it is," said Bethany, tilting her head slightly. "He'd probably like you nearly as much as I do."

Imorean stopped for a moment. There was something in Bethany's tone that caught his attention.

"Beth, are you flirting with me?" asked Imorean.

"I have been for like the past month, but thanks for finally realizing," said Bethany with a mischievous grin and a wink, getting up and picking up her bag. "We can meet up here again if you like? Just let me know when."

Imorean watched her go, a small smile on his face. Bethany had been flirting with him? In all this business of locked gates, unusual classes, and sports practices he supposed he hadn't realized. He nodded to himself. It was time to put all the unimportant material out of his mind. He needed to focus on the here and now.

CHAPTER 20

"Imorean!" called Colton, waving the older boy over.

"Colton." Imorean was panting, having just finished climbing the flights of stairs inside the lecture hall. He was still breathing quite hard when he approached Colton "What is it?"

"Every student in the college has this mythology class. It doesn't matter what major they have, everyone has to take it."

"That's very odd," said Imorean, furrowing his brow.

"I know," said Roxy, walking up behind Colton. "Colton and I checked everyone we came across. There's a lot of unhappy campers."

"Hmm," hummed Imorean. "It must be a mandatory class then, but why? This is an arts and sciences college. Mythology is an odd class to throw in the mix."

"I know," replied Roxy.

"Where's Bethany?" asked Imorean.

"She has this class tomorrow, not today," said Colton.

"Right," nodded Imorean, feeling a bit disheartened that they wouldn't all be having the class together. He liked

Bethany. Much more than he knew he should.

"Hey, guys," said Toddy, appearing at the top of the stairs.

Imorean turned and his eyes opened wide upon seeing his friend. Toddy's eyes were shadowed and his skin looked pale.

"Toddy, what happened to you?" Imorean wiped the surprised expression away from his face.

"I had to get a shot."

"Of what? Poison?" asked Roxy.

"I don't remember," mumbled Toddy.

"You're salivating, Toddy," said Colton.

Toddy raised his brows and wiped his mouth.

"Toddy, I don't think you're well enough to go to class," said Imorean.

"M'fine, really," grinned Toddy. Imorean thought his friend looked as though he was about to throw up.

"No." Imorean shook his head. "You're not. Go back to our dorm. I can take notes for both of us today."

"You sure?" asked Toddy, looking up at Imorean.

"I'm certain. You look as though you're going to puke. I don't want to see you blow chunks in the middle of class, then become the laughingstock of the school."

"Okay," sighed Toddy, blinking heavily then beginning to trudge back to the stairs. "Thanks, Imorean."

"You're welcome!" called Imorean after him.

"He looks like the incarnation of death itself," said Colton.

"I wish I knew what they gave him. I bet it was that EDE shot," said Imorean, shaking his head. "I might see if I can't drag him back to the student health center during lunch. He looked awful."

"I'll help you," said Roxy.

"Thanks, Rox," said Imorean. "Come on, let's see why everyone has been put in this class."

Imorean pushed open the door to the classroom and looked around. It looked very much like the class he had come from earlier. It wasn't decorated, nor was it unique. It was the atmosphere that captured Imorean. There was something inside him that suddenly made him want to be in the classroom.

"Imorean, are you going to keep walking or just stand there?" asked Roxy, pushing him in the back.

"Sorry," said Imorean, stepping forward. He hadn't realized he had stopped walking.

"Idiot," said Roxy, ruffling up his white hair.

Imorean looked around the classroom. There were only about twenty-five students sitting in the room. Perhaps the others would be in a later class. Imorean turned his gaze to the front of the lecture hall. A man stood behind a desk. His hair was graying and his face was tanned and lined, as though he spent a lot of time in the sun. He was scribbling something in one of the many books on the top of the desk. The professor looked up as Imorean and his friends walked in and took their seats. There was something calculating in those brown eyes. It could have been his imagination, but Imorean thought his eyes lingered on him for a fraction of a second longer than the other students. Imorean watched him look away and count the students in the room, then close the book he had been writing in.

"Good morning," said the professor, resting both hands on the desk in front of himself.

"Good morning," chorused the students.

"Welcome to mythology. I am Professor Haroel. Now, I am sure you are all wondering why you have been placed in mythology and what bearing it has on your degree. Believe me, I have had that question many times already this morning. Mythology is merely one of the requirements set by Gracepointe for all of you to graduate. One of this college's many quirks. I hope that you will not find my class too dreadfully boring. Now, if you have not already printed out the syllabus, you will see it projected on the board behind me. Please take a moment to study the course material that we will be covering this semester. Throughout the duration of this class, I urge each and every one of you to try and keep an open mind. Do that, and I assure you, you will not only do well, but perhaps even enjoy this class."

Imorean's eyes skimmed over the words on the board. Most of them were things he had heard of before. Myths, legends, gods, folklore. One section caught his eye. It was a section they would be covering in just a few weeks. Angels and Demons. Imorean's eyes widened slightly. That sounded interesting.

"Seems like a load of crap," muttered Roxy next to Imorean.

"Shh," hissed Imorean.

"Hold on. Surely you're not interested in this stuff."

"I actually am."

"Great. We've lost him, Colton. He's gone completely mad."

"I have not," snapped Imorean.

"I'll wait," said Dr. Haroel from the front of the class. "You two just keep going."

Imorean looked up guiltily. The man must have noticed his and Roxy's hissed argument.

"Sorry, sir," said Imorean, looking down.

"I should hope so," replied Dr. Haroel. The slide behind Dr. Haroel changed, showing the image of a wolf and two children.

"Does anyone know the story projected on the board behind me?" asked Dr. Haroel, scanning the room.

None of the students moved. Imorean was glad he wasn't the only one who felt completely stumped.

"It seems that more of you needed this class than I had

originally thought," said Dr. Haroel.

Imorean leaned back in his seat and listened attentively as Dr. Haroel began to lecture about the picture, which he discovered to be the myth of Romulus and Remus, supposedly the twins who helped found the city of Rome. Despite the unusual subject, Imorean found himself constantly engaged in what Professor Haroel was saying and even found himself feeling interested and wanting to learn more.

"Is that the time?" asked Dr. Haroel, looking up at the clock above the board. "Alright. Your work for tonight is to review the syllabus and gain a deeper understanding of the topics we will be covering. Go to the library, find a few books on ancient myths. Class dismissed."

As usual, there was a mad scramble for the door. Before he exited the room Imorean glanced back up at Dr. Haroel. The man was holding a phone in front of himself and seemed to either be getting ready to call someone or he was texting someone. Imorean shook his head. Dr. Haroel's business was his business.

"What have you got now?" asked Imorean as he and Roxy exited the classroom, Colton in tow.

"I finally have an art class. After sitting through not one, but two classes that have absolutely nothing to do with my degree. You?"

"I've got biology at five. Nothing between now and then. After bio, I have skydiving until seven."

"Imorean," said Roxy, sounding concerned.

"Yes?"

"Are you sure you aren't stretching yourself too thin? I mean, you need some time to study as well. Don't you think you should drop one of your sports?"

"No. I have plenty of time to study."

"If you say so," shrugged Roxy.

"Are your nightmares persisting?" asked Colton.

Imorean stopped in his tracks.

"For the most part," he said stiffly. "I'll be fine, Roxy. I'll see you all later."

"See ya," said Roxy. Imorean didn't turn despite the concern he heard in her voice.

Imorean was glad he had chosen to study on his own in the library for a while after skydiving practice. He had needed the peace and quiet. The teenager glanced at his watch. It was close to ten o'clock in the evening. He grimaced as he pushed open the door to his and Toddy's dorm room. His roommate had come straight to the room after skydiving practice and was already snoring. Imorean breathed a small sigh of relief, glad not to be disturbing him. Maybe Roxy was right, maybe he *was* doing too much.

As he changed into nightclothes, Imorean thought back over his first day in class. He had only had three classes today. The rest would come tomorrow. His Norwegian Literature teacher had been nice enough. She was actually quite sweet, even if Imorean found her class boring. His biology teacher was a small, but quick and clever man, and Imorean had taken an instant liking to him. He was glad the same man taught the biology lab. The professor himself was rather unusual though. Somehow, he looked younger than most of the students and when Imorean had first seen him, he had thought that the professor was simply an intern or even a fellow student.

Imorean frowned as he turned his thoughts to Dr. Haroel. He was a somewhat strange man, but another one that Imorean had found himself liking immediately. Dr. Haroel had gone off on several tangents that had little to no relation to the subject he was teaching, but they were always interesting. That seemed to be the norm here. Unusual but interesting. Imorean found himself feeling a bit disconcerted. He didn't usually take to people in the way he had done here at Gracepointe. Perhaps it was the state of being away from home. Yes, that had to be it.

Imorean sat on his bed and flopped onto his back. Just before he dropped off to sleep though, he heard his laptop *ping*. He had a message. Imorean sat up just far enough so he could see the screen. He had a direct message. From Bethany.

CHAPTER 22

I morean had been grateful for the start of classes, but he was even more grateful for the arrival of the weekend and to be able to wake up late for a change. He checked his watch. It was a little after ten o'clock in the morning. Normally by this time he would be in his first class of the day, but not today. Today, he could do things at his own leisure. Toddy was already gone. Vaguely Imorean wondered where, then shook his head. If Toddy had something to do, it wasn't his business to probe. Imorean sat up in bed and stretched, looking out the window as he did so. He frowned slightly when he saw it was raining. Oh well, he supposed that a lazy, rainy day would be nice.

When he was dressed, Imorean did a bit of his homework, then made his way down to the common room, his laptop nestled in a bag draped over one shoulder. His mother had asked him to video chat her again. Imorean was glad it was around lunchtime and that there were not many other students in the common room. Most of the other residents were already in the cafeteria. He checked his watch. It was almost twelve o'clock. His mother should be up and awake by now.

Imorean sat down in a comfortable arm chair, logged onto his video chat account, and clicked on the icon to call his mother. He smiled, watching as the call connected.

"Hello, Imorean," she said, the black screen on her end lighting up with a video screen. Imorean felt the familiar surge of homesickness upon seeing the living room of his home in North Carolina.

"Hey, Mom," replied Imorean, taking in his mother's appearance. She looked frazzled and tired. Perhaps she had just finished an overnight shift at the clinic.

"My, my, you do look well. What are they feeding you there?"

"Actually, the same stuff as we ate at home. They've been pretty sensitive to the fact that we're from the United States and not here."

"Lovely. How are your classes going? You just started on Monday, didn't you?"

"Yes. They're going really well. I'm enjoying them."

"What are you taking?"

"Biology, the lab that goes with biology, English, Norwegian literature, and mythology."

"Mythology?" asked Amelia, furrowing her brow.

"Yeah," replied Imorean, rolling his eyes. "That's what I said when I saw that I had it on my schedule."

"You didn't ask for it?"

"No. Every student on campus has to take it too. It's weird."

"That is odd. Oh well, some colleges have you take different classes. I suppose that's just one of the ones that Gracepointe wants you to take."

"True. That's what I had in my mind when I heard that everyone had to take it."

"What's that like in the classroom?"

"It's really interesting, actually. This past week we covered famous myths and legends. Next week, it's relations of myths to other narrative forms. I hope that later on in the semester we'll be studying mythological creatures. I think that would be really interesting."

"Doesn't it say it in the syllabus?"

"I'm sure it does, but I don't have it with me right now."

"Of course," replied Amelia, shaking her head. "How are all your friends?"

"They're great. I think Roxy is still asleep. Toddy was gone by the time I got up, but I'm pretty sure he had something to do this morning. They might be in the cafeteria by now though. I've made another friend as well. He's the youngest boy on campus. His name's Colton."

"Oh? How old is he?"

"He's fifteen. He graduated from high school two years early."

"Wow," mused Amelia. "What about the Bethany girl you told me about?"

"She's good. Actually, I didn't realize it, but she's been flirting with me for a few weeks now."

"Imorean, really? You would be one to not notice something like that. Anything come of it yet? Details, details."

"We're just friends, but I don't think I'd mind being something a bit more with her. She's really pretty. I'd like to see where things go."

"Good, good. I can't wait for you to video chat me with her. How about the teams? How are they going? Imagine you getting on the skydiving team? I can barely believe it. When you left you were terrified of heights. You would freak out whenever Rachel or Isaac got up on one of the counters."

Imorean laughed and looked down for a moment.

"Well, I am still scared of heights," he said.

"Then why join the team?" asked Amelia, her thin

eyebrows coming together.

"For right now it's indoor skydiving, so we're going no great height. The highest we've gone so far is ten feet off the ground."

"You're a nutcase, Imorean." Amelia shook her head and smiled, her brown curls brushing over her shoulders. "I am proud of you though, for going outside your comfort zone and doing something new."

"Thanks, Mom," said Imorean, his heart swelling slightly in his chest.

"Is your skydiving coach nice?"

"He has his moments," said Imorean.

"Oh dear. Is he a little strict?"

"He's... he's rude," replied Imorean after a moment. There was truly no other way to describe Michael.

"Oh..." said Amelia. "Who is it?"

"One of the scholarship representatives. It's the older of the two brothers, Michael. Gabriel is the nice one."

"I seem to remember you talking about them after your interview," said Amelia, nodding.

"Yeah. Where are the twins? I haven't seen them yet, not even in the background."

Imorean sat up straighter as his mother looked away, sadness in her eyes. She was hiding something and Imorean was suddenly on high alert.

"Mom?" asked Imorean, prompting an answer.

"They're in Asheville at my sister's house."

"Why?" asked Imorean. His mother and his aunt were not on good terms. Something strange must have happened for her to send them there. Imorean's eyes widened as he saw his mother's lower lip tremble.

"I was going to send them to your grandparents' house for a few days, but on his way to pick them up, Papa had an accident."

"What kind of accident?" asked Imorean, trying to keep the worry out of his voice. "Mom? What kind of accident?"

"He crashed into an animal on the road between here and their house. We assume it was a bear, judging from the condition of the car ... and from him. It was around the same area you wrecked your truck."

"What?" gaped Imorean, his blood running cold. "And you couldn't tell me this? Not even in an email? Why?"

"I didn't want to distract you from your studies, not during the first week," said Amelia, frowning. "I didn't want to break your focus."

"Is Papa okay?" asked Imorean, wishing he was home.

"Yes. He's still in hospital, but he's out of intensive care and the doctors say he's getting better. They say he should make a full recovery. He was very disturbed, Imorean. I was at his bedside and he was rambling about monsters."

Imorean shook his head, looking away from the computer screen. That explained his mother's frazzled appearance. She must have been running between the hospital, her sister's house, and home.

"Are you angry?" asked Amelia, grimacing.

"I just wish you'd told me. Are Isaac and Rachel doing okay?"

"They're fine, just a bit shocked."

"Well, I can see why," snapped Imorean, the words sounding sharper than he had intended for them to.

"I'm sorry," said Amelia, her voice turning sharp as well. "But I only wanted for your attention to be undivided for the first week of school."

"Thanks... I guess," said Imorean. He frowned, knowing that his mother had only acted with his best interests in mind.

"Well... how are you finding the climate over there? I hear it's very different from here," said Amelia, changing the subject.

"It's nice." Imorean heaved a great sigh, but he was glad of the change. "It's a lot cooler and less humid than North Carolina. The first couple of days I was here I had to wear a sweater. It also rains more here than it does at home, but it's kind of nice in a way."

"I wish I could see it," said Amelia with a sigh. "Take some pictures and send them to me via email."

"I will."

"If you happen to see them before you come home for Thanksgiving, take some pictures of the Auroras. I'd love to see them."

Imorean paused. Thanksgiving. Was their Thanksgiving break even still happening? There had been no word from the staff.

"What is it?" asked Amelia.

"I don't know if we get a Thanksgiving break."

"What?"

"It's hard to explain. I'll have to send it in an email. I'll check with the teachers and see if they know anything about the breaks."

"Surely they've given you a calendar."

"All of that kind of thing is on the school's website."

"I see. After we get off chat please check on that. I want to know when I'll next get to see you."

"I will, Mom," replied Imorean, smiling.

"Well…" Amelia gazed at him sadly. "I think I've got to get going. I told Papa I'd be at the hospital today."

"Okay. Tell him I hope he gets better soon." Imorean forced a smile. He really didn't want to say goodbye to his mother so soon.

"Bye, Honey. I'll talk to you soon. I love you," she said, kissing her hand and placing it against the screen.

"I love you too," replied Imorean, copying his mother's motion then ending the call. A feeling of heavy sadness settled around his shoulders as his mother's screen winked black. He was concerned as well. His grandfather was in the hospital. How odd that he had been in a car crash in the same place Imorean had just weeks before, and for the same reason. Imorean shook his head. Sheer coincidence? He didn't think so. There was just something too dark and too precise about the situation. And what about the monsters? Imorean couldn't help but feel that there was something *other* involved.

Imorean arrived at the library later that evening. He was eager to shake off the bad feeling after hearing about his grandfather's accident and had agreed to meet Bethany nearby. He sat on the low stone wall outside the library, half wondering if she had been serious about meeting him.

"Kinda wondered if you'd come, kinda knew you would," said Bethany, approaching. Imorean looked up. So, she had been serious.

"Hey," said Imorean, standing up. He noticed vaguely that she was wearing a new pair of designer shoes. Something struck him as odd, but he couldn't tell what.

"Hi," grinned Bethany.

"What have you been up to today?" asked Imorean, starting to walk.

"Nothing much." Bethany's tone was light and playful. "Just relaxing. You?"

"I video chatted with my mom," said Imorean, noticing her fall into step next to him. He didn't want to bring up his grandfather's accident. It would put a damper on the atmosphere.

"Cool. Dad and I haven't skyped yet, but I'm sure we will eventually."

"So, you've really been flirting with me for the past month, huh?" asked Imorean, tucking his hands into his pockets.

"Well, yeah," smirked Bethany, tucking a lock of her short hair behind her ear. "You're a decent guy and you're by no means average, so naturally I felt drawn to you."

Imorean grinned. "I'm glad to know you think so highly of me. What drew you to me?"

"You're good looking, level headed, and I like your humor. A little on the serious side, but that works on you. You're diligent too. I can tell when you commit to something, you commit, and that's something that's pretty rare in a guy today."

"Seems like you know me pretty well."

"There's something different about you too. Something that runs much deeper than just character traits or appearances. Something I can't quite put my finger on."

Imorean grinned at her. Bethany had leaned ever so slightly closer as she spoke.

"I'm glad *you* can see something else, because I have no idea what you're talking about." Imorean briefly wondered if Bethany's flirty attitude was contagious.

"So, why did you agree to come meet me? Can't have been just because you're my friend. I've seen you glancing at me. I think you're as interested in me as I am in you."

"You're confident, for starters," said Imorean. "You're very pretty and you've got attitude. We also seem to like the same stuff. We both like sports, yet we're at home in a classroom. I'm comfortable with you. We've only just met, but I feel like I've known you much longer."

"The feeling is mutual then." Bethany stopped and looked up at him, batting her eyelashes.

"I'm glad about that." Imorean hardly realized that he had stopped with her.

"So, would you like to get to know me better?" asked Bethany, looking up at him through half-lidded, blue eyes.

Imorean smiled as her pale eyes locked with his brown

ones.

"I would like that very much, Bethany."

"Good."

A flash of surprise leaped through Imorean as she grabbed the front of his shirt, leaned up, and pressed her lips firmly against his.

CHAPTER
22

———— ◆ ————

"Keep your body relaxed, Frayneson! How many times do I have to tell you?" snapped Michael from his position in the doorway to the skydiving tunnel. Imorean, Toddy, and Michael were the only ones left in the gym. All the other members of the team had gone back to their dorms. Imorean could barely believe it was already getting toward September. Classes had been going for almost a month now and everyone was starting to get more involved in their coursework. Most had tests coming up.

Imorean looked up in irritation, glaring at Michael through his goggles. The skydiving coach was in a particularly waspish mood today.

"I don't like the speed of the fans," said Imorean, wobbling in midair and rolling over once. "It's freaking me out."

"As you progress on this team, you need to learn how to deal with higher fan speeds. It is the only way that you will get used to the elements you may encounter on a real jump. Relax, Frayneson."

"I'm trying," called Imorean, raising his voice so he could

be heard over the artificial wind.

"The more relaxed you are, the easier this will be," said Michael.

Imorean panted, trying to listen to what Michael was saying, then his body wobbled again and his feet flipped forward, sending him head over heels. Imorean cried out at the unexpected motion and tensed his entire body. He rolled again and again, continuing to tense his body, wanting to gain purchase on anything to stop the movement. From the door, he heard Michael scoff. There was a whirring thunk as the fans that powered the simulator were turned off. Then Imorean fell, landing heavily on the elastic netting that formed the floor of the skydiving tunnel.

"You disappoint me, Frayneson," said Michael, folding his arms and leaning on the door frame. "You have potential in the air, you could easily become as good of a diver as I am."

"Should I take that as a compliment?"

"It is the closest thing you will get to one," replied Michael. Imorean could feel the man scrutinizing him and lowered his gaze to the floor.

"I'll try again tomorrow, sir."

"I should hope so," said Michael, turning on his heel and exiting the now quiet gym.

"Dude," said Toddy, coming to the wind tunnel doorway. "He had the fan speed up way too high today. Even Bethany was having trouble with it and she's the best skydiver out of all of us."

"Don't I know it," said Imorean, finally finding the strength to climb to his feet. "I wish I knew what his problem was. He can be such a jerk sometimes."

"You disappoint me, Imorean," said Toddy, doing a near perfect impression of Michael's voice. Imorean laughed and shook his head, glad for Toddy's presence.

"You got the quote wrong. He never calls me 'Imorean.' It's

always 'Frayneson.' But seriously, I mean, who actually makes comparisons to themselves?" asked Imorean. "'You could be almost as good as me one day.' It's not like he's perfect or anything."

"He's just being vain," shrugged Toddy, pulling his gym bag further onto his back and passing Imorean his own.

"Thanks," said Imorean with a nod. He checked his watch. It was almost ten o'clock in the evening and was just starting to get dark outside. They normally met Roxy, Bethany, Mandy, and Colton in the library so they could study some of their subjects together. Perhaps it was too late to meet them tonight. Skydiving practice didn't usually go on this long.

"Think they're still there?" asked Toddy, leading the way out of the gym.

"I'm not sure. We can go and have a look. No harm in trying."

"Alright," nodded Toddy.

Imorean was surprised to enter the library and find that Bethany, Mandy, Roxy, and Colton were all still in the building. He and Toddy quietly approached their friends' table, and Bethany looked up as they came near.

"How did you handle the fans?" asked Bethany.

"It was awful," sighed Imorean. "He had the speed too high. We, or at least I, wasn't ready for it. He's pushing us too hard."

"I don't know that he's pushing us too hard. Too fast, maybe."

"Yeah. I thought you all would have gone to bed already."

"Nope," said Roxy, shaking her head. "We're studying for Dr. Haroel's test on Ancient Greek Myths."

"It's going to be rough," said Mandy, shaking her head as she looked up from her book.

"Oh, nice." Imorean deposited his bag on the floor next to their regular table. "When is that again?"

"Imorean," said Roxy. "Get yourself together. I'm the one who's supposed to ask those kinds of questions. The test is tomorrow. Are you ready for it?"

Imorean sucked a breath in through his teeth and darted a glance at Toddy. The expression on his friend's face told him all he needed to know. Neither of them had studied for it. Neither had even known there was one coming up.

"Can I see your notes?" asked Imorean as Toddy sat down next to Colton, starting to read along with the smaller boy in the textbook already lying on the table.

"Honestly, you're lucky I'm playing mother hen right now," said Roxy, sliding her notebook across the table to Imorean and not looking up from the thick textbook she was poring over.

"I certainly am," replied Imorean. He thought he saw her smile slightly. "It won't happen again, Rox."

"I told you, you're spreading yourself too thin," said Roxy, looking up at him. Disappointment and concern were evident in her hazel eyes.

"Sorry," sighed Imorean.

"That's alright. Find me some red dye or red drink powder and we'll call it even," she said.

Imorean saw all the others at the table glance at him in confusion.

"She wants to dye her hair again," explained Imorean with a grin. "Since we're lacking a proper salon here, she's planning on resorting to dip dyeing. I am and always have been her scrounger for hair products."

"He does a very good job, too." Roxy took a second to smile up at him.

"You know we're not supposed to be dyeing our hair unnatural colors," said Colton.

"Oh?" asked Roxy. "Where does it say that?"

"Student handbook, page thirty-five, rule sixty-six,

subsection three, line eight."

"Did you memorize the entire handbook?" asked Imorean, looking up from a page about Perseus and Medusa.

"I had a free afternoon before we came," shrugged Colton.

"In that case," said Roxy. "Imorean, scratch the red, it's too close to my natural hair color and fades too quickly. Find me green, blue, or pink, even better if you can get your hands on all three. I'm going to dye my entire head."

"Are you sure that's a good idea?" asked Imorean, resisting the urge to laugh.

"What are they going to do? Shave my head?"

"I will find red for," said Imorean, rolling his eyes. "Just because I don't want to see you wandering around bald."

"Whatever," shrugged Roxy. She sobered a moment later. "How's Papa doing? Is he out of the hospital yet?"

"Yeah. He's home now, thank God. Mom said in her last video that he was on a ton of pain meds though. I can't help but feel worried."

"I don't blame you. I'm sure he'll be fine though. Your grandpa is a tough guy. He'll be perfectly alright by the time we go home on break, you'll see."

"I hope you're right."

"Can you guys be quiet?" said Toddy. "You're distracting me from Jason and Persephone."

"Toddy," said Imorean, speaking as Colton opened his mouth. "It's Jason and the Argonauts, and Hades and Persephone."

"Well," said Toddy, closing the textbook he had been sharing with Colton and earning a frown from the smaller boy. "I give up. Imorean, I'm cheating off you."

"Don't get caught," replied Imorean, shrugging. "Or else we both lose credit for the test. You might be better off just to try and cram."

"Fine, fine," sighed Toddy, sounding defeated. "Can you

pass me some notes or something?"

"If you get really stuck, I can try to give you some of my answers tomorrow," said Bethany.

"Thanks," sighed Toddy.

Imorean slid Roxy's notes across the table to Toddy.

"Hey, this isn't a read, read, pass circle," said Roxy in mock irritation.

"Sorry." Imorean waved a hand in Roxy's direction and got up from the table to search the library for some other books that he could get information from.

"You don't sound very sorry," called Roxy after him.

Imorean pretended not to hear her. He walked down one of the aisles lined with bookshelves and looked from side to side, scanning the spines for anything he could use. As he walked, one of the books caught his attention. *Cerberus, Black Dogs, and Hell Hounds.* Imorean paused and slid the thin book off the shelf. Cerberus was the three-headed dog that guarded the gates to the Underworld. Would much about him be on the test? He was about to put it back on its shelf when he caught sight of the book's front cover. On it was a big, black dog. Its teeth were bared and its eyes were glowing red. Imorean's breath caught in his throat. The dog on the cover wasn't Cerberus, the dog of the Underworld had multiple heads. This one had a single, distinct head and was built like a giant, black mastiff. From the back of his mind, he heard a soft yet vicious snarl. Following close behind the snarl was something that froze Imorean down to his core. A distant yet familiar peal of female laughter. Imorean quite promptly dropped the book, the air escaping from his lungs. It landed with a heavy smack on the floor.

"Imorean, are you okay?" called Bethany.

"Yeah," replied Imorean, stooping and picking up the book, dusting off the cover before placing it quickly back on its shelf. "I'm fine."

He put one hand against his forehead and took a deep

breath. That growl had been following him in his dreams ever since he had crashed his truck in March. This was the first time since he had heard it while he was awake. Imorean shook his head. He was imagining things. He *had* to be.

CHAPTER 23

I morean was aware of the snarling. Massive creatures circled around him like sharks. Imorean could feel their urgency. He could feel their need to hunt him down. To find him. To catch him.

"They won't kill you," said someone from above. Imorean looked around. He knew that voice. He couldn't place it, but he had heard it before.

"Take flight, little bird," said the voice again. "You might stand a better chance."

Imorean longed to leap away from his pursuers. He could almost feel their hot breath on the back of his neck. They were drawing ever closer. Soon, they would find him. Soon they would catch him.

"You will be found."

Something caught Imorean's attention in the distance. Across a long field was a distant glimmer of emerald. Something about it made Imorean feel safer, but he knew he would only be properly safe if he could reach it. Dimly, he rose out of his hiding place. Only seconds afterward, teeth closed around the back of his neck, ripping, tearing, and bringing him crashing to the ground.

Imorean bolted upright in bed, breathless and drenched in cold sweat. He shook his head. It was a nightmare. Just a nightmare. He touched the tips of his hair. Even they were damp with sweat. He really should take a shower. Yes, a cold shower would do him good. Before he got out of bed, Imorean glanced out of the window. It was just getting light outside. It must be just after five in the morning. This morning of all mornings to wake up early. The test he, Roxy, Toddy, and Colton had been studying for the night before was coming up today. A full night's sleep would have been convenient, but as he was awake, he supposed he could get ahead on some of his homework.

Imorean was just about to step into his and Toddy's ensuite bathroom, when he heard a deep, quiet laugh. This laugh was distinctly male. There was no humor in it, only mockery and cruelty.

"That was real," murmured Imorean, looking over his shoulder. There was no one there. A ghost maybe? Imorean scoffed at the idea.

After he had showered and donned his uniform, Imorean slipped out of his dorm room. He wondered what was causing these nightmares. Never before in his life had anything like this happened to him. Imorean stepped out of the dormitory and into the chilly, early morning air. He wanted to talk to someone, but knew that he had to be careful. He didn't need anyone to think he was nuts.

As he aimlessly wandered the paths around campus, he checked his watch. It was half past six. Would any of the faculty be up yet? The counseling department wasn't open yet. They opened at nine. Would Gabriel be around? No, somehow Imorean doubted it. He knew also from other students that Gabriel had a habit of not being in his office during normal hours.

Imorean looked across the campus common and spotted Baxter with Ryan and several other boys. Imorean smiled slightly as he spotted Dustin from the track team among them. Had they managed to get their football club up and running? It appeared so. In the distance, Baxter turned and raised his hand in a wave. Imorean furrowed his brow in confusion. He didn't understand Baxter. Did he want to be his friend or not? Warily, Imorean raised his own hand to wave back, only to spot Ryan making a rude hand gesture behind Baxter's back. Imorean dropped his hand and shook his head. Baxter, he could probably be friends with, but Imorean didn't think he could deal with Ryan. The boy seemed to hate him.

A few minutes later, Imorean sighed and looked up. He had arrived, seemingly through habit, at the gym. Why here of all places? Imorean was ready to turn and walk in another direction to continue his pondering, when he paused. He could hear the fans of the wind tunnel running. Michael. This must be when Michael practiced his own indoor skydiving.

The teenager grimaced. He still didn't know how he felt about Michael and after hearing his and Gabriel's conversation in the library during his first few days here, he wasn't sure if he trusted him. There was still something about the older Archer brother that set Imorean on edge, even intimidated him.

He glanced over his shoulder, back in the direction of the male dormitory. He didn't think he should allow these nightmares to continue and Michael seemed to be the only member of staff who was awake. Imorean gathered his courage and began to walk toward the gym door.

The noise of the fans covered Imorean's footsteps on the polished wood floor as he approached the skydiving simulator. Sure enough, he could see Michael in the glass wind tunnel. The man was perfectly balanced and was barely moving. His poised body was streamlined as though he was diving into a pool. Then the skydiving coach twisted his body and flipped upward, head over heels. Imorean stopped and smiled, finding himself enjoying Michael's display. Michael descended again, coming back to almost ground level, in complete control of himself as he hovered.

Imorean shook his head. He could barely balance on his stomach, let alone roll over on his back in the way that Michael was doing. It was as though Michael was in control of the artificial winds, bending them to his will rather than himself to theirs. Imorean inclined his head, noticing for the first time that Michael was wearing neither a helmet, nor goggles. Perhaps he was just used to the rush of air. Perhaps it was just another one of Michael's quirks.

Just as Imorean was getting ready to ascend the steps to come to the simulator's doorway, Michael rolled over and locked eyes with him. Imorean expected the man be surprised that he was there, but instead he only quirked one side of his mouth up in an expression akin to a smile.

Imorean stopped on the top step as Michael maneuvered himself to the doorway, then out so he was standing on solid ground. The man turned off the loud fans that powered the simulator, then looked at Imorean.

"Enjoy that little display, Frayneson?" asked Michael.

"Actually, yes, sir," replied Imorean, repressing the familiar surge of irritation that accompanied Michael's use of his last name. "It's always interesting to see someone else in the simulator."

"Well," said Michael, folding his arms and leaning on the glass of the simulator's walls. "That was nothing really. I was just having a bit of fun with the air currents. You should come out on a day when I am actually training for a jump."

"I'll bear that in mind," said Imorean, smiling slightly. Michael seemed to be slightly friendlier when he was on his own.

"You are awake awfully early, Frayneson. What is the occasion?"

"Well, in all truth, I was looking for a member of faculty. Any member of faculty I know pretty well and think I could talk to."

Michael stood up straight and raised one eyebrow. Imorean felt that the man was silently prompting him to continue. Imorean looked down, suddenly feeling guilty or perhaps, embarrassed. He was surprising himself in that he was choosing to trust Michael. Then again, Michael was one of the staff members that Imorean spent most of his time with. Michael was one of the faculty members that Imorean knew best and he supposed that with familiarity came trust.

"Frayneson, I do not have all day."

"I know, sir," said Imorean, tucking his hands into his pockets. "It's only something I've spoken about with close friends."

"For sensitive subjects, I recommend the counseling department."

"They aren't open and I think I have allowed this to go on too long," said Imorean, looking back up at Michael. The man had moved a few paces closer.

"Then say what is on your mind."

"I'm having nightmares," sighed Imorean, feeling more embarrassed. Why should Michael be helpful in this sort of situation?

"Oh? What kind of nightmares?" asked Michael. Imorean wasn't sure, but he thought that Michael's eyes had narrowed ever so slightly.

"There's always a dog or an animal in them."

"Do you fear dogs?"

"I never have before, sir."

"What do these dreams make you feel?" asked Michael. Imorean resisted the urge to widen his eyes. Michael actually seemed to be listening.

"Hunted," said Imorean. "Marked."

"Dreams can show the deepest desires of our hearts or our deepest fears. You understand that, do you not, Imorean?"

Imorean started slightly at the use of his first name. That must be one of the few times he had heard Michael use it.

"There's a voice as well."

"A voice?" asked Michael.

"Yes. Sometimes speaking, sometimes laughing."

"Do you know the sound of said voice or what the voice is saying?"

"It's a man's voice. I don't think I've ever heard it before when I'm awake. It sounds a bit like yours, but it's not yours. He often says 'fetch.'"

"Tell me," said Michael, sounding serious. "What happens in these dreams?"

"There's—there's an air of death in the dreams. Like there's something bad coming."

"I see. If you would like, I will speak impersonally with some of the counselors and see what they think. I thank you for trusting me enough to come to me first. I recommend, as a professor to a student, that you set up an appointment with a member of the counseling department."

"You'll leave my name out of it until I decide what to do?"

"Of course."

Imorean hesitated. "…Then, yes, sir. I—I hope you don't think I'm nuts now."

"Not at all. In ancient times, people used to believe some dreams were prophetic. They are not something to be ignored."

Imorean looked up at his coach. His pale eyes were narrower than usual and there was something *other* flickering behind them. Something Imorean couldn't put his finger on. Yet another oddity that he was unable to completely pin down.

Imorean sat in Dr. Haroel's class, scribbling down answers to the test. He wished he had been more prepared and less tired. He already knew Roxy would be the one to do better than him on the test. Every now and again, Imorean was aware of Toddy's eyes flickering to Roxy's paper. He crossed his fingers that Toddy didn't get caught. Dr. Haroel had a very strict policy on cheating.

Imorean raised his head for a moment to roll the kinks out of his neck. Ryan was sitting on his other side and Imorean scowled as he noticed the other boy's eyes landing on his paper. Imorean hesitated for a moment. He was still stung about Ryan giving him the finger earlier that morning and didn't like the way the other boy spoke to him or his friends. He had also noticed Ryan trying to trip Colton coming into the dining hall that morning. An unusual feeling of maliciousness rose in Imorean.

Giving no sign that he had noticed Ryan's cheating, Imorean leaned forward again and continued his test.

"What took you so long?" asked Roxy as Imorean walked into the dining hall. "We thought you were right behind us."

"I was," said Imorean, feeling self-satisfied. Toddy and Bethany were already seated at the table with Roxy and Mandy. Colton was nowhere in sight. "I had to have a word with Dr. Haroel."

"About?" asked Toddy.

"Hey! D-Bag!" shouted someone, tearing into the dining hall.

Imorean turned, smirking slightly as Ryan approached.

"Hey, Ryan," said Imorean. "How'd your test go?"

"He ripped it up in front of my face," snarled Ryan, slamming his hands down on Imorean's table. "Why the hell did you tell him?"

"Well, you gotta do what's right, you know?" said Imorean, shrugging.

"I might fail Haroel's class because of you! He told Michael too, and said the football club might get suspended."

Imorean folded his arms. "Maybe you should have thought of that."

"Your friends were cheating too!"

"My friends aren't asses," replied Imorean, standing up. A sudden burst of temper had reared its head in Imorean's chest.

"Ryan."

Baxter had come up from behind and placed a hand on his friend's shoulder. Dustin was with him, looking warily from Imorean to Ryan. "Come on. Just leave him. You're making this worse."

"I'll get you, albino boy," said Ryan. "Watch your back."

Imorean curled his upper lip. "Watch your own."

As Ryan followed Baxter and Dustin out of the dining hall, Bethany, Mandy, and Toddy collapsed into laughter. Imorean smirked and sat back down, but his expression fell a moment later when he noticed the disappointed look on Roxy's face.

Imorean was glad to be able to stretch his tense muscles after track practice that evening. The coach had kept all members of the team running sprints around Gracepointe's track. Sprints were not something Imorean took to well and he had a hard time with them.

"Hey."

Imorean looked up to see one of the other track team members. It was Dustin.

"Hey," replied Imorean, standing up straight and stretching his back.

"I think you could use one of these, you look beat," he said, tossing a small package to Imorean.

The white-haired teenager caught the packet and turned it over in his hands, repressing a grin when he saw what it was. Energy drink powder, cherry flavored.

"Where did you get this?" asked Imorean.

"Concession stand behind the bleachers," replied Dustin, motioning over one shoulder.

"Thanks," said Imorean with a grin. He tucked the packet into his sports bag and began walking toward the concession stand. This type of drink powder wasn't exactly what Roxy normally used to dye her hair, but it would have to do. It could also be a good way to make amends.

"So, what happened with you and Ryan today?" asked Dustin.

"I caught him cheating off my paper," said Imorean. "And Haroel said he'd rip up both cheaters' tests if he caught them, so I figured it was better to be safe than sorry."

"Yeah, I guess," shrugged Dustin. "You better watch out, man."

Imorean stopped and narrowed his eyes at Dustin. "Are you threatening me?"

"Not me. Ryan is *pissed*. He's a volatile guy. I'm not tryin' to threaten you, believe me, I'm not. I'm telling you as a friend, watch your back, 'cause Ryan's gonna be watching for an opportunity to kick your ass. The guy was barely passed over for a football scholarship. I wouldn't like to get punched by him."

Imorean inclined his head slightly. There was a genuine concern in Dustin's eyes, and something about it made Imorean more heartened. Dustin was an ally, if not a friend.

"Thanks, Dustin."

"Not a problem. I don't wanna see you get sent to student health 'cause Ryan beat you up."

Imorean laughed halfheartedly. Dustin joined him with even less enthusiasm and Imorean knew that his teammate's warning was real.

CHAPTER 24

I morean couldn't help but notice the change in Michael's temperament in the weeks that followed their early morning conversation in the gym. Where the man had been rather sharp and waspish at times, he now behaved as such *all* the time. Imorean felt that he couldn't do anything right at the indoor skydiving practices anymore. Michael was constantly scrutinizing him and chastising him. The past few weeks on Michael's team had been utter misery for Imorean.

"Have you forgotten everything that I have attempted to teach you, Frayneson?" snapped Michael as Imorean flailed madly in the air. The team had been working on back flips for the past few days. All of them except Imorean had been able to manage them.

"Work with the air, not against it," said Michael, shaking his head.

Imorean glared at him. Perhaps instead of criticizing him, he could offer some help. Behind Michael, Imorean could see Bethany and Toddy looking on in sympathy. It wasn't just Imorean who had been on the receiving end of Michael's temper, although he did seem to be the man's favorite target.

Imorean tried one more time to situate his body properly in the air to perform the flip Michael had asked him to, but he just couldn't manage it. Even now in mid-September, Imorean still hated the fact that he had nothing to hold onto, that he could gain purchase on nothing. He had been on the team for weeks now and his fear of heights was still dogging him. Imorean rolled back into his basic, spread eagle position and hovered.

"That is enough," said Michael, turning the fans off. "We will work on this again tomorrow, Frayneson. For tonight, I have had enough of watching you make a fool of yourself."

Imorean fell heavily down onto the elastic netting and quickly scrambled over to the door before Michael shut it. The surly, skydiving coach frowned at Imorean and shook his head. Imorean opened his mouth to snap a rude comment, but thought better of it at the last moment. Michael was an unpredictable man and he was a faculty member. Imorean didn't think being rude to him would go over very well.

"Come on, Imorean," said Toddy from the bottom of the steps. "We've got studying we need to do."

"I'm coming," said Imorean, not looking back at Michael as he walked down the steps and picked up his bag. The contents had spilled onto the floor and Imorean hurried to pick them up.

"What's his problem?" asked Imorean as he and his friends left the gym.

"What do you mean?" asked Bethany, studying her nails.

"He's been a complete prick for over two weeks now."

"I don't know what the issue is," said Toddy, shrugging and resting a hand of encouragement on Imorean's shoulder.

"I mean if he hates me so much, why doesn't he just kick me off the team? He won't even let me quit."

"Because he can see your potential." Bethany sounded

huffy and had been in a foul mood all day. "Hell, even I can see it. He knows that you could be a really good skydiver, probably even a wingsuit skydiver. I think he just hasn't quite figured out how to teach you to harness your talent though. I don't think he's angry with you. I'm pretty sure he's just frustrated."

"Well, he doesn't have to take it out on me," replied Imorean, holding the door open for his friends as they entered the library. He watched as Bethany passed in front of him. Was she wearing a new set of designer tee shirt and jeans again? Imorean was certain she got new clothes almost every week. Why was it that he found that so strange, he wondered?

Roxy and Colton were already waiting for them at their regular table in the library.

"I still don't get this whole mythology class," snorted Bethany, taking out their textbook.

"None of us do," said Imorean. "I know one thing though, it's driving me up the wall. It's an extra class I really shouldn't be taking and the way Haroel runs it, it should be writing intensive."

"I know," said Colton.

Imorean rested his textbook on the table and looked across at Colton. The younger boy was doing calculus problems with one hand and reading the mythology book when he finished each problem. Imorean shook his head. Colton really did have a unique ability to multitask.

"By the way, Roxy," said Imorean, reaching into his bag again and sliding some packets across the table to his best friend. "This is my payment for borrowing your notes recently."

"Ah!" cried Roxy, looking up from the book she was reading and grabbing hold of the packets. Imorean grinned. She was the only person he knew who could get so excited about powdered drinks.

"I knew you'd pay up eventually." Roxy grinned at him as

she turned the packets over in her hands.

"They took quite a while to find," said Imorean, "but it turns out that they keep them in the sports concession stands."

"You're awesome," beamed Roxy.

"Are we going to study or gossip?" snapped Bethany, leafing through her book. Imorean frowned at her. Bethany could be temperamental, but remaining in a bad mood for several hours was unusual for her.

"We like to do a bit of both," replied Roxy sweetly.

Imorean rolled his eyes. He knew from Roxy's tone that she wasn't intending to be sweet at all. As he placed his binder and his pen on the table, he felt Bethany slip her hand into his. He wasn't sure when they had started holding hands under the table during studying, but he liked it. He was enjoying the quiet, private relationship between them. Not even Roxy knew about it. Yet. Imorean had been planning to tell his friends, he just hadn't quite gotten around to it.

Imorean delved back into his bag for the third time, searching for the book that they were supposed to be reading for Dr. Haroel's class. He frowned. It wasn't there. But he felt certain that he had put it in his bag that afternoon.

"Imorean, everything alright?" asked Roxy, obviously having noticed his expression.

"Does anyone else have a copy of *Osiris and Set?*" asked Imorean, looking around the table. They had recently started their section on Ancient Egyptian Mythology.

"Not with me," Roxy grimaced.

Toddy shook his head. "Mine's back at the dorm."

"Mine too," replied Colton.

"I get my copy tomorrow. I'm on a different schedule from the rest of you." Bethany shrugged, her tone apologetic.

"Are you missing your copy?" asked Toddy.

"Yeah," said Imorean, frowning. "Oh no... my bag spilled

when I set it down in the gym. I bet that's where it is. I need to start reading that book. We're being quizzed on it tomorrow."

"Do you want me to walk with you?" asked Roxy.

"No. No offense, Roxy, but I'll be faster on my own."

"None taken," said Roxy, sitting back down.

"I'll come," offered Bethany. Imorean didn't miss the poisonous glance that Bethany shot Roxy. He felt a twinge of irritation.

"No. I'll go on my own."

Imorean left his book bag next to the table and stood up.

He exited the library, then started to jog quickly from the library back to the gym. He hoped Michael hadn't locked up the building yet. The gym was dark as Imorean approached it. He slowed as he reached the top of the steps. Imorean walked onward and rested a hand on one of the gym's glass doors. He pulled, his heart sinking when he heard the deadbolt clang against the metal frame of the other door. Imorean groaned in exasperation and let his head fall forward against the glass doors.

This day was just not going his way. That morning he had just barely passed one of the tests from Norwegian Literature. Dr. Haroel's lectures were becoming much more involved and complicated. Biology was getting harder and Imorean felt that he barely had enough time to study for it, despite the fact that it was his chosen major. Michael constantly made him feel like an insect under a microscope and never missed a chance to point out his faults. Now he had left the very book he needed to study inside a locked building. Could this day get much worse?

"Can't a guy catch a break?" Imorean asked, tilting his head up and studying the starry sky that stretched overhead.

"Not tonight you can't," said a voice from the shadows.

Imorean turned. That was not a voice he wanted to hear

when he was alone in the dark. Ryan. Imorean remembered Dustin's warning and swallowed hard as he strained his eyes to see in the darkness. This was not how he had imagined the inevitable confrontation.

"Ryan?" asked Imorean, narrowing his eyes and trying to make out a shape he saw lurking in the shadows.

"That's right, albino boy," said Ryan, finally stepping out of the darkness. Imorean's mouth ran dry when he noticed the other two boys with him. Fighting one-on-one was something he could manage, and had done before. Three against one was just unfair. Right now, his chances of stepping away from Ryan with his face intact were not looking good.

"I've been waiting too long for this," said Ryan, grinning.

Imorean resisted the urge to curl his lip. "Yeah, a few weeks is a long time for someone with the attention span of a goldfish."

"You got my football club shut down." Ryan's voice had changed. There was something much more aggressive in it now.

"I wish I could say you didn't deserve it," said Imorean, subconsciously stepping backward. He wanted to put as much space between himself and Ryan as he could. For a moment, Imorean wondered if his friends had noticed how long he had been gone. Maybe. He hoped they had. Imorean rested one hand on the low, stone wall that surrounded the portico in front of the gym.

"You nearly made me lose this scholarship."

"Bitter about that, are you?"

"I don't like your tone, albino boy."

"I hear you got passed over for a football scholarship. I guess they thought you were a girl with how much drama you stir up."

"I'm going to get so much satisfaction out of this," hissed

Ryan.

Imorean watched Ryan's two friends move closer to him from the corners of his vision. When he felt that they had come too close, he tightened his hand on the rough, stone wall and vaulted over it.

A shock ran up and down Imorean's legs when he landed. His landing had been much more uneven than he had expected, but he didn't let that stop him. As soon as he got his bearings, he bolted. Running from a fight wasn't something he had ever done before, but he had never before had to fight with three to one odds.

Behind him, Imorean could hear the pounding footsteps of Ryan and his friends. He was grateful he was a distance runner. He could easily run for longer than they could, but could he beat them for speed? From the way the footsteps were bearing down on him, he didn't think so.

Imorean changed his path and darted between two of the main lecture halls, slipping slightly as he took a tight turn. Perhaps that would be enough to throw them off his trail for a little while. Imorean wished, not for the first time in his life, that he wasn't so easy to spot. A brunet would have a much easier time disappearing into the night, but no, he had to have *white* hair. Ryan and his friends would spot him immediately, no matter how much distance he managed to put between himself and them. Imorean raced around the second corner of the lecture hall and pressed himself flat against the wall, trying not to pant.

"I don't see him," said one of Ryan's friends.

"He can't have just vanished," snapped Ryan. "That guy is owed an ass kicking."

Imorean could tell from their voices that they were close. Instinct told him that moving was his best option, so he listened and inched slowly along the wall. *Crack.* Imorean froze. The sound of him stepping on a loose branch split the night like a gunshot. Curse this campus and all its trees.

Before he really knew it, Imorean took off again, sprinting across one of the campus's many lawns. He knew that Ryan and his friends would be right on his heels. Quickly, Imorean glanced over his shoulder. He came to a screeching halt. There was no one there.

Imorean stopped completely and looked around. Where had they gone? A punch struck the side of his head with dizzying force and Imorean clamped one hand over the point of impact, stumbling. He felt as though he had been hit by a train. He couldn't hear anything, save for a high-pitched whining. The world was spinning. Ryan could hit harder than he had anticipated. A second punch crashed into his cheekbone and Imorean tasted blood in his mouth. Off balance as he was, it didn't take much to send him sprawling on his hands and knees in the grass.

The teenager blinked quickly, trying to look around, to see. He placed one hand against the ground and tried to stand, but a foot collided with his side, sending him rolling a few feet across the lawn. There hadn't been time for him to try to stand and defend himself.

"Don't mess with me again, albino boy and don't you *dare* mention that scholarship ever again," snarled Ryan, kicking Imorean savagely in the ribs. If Imorean hadn't known better, he could have sworn he felt them break. The world whirled in a nonsensical tornado of color and Imorean had a feeling he was rolling over in the grass. He couldn't find the words to reply to Ryan's insult. He was focusing more intently on not vomiting.

"Imorean!" called a dim voice from some distance away. Imorean thought it was Roxy. Thank God she had noticed his absence.

"Let's go," said Ryan.

Relief washed over Imorean, only to be staunched when Ryan stamped down hard on his abdomen, driving the wind from his lungs.

"Imorean! Where are you?" called Roxy again. Imorean wasn't sure, but he thought he heard Toddy's voice as well.

He opened his mouth and tried to answer their cries, but no sound would leave his mouth. He could barely draw breath, let alone cry out for his friends. Imorean wrapped his arms over his stomach and curled into a ball.

Somewhere in the back of his mind, he heard a growl. Imorean opened his eyes and whimpered, still unable to produce much sound. He raised his head slightly and looked around. Were those red eyes that he could see piercing through the shadows or was it just some of the school's lights? That menacing growl came again, accompanied by a rotting smell that made Imorean's stomach turn. He could have sworn he saw a pair of shapes move through the shadows. *'Not now. Not now,'* he begged silently.

Imorean struggled to draw breath into his lungs, coughing as he did so. If he had been frightened earlier, he was terrified now. There was more movement in the shadows and Imorean wondered if there actually was a monster hiding in them. Imorean wanted to move, to get up, to run, as he heard bracken crackling under something's feet. Whatever was there was on the move and it was coming closer.

"Imorean?" called Roxy again. She sounded less distant now.

"Rox," croaked Imorean, looking around. He still didn't want to move very much.

"Imorean," said Toddy.

Imorean was able to hear footsteps now. There were two sets of them and it sounded as though they were running. He felt a bit more able to breathe now, air gracing his lungs with more ease.

"We thought you were going to find a book, you fool," said Roxy, kneeling next to him and resting his head in her lap. Imorean could see Toddy leaning over her shoulder, his eyes wide with concern.

"I was," replied Imorean. His voice was strained and he tried to focus on his friends. To Imorean, it seemed as though they had both turned into liquid and were swimming back and forth before his very eyes.

"Well that obviously didn't go very well, did it? You couldn't even find your way to the gym," huffed Roxy, shaking her head. "What happened?"

"Ryan happened," muttered Imorean. He wasn't quite sure if he had even said the words aloud.

"Imorean, you shouldn't have kicked the hornet's nest," said Roxy. "Now look what you've done. This is your own fault, you know."

"Come on," said Toddy. "Let's get him back to the dorm."

'Yes, good idea, Toddy,' thought Imorean. He didn't want to speak aloud. Speaking hurt his head and made everything spin more than it already was.

"Come on," said Roxy, grabbing hold of Imorean's arm and looping it over her shoulders.

"Can you stand?" asked Toddy as he helped Imorean scramble up.

"I'm not sure," mumbled Imorean, blinking hard.

"Okay," replied Roxy, rubbing his forearm in a reassuring gesture. "That's fine. We'll just drag you across campus."

Imorean quirked a small smile, but felt he was unable to reply.

The white-haired teenager felt an unusual rush of affection when he was dumped unceremoniously onto his mattress. His friends had gotten him back here as safely as they could.

"Are you going to be okay?" asked Roxy, pausing in the doorway.

"Yeah, I think so," replied Imorean, kicking off his shoes and taking the set of pajamas that Toddy was holding out for him.

"Okay," nodded Roxy. "Toddy?"

"Yeah?"

"Please take him to the student health center if he doesn't feel better tomorrow, would you? I don't like the look of that knot on his head. He might have a concussion."

"I will."

Imorean sighed as he listened to their conversation. He hoped he would feel right by the next morning. He really didn't want to pay the student health center another visit.

"Goodnight," said Roxy, closing the door as she exited.

"Where's my bag and everything?" asked Imorean, looking up at Toddy. Even the low light in the room and the sudden movement was hurting his head.

"I brought it," replied Toddy.

"Where's Colton?" asked Imorean. "And Bethany and Mandy?"

"They're still in the library. Bethany and Mandy said they'd walk with Colton later. I doubt Ryan would try and tackle three of them. Besides, he doesn't have any issues with any of them."

"I hope not," replied Imorean. He found himself wishing for an icepack to press against his head.

After he had changed into the pajamas, Imorean laid back down on his bed and drifted into sleep almost as soon as his head hit the pillow.

There was a strong wind blowing. One that Imorean didn't like. He felt that it could knock him clear out of the sky. Air rushed past him at almost two hundred miles an hour. Imorean had no idea why he had consented to skydiving with Michael. Something about redeeming himself. Imorean couldn't remember. Beginnings were always so hazy. A thick, green forest raced up to meet him and Imorean pulled on his parachute cord, confident it would deploy. It did not. Imorean yelped and pulled again, harder this time. Still nothing. Again. Nothing. Imorean could see the branches on the trees now. If his parachute didn't deploy soon he would be speared on the treetops. Imorean wailed and pulled his parachute cord with both hands. At the very last minute, the chute deployed, slowing his fall. It was too late though to navigate away from the forest. Imorean had no choice but to land amongst the trees. The white-haired teenager cried out as sharp twigs and branches scraped his legs and arm, his clothing doing little to protect his skin as he barreled down through the canopy. With a jerk, Imorean stopped. He was still over ten feet above the ground, just dangling. Imorean turned to see what had stopped his controlled fall. His parachute was caught on a large tree limb. If he didn't unbuckle from his chute, he wouldn't be going anywhere anytime soon.

With shaking fingers, Imorean undid the straps that kept him tethered to his parachute. As the last one came undone, Imorean fell, plummeting again. He landed heavily on the ground, feeling stunned. For a moment, he lay still, trying to regain his bearings. When he sat up, his head spun sickeningly. He didn't want to move anywhere. Then he heard it. Through the thick forest came a savage, hungry growl. Imorean scrabbled to get to his feet. As he turned, he came nose to nose with a massive, salivating, black dog. Its red eyes bored into his own, paralyzing him. The eyes seemed to burn vivid red, lit by the fires of a raging furnace. As Imorean looked into the monster's eyes, it seemed to be saying something. I'm close. I'm close. Marked. Marked. Marked. Imorean trembled. He willed his body to run, to move. Then the creature's jaws opened, showing bloodied teeth the size of butcher knives.

Imorean yelped aloud and sat upright in bed. His body was trembling. This time, the memories from his nightmare were more vivid. More so than usual. They felt more real. His chest felt tight with fear and his hands were shaking. His teeth chattered together and he placed one hand over his eyes. The dream this time had been so lifelike, so solid. It was as though everything had actually been happening.

"Are you okay?" asked Toddy from across the room. Imorean looked over to see the younger boy sitting upright in bed.

"Did I wake you up?" asked Imorean, not answering the other boy's question.

"That's not important." Imorean saw Toddy shake his head in the darkness. "Are you okay?"

"Yes," lied Imorean. "Yes, I'm fine."

"You don't look fine. You've been more tired lately, Imorean. Is this why?"

Imorean looked away. The fewer people who knew about his nightmares and the black dog, the better.

"Everyone gets nightmares." Toddy's voice had a reassuring tone to it, but it did nothing to soothe Imorean. "I used to get them a lot."

"It's nothing," replied Imorean, pulling his blankets higher on his shoulders.

"Was it about what Ryan did to you?"

Imorean repressed a laugh. "No. No, nothing like that."

"Then what?"

Imorean put his head back down on the pillow. "Goodnight, Tod."

He feigned sleep, even though he knew he wouldn't find it. Not now. Not after the newest terror with the dog. Why was it always a dog? He had never been afraid of dogs before. He didn't think he was afraid of dogs now, just the one he kept seeing in his dreams. Then again, he wasn't altogether sure that that it *was* a dog. It was a monster, that was for sure.

CHAPTER
25

Imorean yawned as he sat down at his regular table with his friends that morning. Bethany had cornered him outside the dining hall earlier and fussed over him for several minutes. Imorean couldn't help but feel warmed by her affection. Her foul mood from the night before seemed to have vanished.

"How are you feeling?" asked Roxy, taking a second to stop eating and look up at him in concern.

"I'm fine," replied Imorean, rubbing the side of his head. He could still taste blood in his mouth. He had noticed earlier that morning that he had a few dark bruises on his ribs and a lump on the side of his head, but other than that he was unharmed. The most noticeable bruise was the vivid, purple one on his cheekbone.

"Toddy says you had a bad night last night," said Roxy, taking a bite of food.

"Don't talk with your mouth full," chided Imorean as Toddy, Colton, and Mandy made their way to the table. He smiled as Roxy glared at him in mock irritation. She elbowed him sharply, prompting his answer.

"Ouch," said Imorean, putting one hand over the area where her elbow had landed. "You've got really sharp elbows you know, Roxy. But he's right. I didn't sleep well last night."

"Any idea why?" asked Roxy. Imorean wordlessly passed her a napkin, making her roll her eyes. "Why are you such a stickler for table manners?"

"I was raised properly."

"Oh, and I was raised like a savage, was I?"

Imorean caught Roxy's elbow before it snapped into his side for the second time that morning.

"I never said that."

"You were thinking it." Roxy grinned. She sobered a moment later. "Really though, what's going on?"

"Nothing, I'm just not sleeping well."

Roxy rolled her eyes. "If you say so."

The chatter in the dining hall lulled for a moment as the door opened. Imorean turned, wondering what had caused the sudden quiet. He felt mildly surprised to see Michael and Gabriel breeze through the doors. It wasn't unusual for the teachers to eat in the dining hall with the students, but Imorean couldn't think of a time that both Michael and Gabriel had done so with them. The volume of chattering students returned to normal, forgetting the abnormal presence of the two brothers. Imorean though, stayed looking at the two men for a moment more, curious as to why they were here. Gabriel was talking animatedly to his older brother, but Michael seemed to be more focused on his phone. It looked as though he was typing a text message.

Imorean began to turn away, but shuddered slightly as an unnatural rush of warm air landed on the back of his neck. It felt as though someone was breathing down the collar of his shirt. Imorean watched as Michael's head snapped upward and he began to scan the dining hall, as though he was looking for something. Then Michael's jade green eyes locked with Imorean's chocolate brown ones and the man quite promptly dropped his phone. Imorean thought he saw a sense of urgency in Michael's eyes, but he was too far away to be sure.

"Stop doing that," said Roxy, putting one hand on Imorean's shoulder and shaking him.

"Doing what?" snapped Imorean, turning away from Michael to look back at his friends.

"Ogling Michael. We all see you doing it and it's a little worrying."

"Making me feel a little jealous," Bethany muttered, sitting down next to Imorean.

"Oh, shut up. I do not ogle him."

"Yeah, you actually do," said Mandy, smiling.

"I do not," replied Imorean, returning to his breakfast. He vaguely noticed Roxy's eyes narrow in suspicion. The expression was gone a moment later.

"We're only calling what we see," called Roxy in a sing-song voice.

Imorean got up from the table. "And on that note, I'm going to the library. I'll see you guys in Haroel's class."

"See ya." Roxy waved him away, but Imorean barely noticed.

Imorean blinked hard at Dr. Haroel, struggling to keep his eyes open. After his first class of the day, he had started feeling tired, probably the effects of having had constant nightmares for the past week. The black dog was always woven somehow into the dreams.

Imorean's mind wandered. He found it hard to believe it was already almost October. Autumn was upon them. He still had to find out if they were so much as getting a Thanksgiving break. What about Gabriel and Michael? The two brothers were up to something, that Imorean was sure of.

Though, as to what, he had no idea. Not yet.

Imorean's eyelids grew heavier as his thoughts wandered further and further from the topic that Dr. Haroel was lecturing about. How long had he been in this class now? Ten minutes? Fifteen? Perhaps a little longer.

"Imorean, am I still holding your attention?" asked Dr. Haroel, pausing in his lecture.

"Yes, sir," replied Imorean. Had he nodded off during Dr. Haroel's lecture? "Sorry, sir."

"As I was saying," said Dr. Haroel, looking back at the rest of the class. "Each culture from around the world has its own mythical creatures. The Loch Ness Monster from Scotland, the Chupacabra from Central America, the Black Shuck from England. All are creatures specific to those areas. There are some legends of creatures though, that span the world. I know, I know, you must be thinking what on earth does this have to do with the introduction to our section on angels and demons? I assure you though, that this discussion does relate back to this class."

"In his mind," muttered Roxy from her position next to Imorean.

"Roxy," said Imorean, glaring at her slightly. He couldn't fathom why she disliked Dr. Haroel's class so much. Imorean shook his head and shrugged, making a small attempt to shake off his tiredness. Roxy's irritation could, of course, have stemmed from Dr. Haroel's blatant refusal to use her nickname.

"Sir?" said Colton, raising a hand.

"Yes, Colton," said Dr. Haroel.

"All of those other creatures I have heard of, except for the Black Shuck. What's that?"

"According to legend, it was a monstrous dog that terrorized parts of England during the sixteenth century. It was said to have stood at seven feet tall, had black fur, and glowing red eyes."

Imorean's eyes widened. The Black Shuck sounded terrifyingly similar to the demon dogs he had been seeing in his dreams and to the black dog of Valle Crucis. He swallowed hard and listened as Dr. Haroel continued.

"The Black Shuck itself is interesting in that there are other legends that also involve a black dog. They are few and far between, but if one looks hard enough they can find legends in which black dogs exist in other parts of the world.

"Creatures like The Black Shuck may be known by other names, black dogs, Hellhounds, ghost dogs, and bearers of death. Some legends even go so far as to state that they can cause people to die. In other cultures though, black dogs are said to be benign. The legend really can go either way. Now, as we are on the topic of black dogs and supernatural beings like them, there are other creatures that span most cultures as well. Can anyone venture a guess at what they are?"

"Sir?"

Imorean looked up in surprise to see Roxy raising a hand.

"Roxanne," said Dr. Haroel, pointing at her.

"Is one of the answers demons?"

"Perfect. Your classmate is right. There is lore about demons worldwide and it is common. A few keywords on the internet can take you directly to demon lore.

"Some cultures say that demons are non-corporeal creatures. However, others say they are able to take on a physical shape."

"Sir," said Toddy, raising a hand. "Where do angels come into all this?"

"Angels," said Dr. Haroel. The slide on the board behind the teacher changed, revealing a new slide. A child, dressed in white, complete with fluffy, downy wings. There was no other word for it but cuddly. "These creatures are the opposite of demons. Where demons stand for everything that is evil, wicked, and hateful in the world, angels stand for the opposite. They represent everything good, holy."

The professor's eyes swept the classroom and a small smile formed on his face.

"And divine."

"Where do demons come from?" asked Imorean, the question tumbling out of his mouth before he raised his hand.

"Hand raised next time please, Imorean," said Dr. Haroel. "But good question. There is history behind where demons come from. The shortened version is that many millennia ago, there was a war in heaven between the angels who were loyal to God and the ones who wanted to rebel. When the angels who rebelled were punished, their divine nature was taken and they were cast out of heaven. They became fallen angels, creatures better known as demons."

Tentatively, Imorean raised his hand.

"Yes?"

"You said earlier that the Black Shuck and beasts like it were known as black dogs, demon dogs, and Hellhounds. What's the connection between the angels who were cast out of heaven and the dogs?"

"Hellhounds are said to guard the entrances to the world of the dead, much like Cerberus does in Greek Mythology. Many accounts throughout history say that people have spotted large, black dogs roaming graveyards or burial grounds by night. Some say that Hellhounds are used to guard treasure, but others say that they are sent out to hunt down lost souls. A sort of devilish bounty hunter. Old folklore says that if one stares into a Hellhound's eyes twice they are sure to die, other lore says that just hearing one is an omen of death," finished Dr. Haroel, leaning on his desk.

The class was quiet. Quieter than usual. Imorean was certain the other students could hear the pounding of his heart. He was not a superstitious person. He could enjoy a good horror movie and not feel too spooked afterward, but now, he felt terrified. Surely a mythical apparition could have no bearing in this mortal world. Imorean reminded himself that this was a mythology class. It had no bearing on what he had been seeing in his dreams. It was just coincidence. Nothing more.

"What about angels, sir?" said Colton.

"What about them?" asked Dr. Haroel, inclining his head.

"Well, what sort of bearing do they have on demons and Hellhounds?"

"Lore states that to this day there is still war raging between the two supernatural powers and it will only stop when one side wins. A few legends state that humanity itself hangs in the balance of the war. Which brings me to your essay topic for this week. Write a three-thousand-word essay on an angel or a demon, the culture or religion it exists in, whether it is evil or benign, and what its purpose is. Also, in relation to the war, give me your ideas on which side would win and why."

Imorean couldn't repress the groan that escaped him. He was glad that the rest of the class's drowned his own out. Dr. Haroel, though being one of the best teachers Imorean had had so far at any institution, liked to hand out reports and essays way too much.

Imorean got up to leave the class more slowly than Roxy, Toddy, and Colton. He had a question he wanted to ask Dr. Haroel. The teenager's friends were already at the door by the time Imorean had finished packing up his books.

"Are you coming, slowpoke?" asked Roxy, pausing in the threshold.

"I'll be along in a minute," replied Imorean. "I'll meet you in the dining hall."

"Suit yourself."

Imorean frowned and made his way to the front of the classroom to where Dr. Haroel now sat behind his desk, half hidden by a mountain of paper. Imorean quirked a smile.

Hopefully it was all the essays they had had to write last week. At least Dr. Haroel could have the fun of grading them.

"Dr. Haroel," said Imorean.

"Yes?" asked the professor, looking up. His gaze hardened slightly when he saw Imorean. "Ah, my sleepy student. What can I do for you, Imorean?"

"Sorry, sir. I have a question for you."

"That is?" prompted the man.

"Are angels, demons, and Hellhounds... things like that... are they *real?*"

"That's an unusual question certainly," replied the professor, smiling and putting down his pen. "Frankly, Imorean, I think that the existence or not of angels and demons is a matter of opinion, don't you? It's not exactly my job or my place to tell you what is real and what is not. I am your teacher. I am here solely to impart knowledge, not to tell you what to believe."

"I suppose so, sir," said Imorean, frowning in confusion. That didn't exactly answer his question.

"You look discontented with my answer."

"I don't know, sir."

"Do you believe in them?" asked Dr. Haroel.

"I don't think so. They're mythical creatures. It's all just a bit too farfetched for me, sir," said Imorean, shaking his head. His tongue felt leaden in his mouth, as though he was lying.

"Go to the library, Imorean," said Dr. Haroel, quirking a small smile. "I'm sure your answer will be lurking somewhere between the bookshelves. For now, theology, the existence of demons, Hellhounds, God, and angels is a massive can of worms that perhaps a young man like yourself should not be too worried about opening. I prefer to focus myself on the mythological and literary aspects of the legends. We may delve into some theology later on in the semester, but not yet. Focus on your essay for now."

"Yes, sir." Imorean didn't feel convinced. As far as he was concerned, the only answer lurking and lying in wait was the black dog of his nightmares and that was starting to feel more real than he would like to admit.

"Now, I will have to excuse myself. I am on a much-needed lunch break, and so, hopefully, are you. If you find yourself with further questions, please come to me during my office hours."

"Yes, sir."

The white-haired boy made his way out of the classroom and began the walk down the stairs. When he got to the bottom, he heard a voice coming down the hallway from the other direction. He quickened his steps slightly and started to cross the large foyer, making his way to the door at the other end of the floor. It was lunch time and he was starting to feel hungry.

"Let me guess," snapped the voice.

Imorean checked his steps. That was Michael. He recognized the irritation in the tone.

"It was Frayneson, was it not?" Michael snarled, sounding livid.

Imorean stumbled to a halt. He had never heard Michael say his name with so much anger in the tone. For a moment, he wasn't sure if he was being spoken to or not, and he stayed quiet.

"Is he asking about them?" asked Michael. His voice was concerned now. "You have got to be kidding. They have only been here a matter of weeks. It is just now turning October. *How* have they caught on so quickly? Then again, that one has his nose into everything. He even found out about the gates within a few hours of being here... All right, all right! I will meet with Gabriel and Afriel as soon as possible and see what we should do. This is not good, Haroel. Taking them out of the United States was the entire point of this endeavor!"

There was a pause. Imorean stood pressed flat against the

wall. It sounded as though Michael was just around the corner in the next hallway. His heart was racing. The gates. Michael had mentioned the gates and the students' removal from the United States. Why was it always him overhearing conversations he wasn't supposed to? Why, oh why, just for a change, couldn't it be Roxy or Toddy?

"No, you are misreading me. I am not angry at you... No, I am not angry at him either. It is not his fault he is clever. Try and keep the students reined in for a week more. I wanted to do as Gabriel asked and bide our time just a bit longer. Yes, you are correct, there is too much at stake here. If you do not have an evening class today, we will try and get the meeting tonight in as early as possible. Hopefully, nothing else will happen between now and then. All right. All right. I will see you later. No, that is not necessary. I will deal with Mr. Frayneson myself."

Imorean's breath hitched in his throat as he heard footsteps coming towards him. He couldn't make it to the door from here. He would be spotted and he couldn't go back up the stairs. Surely Dr. Haroel would be coming down them by now. Imorean closed his eyes and clenched his teeth as the footsteps drew closer and closer. The precise rap of Michael's shoes on the floor rang out like a siren. There was nowhere to go. If he had only gone with his friends, he wouldn't have overheard this.

Imorean backed up a few paces, trying to keep his steps light, then Michael rounded the corner. Imorean froze and locked eyes with the skydiving coach.

CHAPTER 26

———— ❦ ————

Imorean's blood seemed to freeze in his veins as his brown eyes and Michael's pale, peridot ones bored into each other. There was an odd, equal mixture of surprise and anger in Michael's eyes. Imorean swallowed hard and opened his mouth to speak, but no words would come out.

"Imorean," said Michael, shaking his head and smiling. "You look like you have been in a fight. Are you all right?"

Imorean didn't respond. Something in that smile looked feral and fear overrode any answer he might have given Michael. The tension that should have been broken by Michael's question was only heightened. Michael's eyes flashed and Imorean repressed a shiver. There was a dangerous aura flickering around him. He felt for a moment that Michael was sensing more than he should have been able, as though the coach knew that he had overheard the phone call. Imorean took another step back, putting space between himself and Michael. The flimsy trust he had built in the skydiving coach was trickling away like sand through an hourglass. For the first time, he felt afraid of the man. Truly afraid.

"Imorean, it is all right," said Michael, stepping forward again.

Imorean stepped back.

"What's going on?" asked the teenager. He hated the way his voice hitched at the end of his sentence.

"I do not understand what you mean," said Michael.

"Yes. You do," said Imorean, backing down even more. Surely there was another way out of this building other than the main door. There had to be a nearby fire exit or something, but, inside, Imorean knew better. He knew the layout of the building. Michael was standing between him and the nearest way out. It seemed almost intentional.

"Imorean," said Michael, raising both hands in a calming gesture.

Imorean flinched backwards, tensing his body and feeling ready to run. Fight or flight was kicking in. Michael sighed in irritation and dropped his hands back to his sides.

"There's something going on here that we aren't being told, isn't there?" asked Imorean, narrowing his eyes. He felt as though he was perching on his toes, escape imminent.

"Yes, Imorean," replied Michael at last. "Yes, there is."

"What is it? Tell me or I call the police."

"I think you will find that all electronic communications in and out of Gracepointe," began Michael, raising his hand and slowly lowering it. "Have suddenly gone out."

As the man spoke, there was a flicker of light overhead. Imorean swallowed hard and looked around.

"I'm going to call the police," said Imorean again. He was glad that his voice sounded firm this time.

"Try," said Michael, holding his cell phone out to Imorean. "Norwegian police number, if you didn't know, is 112."

Imorean warily took Michael's phone and flipped it open, finding the screen to be nothing but static. Michael shrugged and smirked.

"What are you doing? To this place? To me and my fellow students?"

"Relax, Frayneson," said Michael, taking his phone back. "It is nothing you have to concern yourself about."

"I think I do. I'm a student here. Me and the rest of the students are caught in the thick of this. What's at stake? And why did we have to be taken out of the United States? What did you mean deal with me yourself?" panted Imorean, fear spiking in his blood.

"Imorean, you will get yourself in trouble with all these questions. It is best not to ask."

"Answer me!" demanded Imorean, his fear suddenly giving way to anger.

"No," replied Michael, shaking his head. "I refuse."

"What's going on here?"

"Leave well enough alone, Imorean."

"I don't know what you're planning, but I'm not going to stop pushing until I find out what you're hiding. I'll tell the rest of the students what I heard!"

"Then you are leaving me no choice. I must deal with you now and hang the consequences."

Imorean dropped his backpack as Michael swung at him, aiming to grab his arm. Imorean's eyes widened and he jumped back, accidentally slamming himself into an interior wall. Michael was moving fast, faster than any person should be able to move naturally. The grip that landed on the bare skin of Imorean's wrist was strong as iron and it felt as though the bones were being crushed. Imorean's vision flashed green, and for a second it was as though the air had been punched out of him. Vision flashed white, green, white, green. Brown eyes rolled in Imorean's head. A weight rolled off his shoulders and for a split second, he felt as though he was being lifted from the floor. Something in the back of Imorean's mind shattered. His eyes snapped open. Surely, he had to be imagining the ethereal green glow surrounding them both. Surely, the sound of windows rattling so hard that it seemed they would splinter in their frames was a trick of his fear. The lights flickering overhead had to be nothing more than an issue with the wiring. His senses were alight. Sound too much. Light too much. Scent, taste, touch. It was all too much. Panic and pain burrowed into him. Imorean screamed. Surely there were other students somewhere in the building! Away, away, away, he had to get *away*. He turned to pull free, tugging to get his arm out of Michael's hold. Adrenalin set his blood cold and for a second, he could have sworn the man's grip slipped.

"Be still!"

"Get off me!" shouted Imorean, raising his voice as high as he could. He needed to attract as much attention as possible. He launched toward Michael, lowering his shoulder and driving it straight into the center of Michael's chest. Anything to get away. Anything at all.

Imorean realized too late though, that he had made a mistake. He lost his balance as Michael spun him around, placing them back to chest, and trapped his arm between them. Then there was an arm around Imorean's throat, gently pressing tighter and cutting off air to his lungs. Panic broke in Imorean and he screamed again before Michael could stifle it in his throat. With his free hand, he pulled and tore at Michael's arm, trying to get away. He jumped up, and gasped loudly as Michael's grip was jostled looser. A hand clamped down over his mouth, and the arm redoubled its tight hold. Imorean thrashed. He didn't stand a chance of winning against Michael. The skydiving coach was much older, bigger, and stronger than he was, but that did not mean that Imorean was not willing to fight. He bit down hard on Michael's palm. Surely, that would be enough to force Michael's hand away. Another green flash tore across Imorean's vision as something clocked him hard on the side of his head. Both of Michael's hands were occupied, so where the blow had come from, Imorean had no idea. The strength of the impact caused Imorean to tighten his teeth on Michael's hand and he thought he tasted blood in his mouth.

Michael hissed loudly, but tightened his grip. "I do not want to do this, Imorean, but you endanger everything we are doing and you must be dealt with."

Imorean found sheer panic in those words. His world was starting to go black and was fading away. His ears were ringing and filling with rushing water. His head felt slow and dull, like it was filled with cotton. What would Michael do with him when he was unconscious? Michael's hand dropped away from his mouth and Imorean gasped raggedly for breath, spitting between gulps. Even the fresh air could not beat back the rising tide of darkness that was slowly starting to force him down. His knees were weakening. The blood flow to his brain was being cut off. Dimly, Imorean knew that the only thing that would save him from losing consciousness would be Michael letting him out of the chokehold. He had to rise back up. He had to get away. Through the shadows that were clouding over his vision, Imorean spotted a glimmer of unnatural, white light gathering at the tips of Michael's fingers. Fingers that were now moving toward his forehead. Imorean thrashed weakly, still pushing for freedom.

Then something sharp, something metallic, cut through the skin of his trapped arm, and Imorean felt as though he had been jarred back to life. Inside, he gathered all the energy he had left, planted his feet firmly on the floor and reared backwards, shoving with everything he had. A flash of white cleared his darkening vision and Imorean felt as though all his energy had flown out of him in a pulse.

The pressure of Michael's arm around his neck was gone and Imorean collapsed, the world clearing as he lay on his side, heaving air back into his lungs. He looked up. Michael was lying face down several yards away, weakly lifting his head. Green eyes were unfocused. He seemed stunned and confused. Imorean scrambled to his feet, tottering as he did so, and grabbed his fallen backpack. He hissed as his arm brushed his side. The skin on the underside of his forearm looked as though it had been burned. There was a long, angry line of red marring his arm from elbow to wrist. Imorean held his arm against his chest as he gathered his strength and walked on. His feet were sluggish and the world was spinning as he stumbled toward the exit, leaning on the wall as he walked. He needed help.

Imorean gathered himself and breathed deeply as he jumped down the sets of steps and landed unevenly on the pavement. He was still very dizzy and his mind felt out of focus. His arm felt as though it was on fire and the burn seemed to be spreading under his skin. Fear was spreading too and he knew he had to put as much space between himself and Michael as possible. Imorean was a good runner, but it had been a long time since he had run out of true panic and never had he needed to run after being nearly knocked out. His steps felt hesitant and uneven. He tripped more. He needed help. He needed his friends. His breath tore at his raw throat in sobs as he raced across the campus, heading toward the cafeteria. From there he could get Roxy, Mandy, Toddy, Bethany, and Colton and they would run away from here. They could figure something out together. He wanted his friends more than anything else. He wanted their help, their support. He needed them. He needed them desperately.

Suddenly, Imorean skidded to a halt and dragged more air into his lungs. He could see two faculty members were standing at the top of the steps to the dining hall. They were looking out over the common grounds, as though they were searching for someone. What if Michael had somehow told them to look for him? Imorean didn't think he could take the risk of it being him that they were searching for, if they were searching at all. Quickly, Imorean backpedaled and tore toward the male dormitory. Maybe Toddy, Colton, Dustin, Baxter or even Ryan, by some miracle, would be there. He needed help and now, he would settle for anyone.

Imorean slammed the door to his dorm room shut and slithered to the floor, panting raggedly. Every breath tore at his throat. The lobby had been deserted, and the rest of the building had been quiet. Imorean's bag slid off his shoulder and came to rest on the floor. His entire body was shaking and his eyes were rooted to the floor as he desperately tried to process everything. Michael... Michael had attacked him. A member of staff had attacked a student. Imorean gritted his teeth and shut his eyes tight. Michael could have killed him. But why...?

"What the hell is going on?" asked Imorean, his voice was ragged and quivered as he spoke. "Toddy? Are you in?"

The only response was a soft rush of air and a shadow falling across the floor as a figure crossed in front of the window.

"They aren't here and I believe the correct question is 'what in Heaven's name is going on?,'" said a voice.

Imorean jumped in surprise, his eyes snapping open as he raised his head and looked up sharply. Someone was leaning on the dresser in front of the window between Imorean and Toddy's beds. For a split second sheer panic tore through him. Michael! How had Michael gotten here? Then he saw hazel eyes rather than green ones. Gabriel. The best help he could possibly wish for. Relief flooded Imorean. Gabriel was one of the staff members he knew he could trust... but *why* was he here? How had Imorean not noticed him in the room before now?

"Remember, Michael doesn't like profanity on campus," Gabriel said, standing up.

"How did you get in here?" asked Imorean, shakily pushing himself to his feet.

"I have a spare set of keys to all the male dormitories. I came here after I received a rather odd message from my twin brother. You had placed him in a position that would require more finesse to resolve than he was capable of giving. Is that true?" asked Gabriel, inclining his head.

"How did you know to come here? Your brother said all tech was down."

"Almost all," replied Gabriel with a grimace. "Not ours. I suppose you could say that the faculty works on a different network to the students."

"Mr. Archer, what's happening? Please. I have to know. Your brother attacked me!" said Imorean, his brow furrowed deeply.

"I know he did, but I can't tell you why, Imorean. Not yet. My brother's orders."

"He's not a soldier," protested Imorean, his voice rising in pitch. Had the two Archer brothers turned on the students? But why? There was no reason to.

Gabriel chuckled humorlessly and smiled.

"I'm sorry about this, Imorean. Really, I am. I hope you can believe that. I would have liked to wait longer," he said apologetically as he stood upright and stepped closer to Imorean.

Imorean backed into the door behind him and reached for the handle, ready to race off again. He would run for the gates this time. He wouldn't stop until he reached someone who could help him. Gabriel frowned and snapped his fingers. Imorean yelped and jumped forward as the door locked on its own. He looked up at Gabriel with wide, fearful eyes. What manner of man was this? Was Gabriel Archer even a man?

"Please, Mr. Archer, please, if you can't tell me what's going on, let me leave."

"That isn't possible, Imorean. I'm sorry."

"Why?! Why are you keeping all of us here?"

"Soon you'll know. Now, be still," said Gabriel, closing most of the space between them.

Imorean was too scared to move and the last of his energy

was being swept away as the adrenaline in his blood vanished. He pressed himself flush against the door and could only watch in wide-eyed fear as Gabriel raised one hand. Again, he saw ethereal, white light gathering at Gabriel's fingertips. He shook his head, silently pleading. There was not so much as a flicker of sympathy in Gabriel's eyes. There was light pressure as the man pressed his index and middle finger firmly to the area between Imorean's eyes. Imorean whimpered aloud as the room spun and his knees lost their strength, trembling beneath him. He swayed on his feet, raising his eyes to Gabriel's. Utter betrayal. All around him, the world blurred, as though his eyes were not working properly. Water was rushing in his ears. His senses were distorting. Colors blurred together, separated and blurred back, melting together. He gasped for breath as his chest tightened and panic started to rule him. He could trust none of the faculty here. Everything had been a lie... and he had believed it.

"That's it. That's it. Relax. Just relax," said Gabriel. "You're fine. You're fine. This'll be over soon."

Imorean felt the man catch him as his legs lost their strength and he slumped forward. He had no energy left to fight. He was spent. Imorean grabbed hold of Gabriel's shirt, trying to find something, anything, to keep him on his feet. Everything felt foggy and distant. He flared his nostrils and panted, feeling as though there wasn't enough air entering his lungs. This was even worse than when Michael had been choking him. This was not something he could fight. Whatever was happening was already inside him. His entire body was hot. He felt drunk, slow, and incapable.

"Just relax now, Imorean," said Gabriel. "We'll tell you everything you want to know when you wake up. I promise."

"Am I going to wake up?" asked Imorean, fear tearing through his body. Sluggishly, he struggled and tried to pull his feet back beneath his body. He wanted to rise, he wanted to run.

"Yes, we hope so," replied Gabriel.

"Are you sure?" asked Imorean, his words slurring as he spoke. What Gabriel had said was hardly reassuring. He felt Gabriel lowering him the rest of the way to the floor. His body felt as though it was lying down, but Imorean couldn't be sure. Everything felt very distant, almost unreal, as though he was a fading light in a world of darkening shadows. Through his blurring vision, Imorean saw Gabriel smile sympathetically.

"I promise," replied Gabriel.

Imorean's eyelids fluttered and he panted to try and catch his breath.

"Okay," mumbled Imorean, his hold on Gabriel's shirt loosening. The last thing the white-haired teenager knew was the feeling of his hand thudding onto the carpeted floor. Then the world was gone.

CHAPTER
27

———————

Pine branches burnt orange under sunset glow. No birds called. The world was unearthly still. Imorean breathed deep. He was not alone.

"I tried to warn you. Tried to tell you what they're really like."

Brown eyes looked up. The ethereally beautiful man who had haunted his dreams was back. He was flanked on both sides by demon dogs, jaws dripping saliva and eyes glittering maliciously. A wall of darkness lay behind the man, gathering at his feet and growing. Imorean trembled. Sheer loathing rolled from the man in waves. The darkness was fearful. The hounds were terrifying. They had haunted him for months, but it was the sense of monstrous intent from the man that scared Imorean more than anything else. The man who carried himself like royalty and seemed to know and understand more than anyone else by far.

Imorean swallowed hard. "You never told me anything."

The man smirked, his black hair shining under the bloody light of the setting sun. "You do not heed your dreams. Alas, just like before, you are choosing your side. Not that you really have much choice this time..."

"My side?"

The dark-haired head cocked to one side. "Oh, Imorean, you still don't know who you are? Incredible."

A hiss was torn from Imorean's mouth as something chilled his blood. He gripped the center of his chest. He knew he should recognize the tone of the man's words. There was a huge piece of this intricate puzzle missing.

"When we meet, I will give you one last chance."

"One chance for what?"

"To change the future... and erase the past. One chance."

Imorean looked around wildly as the two demon dogs started to advance on him. Slow and predatory they came. Hunting.

Brown eyes locked once more on the black-haired man. There was a terrible knowing in those stony gray eyes, as though he already knew the future. Imorean ventured a question.

"What do you mean?"

"See you soon, Imorean."

"Imorean," said a quiet voice.

Imorean's eyelids flickered. The sound of his name jerked him back to the real world, leaving the dream behind to fade into non-being. He didn't want to wake up. His entire body felt exhausted and drained. He was sure that if he slept for a little while longer he would feel better.

"Imorean," said the voice again, more insistently this time. "You need to wake up. Come on. I know you can hear me."

Imorean tried to open his eyes, he really did, but they just felt too heavy. He was in pain. A lot of pain. The attack he had sustained from Ryan some time ago felt like nothing by comparison to this. Now, it was as though every bone in his body had been broken, reshaped, then mended. He could taste blood in the back of his mouth, clinging to his throat. His body was on fire, from the ends of his fingers to the tips of his toes.

"Perhaps we should just throw a bucket of water on him," suggested someone. Imorean thought it sounded like Michael.

"Do you *want* to get bitten again?" chuckled a third voice somewhere to Imorean's right. It was a voice Imorean had only heard once before and couldn't place in his head. A low groan escaped Imorean's mouth as his blood ran cold in his veins.

"Do you not have work to do, Dr. Hall?" snapped Michael.

"Oh, I do. I had to replace Imorean's fluids… and I wanted to ask how your hand is," snorted the doctor. "You should have known better."

Michael made a noise of disgust. Imorean held his eyes shut as he heard footsteps.

"Something you'll be interested in, Michael. He has a birthmark on his chest."

"Oh?"

"Mmm. Two inches long. Perfect, narrow diamond. Dead center of his chest."

"I wonder…"

"Stranger things have happened."

"How's his recovery going?" interrupted the first voice. Imorean was almost certain it was Gabriel. Was that genuine concern he could hear?

There were more footsteps, followed by the rattle of metal on metal. Dr. Hall spoke again. "His vital signs are fine. I'm sure he'll be coming around very soon. If he does, I highly doubt he'll want food. As you know, the transition has a tendency to alter their appetite for a few days. Some adjust quicker than others. If he doesn't wake up now I think you should just come back again tomorrow. He'll certainly be awake by then. I have to go and check the others. Are either of you coming?"

"I'll stay with him a little longer," said Gabriel.

"Then we will see you in a few minutes. Lead on, Hall," replied Michael. Imorean heard the sounds of movement and two sets of fading footsteps, then he opened his eyes.

"Where am I?" asked Imorean. His voice didn't sound like his own. It sounded rough and his throat felt raw. As soon as the words left his mouth he regretted speaking. His chest hurt. The only time he could liken any feeling to this was when he and Roxy had gone to a concert and he had lost his voice from cheering so much. Had he been screaming this time?

"Thank Heaven," said Gabriel, breathing an audible sigh of relief.

Imorean opened his eyes blearily and found himself gazing at a high, stone ceiling. His eyes felt swollen, as though he had been crying hard for some time. Imorean looked down in surprise. There was an IV sticking out of a vein in his arm. It was connected to a drip next to him. Fearful nausea rose in his empty stomach, and he looked away.

"Mr. Archer?" asked Imorean. His voice was shaking. He raised his head and looked over at Gabriel. Imorean's entire body trembled and he dropped his head back to his pillow, feeling dizzy with exhaustion. Gabriel was sitting on a low stool next to his bed, brow furrowed in concern. Imorean raised his head again, not content to lie still. He and Gabriel were surrounded by high, white curtains that offered a vague sense of privacy.

"You pulled through," said Gabriel. "Well done. Very well done indeed. That's the first step."

"What's going on?" asked Imorean, coughing hard. His throat burned as he did so. His chest and back throbbed painfully. Yes, he had definitely been screaming, but why? Why didn't he remember the reason?

"I did say I'd tell you everything when you woke up, didn't I?"

Imorean nodded, regretting it as soon as he did so. The room spun in a sickening way and he leaned his head back on the pillow. He felt queasy and knew he should have vomited, but there was nothing in his stomach. He couldn't look at the drip next to him. It would only make him feel worse and more afraid.

"Don't strain yourself," said Gabriel. "And refrain from moving as much as you can."

"Okay," replied Imorean. He felt all too happy to comply with Gabriel's wishes. He rested his head back on the pillow and looked toward Gabriel, away from the IV and drip. He didn't want to think about what was being injected into his veins.

"Your questions." Gabriel leaned forward and rested his elbows on the bed. The man's hazel eyes seemed troubled. Was that guilt that Imorean was reading in his expressions?

"Are you going to answer them now?"

"If I wasn't, I wouldn't have asked," replied Gabriel, smiling slightly. "I will tell you as much as I think you can manage to hear."

"What am I..." Imorean swallowed. "What am I being given?"

"We were giving you a heavy sedative until this morning," said Gabriel. "You've been given morphine regularly for the last few hours. After something like... what has happened, it makes coming back around much easier. Now that you are awake, I assume that Dr. Hall will take you off it."

"If I'm on morphine, why am I hurting so much?"

"Morphine will help kill pain, but not pain of this caliber. Manmade medicines don't work on... well, something like this."

"What's going on? You know that I overheard your

conversation with Michael in the library back in July. Is this what that was about?"

Imorean swallowed hard. His voice felt thick, and he knew he sounded afraid.

"The truth... yes, that conversation was in reference to this. You are part of a plan that we have had to enact much earlier than we would have liked to. My brother was pushing for an earlier start to the plan. I, on the other hand, wanted you and your classmates to have at least one vacation at home before the plan was begun."

"What plan?"

"I'll tell you after the drugs have worn off. When you can walk, alright?" asked Gabriel. There were undertones of hesitation and vagueness in his voice. "With the way you recovered from this, that shouldn't take too long. A few hours, if that."

"How long have I been asleep?" asked Imorean.

"...Four nights, five days," replied Gabriel.

"What?" cried Imorean, flinching and closing his eyes as he did so. His own voice seemed to be too loud in his ears.

"Four nights, five days."

"Why are we here? Why did we have to be taken out of the United States? The locked gates?"

"Quite frankly, it was so you couldn't leave, couldn't go home. We needed you all to remain here."

Imorean glared. "So, you and the rest of this college has kidnapped us?"

"We here at Gracepointe have done nothing without your consent," replied Gabriel. "Everything we have done here has been completely legal. We have not kidnapped you. You gave us your written consent to temporarily hold you here."

"What do you mean, with our consent?"

"Do you remember those packets of forms that we sent home for you to sign?"

"Yes."

"Did you read the terms and conditions?"

"...No," said Imorean.

"No one ever seems to," said Gabriel, rolling his eyes. "In the terms and conditions that you legally signed and agreed to, you were asked if you agreed to us, oh what was the wording... be a part of an education in a foreign nation of a foreign culture. One of the ways in which we ensure this happens is to cut off a direct route home."

Imorean gathered all his remaining energy as anger rose in him. "I don't see the connection between me lying in the hospital after being attacked by staff and 'education in a foreign nation.'"

A breath of humorless laughter escaped Gabriel. "Perhaps our definitions of education are slightly different."

"What happened to me?"

"I'll tell you that when you can walk. Here, Imorean," said Gabriel, resting a hand on Imorean's shoulder for a second. "Go back to sleep for a few hours. I have some errands I need to do. When they're finished I'll come back and we'll see if you're ready to get back on your feet."

"Alright," replied Imorean, furrowing his brow. He felt warmer than usual somehow. Calm. Overwhelmingly calm and quiet, as though sleep had hold of his ankles and was dragging him down.

"Sleep well," said Gabriel, standing up and pulling back one of the white curtains. Imorean glanced out and for a split second was certain he could see Roxy lying on a bed across the room. He looked up at Gabriel with wide eyes.

"Don't worry. We have everything under control," said Gabriel, stepping off and allowing the curtain to drop.

Imorean sighed heavily and closed his eyes once again. He was going to go to sleep, and all too soon. He wanted to get up, to find out what had been done, to stand in the clear and to know, but exhaustion tugged insistently at his strength. He leaned his head back on the pillow and moved to lie more comfortably on the mattress. Suddenly, raw, electric pain spiked up from somewhere beyond his shoulder blades, down his back, and all the way to his hips. It was pain so acute, Imorean could taste it in his mouth, metallic and bitter. Imorean felt again that he was going to be sick. Had he injured his back? Was that why he was in so much pain? For a few horrible seconds, Imorean wondered if he was paralyzed. Would he be able to move as much as he already had if he was paralyzed? He felt as though he needed to stand up and have a proper look, but his body was just too exhausted. Finally, Imorean closed his eyes again, glad to shut out the sight of the IV. His back still throbbed horrifically, but somehow, Imorean was able to drift away into a dreamless sleep.

CHAPTER 28

The light in the room was much lower when Imorean opened his eyes again. He felt slightly more comfortable and was grateful for the lower light. He had a feeling that it was evening. He looked at his arm. The IV was gone, as was the drip that had been at his bedside. All that remained on his arm was a white bandage.

"You're awake," said Gabriel, pushing the curtain back. "That was perfect timing, I think."

"It was," replied Imorean, yawning. "I've just woken up."

"Good," said Gabriel, smiling slightly. "How are you feeling?"

"Stronger," replied Imorean, being careful not to nod as well. His body did feel much stronger and he felt more as though he would be able to get up and do things.

Gabriel nodded. "Good, good. Alright then. I'll help you get to your feet."

"Thank you," said Imorean, worried about what would happen when he tried to stand. He wasn't quite sure that his body was as strong as he thought. He swallowed hard as

Gabriel came to the side of his bed. The older man offered a hand to him and Imorean glared for a moment, before taking hold of it. Imorean swallowed hard as he stood up, bare feet coming into contact with the cold stone floor. The room spun and shards of pain raced down his spine. His knees sagged beneath him and he felt his balance slip. Gabriel was immediately supporting him from under his shoulder, steadying him. For another awful moment, Imorean thought he might have broken his back, but how? The room was still spinning slightly, but after a few moments of standing upright it stopped. Relief welled up in him. He could feel the floor beneath his feet. He hadn't broken his back... but what had really happened?

"Can you walk?" asked Gabriel.

"I think so," replied Imorean, taking note of what he was wearing. A pair of blue and yellow pajama trousers, provided by the school, and a very loose tee shirt that felt as though there were holes cut into the back of it. He could feel cool air slipping through the fabric to touch the skin on his back. The air felt blocked somehow though. His shoulders and back were starting to throb painfully and Imorean resisted the urge to groan.

"Come on then," said Gabriel, removing his support to step forward and lead Imorean out from behind the white curtains.

The teenager looked around. It seemed as though every bed in the room was occupied. Each one was surrounded by its own wall of white curtain.

"Where is this place?"

"It's part of the student health center. This is our on-campus hospital. Actually, it is the oldest building on Gracepointe's campus, equipped with everything the university could need."

"I'm dropping the scholarship," said Imorean as Gabriel led him out of a large, oaken door at the end of the room.

Imorean realized as he walked that he felt slightly heavier than usual, as though there was a great weight pressing down on him, just behind his shoulders.

Gabriel snorted. "I'm sure."

"I'm serious," insisted Imorean as they slowly ascended a wide, sweeping stone staircase. "I don't care how much I have to pay back. I don't want to be here anymore."

"Of course." Gabriel's smile had not faded.

Imorean glared at the man. Who was he to smile at a time like this? Just who did he think he was? He and his classmates had just been the victims of a mysterious, vicious plan that Gabriel and Michael had concocted, and the man was *smiling?* Imorean stumbled slightly as Gabriel came to a sharp halt and pulled a door open.

"This is an office," said Imorean, looking into the room.

Gabriel snickered. "Very observant. Not just anyone's office though."

"It's not yours. Yours is on West Campus."

"Quite right," nodded Gabriel, motioning for Imorean to go in.

Imorean stepped hesitantly into the office and looked around. It was almost medieval in its decor. The windows of the office were high and reached the ceiling. There were intricate tapestries and paintings on the walls, leaving almost no bare spots. Books were piled neatly on bookshelves, making the room look unnaturally neat. The two most noticeable things in the office were a large, full length mirror, running the length of an entire wall, and a huge, ornate desk in the center of the room. Imorean frowned for a second. Was that gold inlay on the front? There were two chairs between Imorean and the desk.

"This is *my* office."

Imorean flinched and looked up as Michael appeared out of a side room. Imorean tensed his body to run again, the memory of what Michael had last done still very fresh in his mind. He hesitated though, when he saw what was in Michael's hands. He was carrying a bottle of amber liquid and three small glasses. A flash of satisfaction tore through Imorean as he spotted the white bandage around one of Michael's hands.

"Good to see you back on your feet, Imorean," said Michael, setting the glasses and bottle down on his desktop. Imorean felt slightly taken aback and he relaxed marginally. There was no venom or aggression in Michael's tone now. The man gave no indication that only four days ago he tried to strangle a student or that said student had bitten him.

"It's good to be up... sir," replied Imorean warily, deciding it was probably best to be polite until he knew exactly what was going on.

"Sit down if you would like," said Michael, motioning to the chairs on Gabriel and Imorean's side of the desk.

"Thanks, Brother." Gabriel sighed heavily as he sat down on one of the chairs. "How long has that aged for?"

"This whiskey aged ten years. Do you drink, Imorean?"

"I'm underage, sir," replied Imorean. He had drunk his fair share of alcohol during his senior year, but he wasn't going to tell Michael that.

"Not here," said Michael, pouring a bit of the whiskey into each of the glasses. "Drinking age in Norway is eighteen. You *are* eighteen, are you not? Normally, I would not have to ask, but I do not happen to have your file with me right now."

"Yes, sir."

"Then drink this. You will want it, believe me."

"Why?" asked Imorean, taking the small glass and holding it between two fingers. He didn't put it past Michael to want to poison him.

"Drink, then we will talk," ordered Michael, taking his own glass and tipping it quickly back.

"Can I drink it after having so many drugs pumped into me?"

Michael looked at Gabriel and both brothers chuckled. An identical sound.

It was Gabriel who replied. "Oh, yes, Imorean. You will be perfectly safe. The way I see it, there is not much that can hurt you at all anymore."

Imorean looked at Gabriel hesitantly, and watched as the smaller man knocked back his own shot of liquor. Imorean swallowed hard then raised the glass to his lips and tipped it back. The whiskey burned furiously on the way down and Imorean scrunched up his face at the bitter aftertaste. He had never liked whiskey, preferring to stick to clear alcohol.

"It has a bite," said Michael, taking the glass from Imorean and replacing it on his desk. "Another?"

Imorean shuddered and shook his head. "It's gross."

"It's a bit of an acquired taste," smiled Gabriel, elbowing Imorean slightly.

Imorean couldn't help himself from recoiling slightly, watching as Gabriel settled himself more comfortably in the chair next to his own. It was the same lighthearted joviality that had drawn him to Gabriel in the first place that now disgusted him. What right did Gabriel have to behave as though nothing was wrong?

Michael finally sat down behind his desk and folded his hands together.

"Now, what do you want to know?"

"Why did you give me whiskey?"

"The alcohol helps people to relax. In approximately five to ten minutes you are going to receive a rather large shock, so I decided to do anything I could to make you more comfortable."

"What shock? What did you do to me to make me go to sleep for four days? How many other students are down in the hospital? What is going on here?" asked Imorean, the questions tumbling out of his mouth. He stopped quickly when Michael held up a hand, wordlessly silencing him.

"The entire school is currently in the hospital with the exception of the staff. All your friends are down there, but do not fret. They are well taken care of."

"What are you doing to us all?"

"You would not happen to have any other questions before I answer that, would you? I will have to show you the answer to that one."

"I want to know exactly what's going on," replied Imorean, narrowing his brown eyes.

"Come on then," said Michael.

Imorean watched the man stand up, then motion for him to do so as well. He hesitated. Should he do as Michael ordered? Slowly, Imorean did as Michael asked. His body still hurt as he stood, his back throbbing painfully. What had been done to him?

"It's alright."

Imorean looked up at the sound of Gabriel's voice. The smaller man was standing as well and was smiling in a comforting yet sympathetic way. Imorean was repulsed. He didn't want Gabriel's pity, his sympathy, or his compassion. He just wanted to go home.

"Come here," ordered Michael.

Imorean turned his head and saw Michael standing in front of the large, full length mirror. Warily, Imorean crossed the room and stood next to Michael. He couldn't help but feel a bit trapped as Gabriel stood on his other side, sandwiching him between the two men. Imorean furrowed his brow as Michael raised one hand over his head then swept it down quickly. It felt to Imorean as though a veil had been removed from over his eyes and for the first time in his life he could see, *really* see. His breath caught in his throat. For a moment, Imorean couldn't breathe. He choked for air. His lungs couldn't remember how to work.

"This is what we did," said Michael, turning his intense, pale gaze to Imorean.

Imorean leaped backwards, a loud gasp leaving his mouth as he did so.

A pair of massive, emerald-feathered wings fanned out from Michael's shoulder blades and arced impressively above the man's head. Imorean shook his head as the wings stretched straight out, revealing a span of what must have been close to twelve feet. A second, much smaller pair flared from the center of his back and flexed a few times.

"These have been so cramped," mused Michael, shuffling the smaller wings and folding the large ones back to a resting position. The structures were so large that the bend of each wing was visible behind Michael's shoulders and the primary flight feathers almost reached down to the backs of the man's knees. Imorean refused to believe that the wings actually *belonged* to Michael. It was impossible. Surely, this had to be some kind of joke. A sick, cruel, twisted joke. He felt nauseous and scared. This wasn't real. This wasn't real. It couldn't be real.

Imorean wanted to step further away as Michael looked back at him, but he couldn't go anywhere. Gabriel was still standing firmly on his other side.

"If I were you, I would take your eyes away from me and take a moment to look at yourself," said Michael, resting a heavy hand on Imorean's head and forcing him to look back at the mirror.

Imorean's jaw dropped. He felt as though he had been punched in the chest. Two, white, feathered *objects* were arcing up from the area between his own spine and his shoulder blades, flared out from his sides ever so slightly. This sort of thing only happened in science-fiction movies. Imorean studied the feathery structures in shock and horror. Impossible. His knees felt weak and his heartbeat felt faint.

He resisted the urge to vomit. Were they what he thought they were…? No, they couldn't be, could they?

Vaguely, Imorean saw Michael smile. "Welcome, Imorean, to the newest battalion of Heaven's angel foot soldiers."

"No," whispered Imorean. "No, no, no, no, no…"

With a trembling hand, Imorean reached to one side. His fingers met real feather and real muscle. What was more, through the wings, he could feel his own fingers skimming over the feathers. Surely, they weren't attached to him. They couldn't be. They just couldn't be. He couldn't have… wings. Real wings.

End of Book One

The story continues in

Book Two: Angels Soaring,

available late 2017.

Make sure to follow me on Facebook to be notified when the
next book is released!

www.facebook.com/HarrietCarltonAuthor/

54153112R00153

Made in the USA
San Bernardino, CA
09 October 2017